"I wanted to go with you tonight."

Michael parked the van and cut the engine. "I'm not here just to kill some time. I want to be a part of this ministry."

The back door of the van opened and the kids piled out, leaving them alone. He wondered about their actions.

Did teenagers play at matchmaking?

He turned to face Maggie and caught her watching him, her eyes sparkling like sapphires. Mesmerized, he leaned toward her.

The wary look that crossed her features stopped him. For a second it looked like panic. He leaned back into his seat, letting the moment pass.

"I'm sorry. I shouldn't push my way into your life." He tried to explain, reaching to tug at the tendril of hair that had fallen loose from her ponytail. But what he meant as a playful gesture became something more intimate.

"I need to go. Thank you for helping tonight. We couldn't have done this without you."

"Maggie, wait."

She shook her head. "No, Michael. It isn't you. It's me."

BRENDA MINTON

started creating stories to entertain herself during hour-long rides on the school bus. In high school she wrote romance novels to entertain her friends. The dream grew and so did her aspirations to become an author. She started with notebooks, handwritten manuscripts and characters that refused to go away until their stories were told. Eventually she put away the pen and paper and got down to business with the computer. The journey took a few years, with some encouragement and rejection along the way—as well as a lot of stubbornness on her part. In 2006, her dream to write for the Steeple Hill Love Inspired line came true.

Brenda lives in the rural Ozarks with her husband, three kids and an abundance of cats and dogs. She enjoys a chaotic life that she wouldn't trade for anything—except, on occasion, a beach house in Texas. You can stop by and visit her (not at the beach house) at her Web site: www.brendaminton.net.

Trusting Him
Brenda Minton

Steeple
Hill®

Published by Steeple Hill Books™

STEEPLE HILL BOOKS

Steeple
Hill®

ISBN-13: 978-0-373-87446-0
ISBN-10:   0-373-87446-4

TRUSTING HIM

Trust in the Lord with all your heart, and lean not on your own understanding; In all your ways acknowledge Him and He shall direct your paths.
—*Proverbs* 3: 5–6

This book is dedicated to Doug for always believing I could do this, and for giving me the time and the support. Thank you for letting me dream big. To the kids, for putting up with mac and cheese, digging socks out of the basket and for reminding me (more than once) that it was time to eat.

To my family and friends, for encouraging me, reading for me, and for the critiques that made it all come together. I love you all. Ellen, Keri, Steph, Dawn, Angela, Shirlee, Cheryl, Barbara, Lori, Jill, Karla and Patsy. To the ladies at Crossroads, for love and prayers. You prayed, God heard.

To my agent, Janet Benrey. I can't say enough about what you mean to me. Thank you for putting up with me, listening to me, and for all of the valuable advice. And did I mention...for putting up with me. Onward and Upward.

And to my editor, Melissa Endlich. You rock!! I'm so glad you were the editor who took the chance on a new author. You've taught me so much. You've encouraged me. You've helped me to believe in myself as a writer. This one is for you.

Chapter One

Afternoon sunlight filtered through the living-room windows of the trailer, dispelling the gloom but not the tight feeling of dread in Maggie Simmons's stomach. She felt it to the very core, twisting and wrenching—a six-year-old ache that had healed but left scars. She didn't want to be here, not alone, not when shadows drifted into the corners and every noise, even the slightest creak, sounded ominous.

Something scurried across the floor, taking cover under the couch. Maggie shrieked and jumped back, feeling silly afterward. A mouse. Good thing nobody witnessed the little dance she had done when it ran past her.

The new tenant would have to deal with the old tenant, the one who probably lived somewhere inside the used plaid sofa the church had bought for the trailer some years ago, back when the place served as a parsonage for their pastor. The way Maggie saw it, the mouse had squatter's rights. The trailer *had* been empty for six months.

She walked to the back bedroom armed with a dust rag, broom and furniture polish.

Michael Carson. The new tenant. She had to stop thinking of him as a tenant renting from the church. He planned on being more than that. She bristled when she thought back on the conversation with Pastor Banks, the one where he had told her that Michael Carson would be attending their church, and that eventually he would like to help with the after-school project.

"What are you snarling about?"

Maggie jerked back from the dresser she was dusting and turned. She didn't have to guess how her friend, Faith, had found her. Maggie's grandmother would have told her, and probably would have even asked Faith to check on her.

"I'm not snarling. I'm cleaning. It never makes me happy. And you shouldn't sneak in and scare a person like that."

"You're a clean freak. Of course cleaning makes you happy. You like to send those dust bunnies on the run. I think you're snarling because your granny has some awesome fried chicken on the stove, and she invited me to eat with the two of you. And you know I can eat more than you."

"Yes, that's it. I'm snarling because my best friend is a bottomless pit with a stinkingly fast metabolism."

"All part of my charm." Faith grabbed the broom and started to sweep the hallway. "And you're upset because you are going to have an uninvited guest in your life. He's suspect, I'm telling you that much. I wouldn't trust him at all."

Maggie shook her head and walked away. Faith followed.

"It isn't that I don't trust him." Maggie dusted the ceiling light in the living room, sending dust and cobwebs floating to the floor to be swept up later. She brushed a strand of web off her cheek and blew at the dust floating in front of her face. "I just want the best thing for the after-school program. We've managed to get the neighborhood kids off the street. We're teaching them to care about others, and to have goals."

Kids could come to the church after school, knowing that someone would be there for them. They were given snacks, homework help and roles in community projects so that they could learn to help others. In the summer she planned boating, hiking and other activities to keep them out of trouble.

Members of the church had even volunteered to mentor and teach the kids different skills that they might not learn at home. One taught sewing, another cooking, one gentleman taught the boys about cars and another taught gardening.

It was about more than going to church. It showed them the importance of fellowship and helping others. They were growing.

Years ago Maggie had been one of these kids, she knew what they needed. She wanted to be the person who was there for them.

Faith walked up behind her, resting her chin on Maggie's shoulder. "It'll work out, Mags. I know this is hard for you, letting this guy in—not just into your ministry, but into your life. But even you've said that you needed help. Maybe this is God's—"

"Plan? Yeah, maybe so. Don't worry, I'm not going to run him off. I'll give him the chance he deserves."

"You're a strong woman, Maggie. You'll get through this."

Maggie nodded and walked to the door. She expected to see them driving up at any moment. Pastor Banks had driven the few hours to the state prison in central Missouri to pick up Michael because he had asked his family for one day to get settled before seeing them. It was nearly five o'clock. It wouldn't be much longer.

"I'll be back in a sec. I have a cooler of bottled water in my car. I thought maybe you'd need something to drink, and I figured you forgot to bring something." Faith slid past her and out the front door.

Maggie watched Faith leave. Faith had asked her the same question as Pastor Banks. What bothered her about this? Michael Carson's past didn't upset her. Most people had a past. Not everyone had made mistakes as big as his, but hadn't they all made mistakes?

It wasn't his past. It was hers that made this so difficult. Her memories of a mother who could never seem to quit using drugs, followed by Maggie's own years of rebellion, were the real problem. Choices she had made, wrong decisions—those things haunted her. A night that she couldn't reclaim added to the heap. A dark road, a guy she had trusted, pushing her to go where she hadn't wanted to go.

She walked away from the door, her heart racing as the memory continued to flash through her mind, an instant replay that had dulled with time but hadn't faded.

Greg had taken what she hadn't wanted to give. She had trusted him, even considered that they might have a future together. Their future ended that night, sending her life on a completely different path.

The door to the trailer rattled as it opened. Maggie jumped and turned, Faith's red head peeked in. She smiled and held up the cooler.

"Relax, it's just me."

"I knew that."

Faith carried the cooler into the kitchen. "Nice place."

"He doesn't have to live here." Maggie took the bottle of water that her friend held out to her. "His parents have a home in River Oaks Estates. On the ninth hole of the golf course, I think."

"Claws, my friend? That isn't like you." Faith opened her bottle of water. "Sit down with me."

"I need to finish sweeping."

Faith backed up to the counter and with a hop she was sitting, the bottle of water next to her. "Why clean it for him if you dislike him so much?"

Maggie shrugged. "Because I'm a nice person. And because I don't dislike him. I don't know him."

"You're too sweet, Mags. And you gotta admire that he would want to live here, and not with his parents."

"Yes, that's something to admire."

"So—" Faith looked down at the bottle of water she had picked up "—so maybe he isn't another rich guy who takes what he wants without thinking of the consequences. Isn't that what you're thinking? You think he's using his money to get what he wants. He's out of prison, has a second chance, and now he's going to walk in here and make it all better by doing a good deed."

Maggie looked out the window, concentrating on a sparrow that had landed on the railing of the deck. Was Faith right? Maggie sipped from her bottle of water, shrugging as she turned to face her friend.

"Thanks for that, now I really feel like a heel. Yes, maybe that is what I've been thinking. I haven't even met the guy but already I've put him in the box with other people who have let me down. I'll work through it."

"Money or not, his life isn't going to be a walk in the park."

"Life rarely is a walk in the park." Maggie smiled at her friend. "But I guess we both know that, right?"

Faith was a cancer survivor. Maggie had survived her

father's abandonment before her birth, her mother's death and Greg. They had made a pact a long time ago to not dwell on darker days, but to move forward. But sometimes that was easier said than done. Sometimes life tossed in a few obstacles, just to keep them on their toes.

Maggie wanted to think that Michael Carson was a temporary obstacle. He would get settled, get back on his feet and move on.

"We're both survivors, Maggie. Which is why, even though it hurts, you're going to give Michael Carson a chance."

"Yes, I'm going to give him a chance. Mercy, isn't that a key ingredient to living our faith?"

"You got it, sweetie. We all need mercy, a little forgiveness and a second, sometimes a third, chance."

Maggie smiled, the appropriate response. She had received enough mercy, and more than one second chance of her own. But Michael Carson, this faceless entity, in her life and in her ministry?

"Faith, I'm fine. You don't have to babysit me. It's been six years. I'm nearly twenty-seven, which makes me a grown-up. I'm not afraid to be here alone."

"I know, but I want to be here for you." Faith smiled, her eyes sparkling with humor.

Maggie got it then, and she felt like an idiot for not getting it sooner. "You're not here for me. You're here because your curiosity got the best of you. You just want to see him."

Faith put a hand on her chest, her eyes widening in an overly sincere fashion. "Mags, I can't believe you think that of me. Honey, I'm hurt."

"And I'm right."

"Okay, I admit that idle curiosity might have something to do with my being here. I'm a writer, you know, I do like to study people. And I do care about you."

"The world is your…" For the life of her, she couldn't think of the word. "Whatever."

"Stage?" Faith supplied. "No, not really. I think that would make me an actress." She hopped down from the counter. "Let's get some fresh air. This place smells like pine cleaner and bug spray. And I think I just saw a mouse."

"Yeah, I think he lives under the couch. Let me grab my purse and we can go."

Faith's hand on her arm stopped her. Maggie turned, catching the compassionate look in Faith's green eyes.

"Maggie, remember, he's not Greg, and he isn't your dad."

"Yes, I know. I'm not judging him, Faith. I know all about making mistakes."

A car engine rumbled to a stop in the driveway. Maggie looked out the window, Faith nudging in right behind her. Pastor Banks got out of the car first. Michael Carson followed, exiting from the passenger side.

Maggie pushed aside the lecturing voice inside her mind, the one that told her she was behaving like a teenager. Faith whistled softly, obviously not getting the same mental lecture.

"You are in big, big trouble, Maggie Simmons."

Maggie shrugged off the warning as Michael Carson reached into the back of the car and pulled out a battered duffel bag. He turned to stare at the trailer, his stance casual, but his shoulders looking tense beneath a snug, dusky-blue sweater, a white T-shirt showing at the neck. He didn't pose a threat to her. He looked like other men she knew. His jeans were faded, his brown hair a little too long; he didn't bother her at all.

He didn't bother her until he walked through the door, taking up too much space in the narrow room, and slamming headlong into her resolve with hazel eyes that connected directly with hers.

She saw then that Michael Carson wasn't at all what she had expected, or told herself he would be. He wasn't a hardened criminal. He didn't have cold eyes. He had eyes that challenged her to doubt him.

The two women standing in front of him didn't move. Michael Carson suspected that if he jumped or yelled "boo," they would probably scream and run. Were they expecting him to do something suspicious, criminal or thuglike? He hoped not.

He had been afraid of this reaction, and thought it would be more the norm than the exception. Being prepared didn't make it easier to accept.

The smaller of the two women, a blonde with twilight-blue eyes and a complexion that reminded him of summer sunshine, wore a wary look. The redhead, she was more curious than wary. She smiled, managing to look a lot like someone who was up to something. His attention turned back to the blonde.

"Michael Carson, let me introduce you to Maggie Simmons, our youth worker." Pastor Banks smiled and nodded toward the blonde. "And her incorrigible friend, Faith Lane." The redhead.

Michael thought the introduction he had learned in his support group might be in order: *My name is Michael Carson and I'm a recovering drug addict.* Maggie Simmons looked as though she expected that from him. Or less. Definitely not more.

He didn't want to let her down.

Pushing past sarcasm, he realized that he honestly didn't want to let her down. But not just her—he didn't want to let anyone down. Not even himself. And since he'd walked out of prison—his home for the last four years—one thought had been taunting him. He could slip so easily.

Concentrate on something else. Don't get sucked into doubt. He glanced around the sparsely furnished trailer. It smelled of cleaners and bug spray. The broom leaning against the counter was further proof that someone had been cleaning.

Maggie Simmons had done the cleaning. She wore the evidence on her white T-shirt, smudged with dust. Eyes full of doubt, she watched him as though she didn't know what he was doing in her life, and yet she'd done this.

"Thank you for cleaning the place up." He shot her a smile, hoping for something similar from her. "I hadn't expected that."

"It always helps to come home to something clean," Maggie returned, and she even smiled. Her smile was definitely sunshine and hope. Or maybe four years of prison, four years with few feminine contacts, had left him a little fanciful.

He didn't know what to say. He dropped his duffel bag on the floor and stepped farther into the living room.

"It isn't much, but it's a start." She continued to talk, her tone apologetic.

A start. Exactly what he'd thought when Pastor Banks offered to rent him this place. He needed somewhere to get his life in order. This would be easier than in his parents' home in Springfield, and in their world of constant social activity and polite gossip that would keep him in the gutter.

His mom and dad believed in him. But they were two

people, three including his brother, and he needed more than that. He knew he would need the support of the church in Galloway, and the pastor who had been visiting him for almost three years.

Pastor Banks, tall and burly, with a tender heart and a smile that exploded across his face. He believed in everyone, and in the ability of God to redeem and give second chances. He preached mercy, and he meant it.

His ministry had changed Michael's life.

It had truly changed him. Maggie Simmons looked like she might doubt that. She moved away from him, to a brown bag of groceries on the counter. He watched, wondering what her story was, and knowing instinctively that she had one.

"I bought a few things to get you started." She flashed a look over her shoulder that didn't quite become a smile as she took canned items from the bag. "I wasn't sure what you'd want."

"You didn't have to do that." He started to move toward her but stopped. She wasn't wearing a sign that said, Let's Be Friends. More like a sign that said, Keep Out. "Thank you."

"You're welcome." She opened the refrigerator door and stuck something on the shelf.

Pastor Banks jumped back a step, drawing Michael's attention from the nervous youth worker. "What's the matter with you?"

"I think I just saw a mouse."

Maggie Simmons actually laughed.

Chapter Two

A sliver of light broke through the curtains of the bedroom, waking Michael from what had only recently become a sound sleep. The night had been long and too quiet. No fights had broken out, not one door had slammed and nobody had snored. It had been only him, the occasional bark of a dog and something scurrying inside the wall.

He glanced across the room, squinting to read the clock on the dresser. Barely six. His normal waking time. Disappointed by that, he considered rolling over, covering his head with the pillow and going back to sleep. He had really planned to sleep in, at least until eight. His internal alarm clock hadn't gotten that memo.

Instead of giving in and going back to sleep, he laid there, relishing freedom. No prison guard would show up and tell him to get busy. He could stay in bed as long as he wanted, in a room with no lock on the door and no bars on the windows.

His own bed. His own home. Nobody here would tell him to get to work. Nobody would tell him to head for chow. And nobody would keep him from messing up.

What if he couldn't handle freedom?

Get out of bed, do something. He pushed himself to leave the comfort of the mattress that had swallowed him in its softness the night before. Down the narrow paneled hall, to the sunlit kitchen. He paused at the window over the sink and looked out at hay fields across the road.

This place was perfect. He was glad he'd taken Pastor Banks up on the offer to rent from the church. Here he could get his bearings. He wouldn't have to worry about his parents and how to protect them. He needed this time alone.

For four years he'd had very little time on his own, without someone watching, listening. He had once heard that the Chinese people didn't have a word for "alone." There was no concept of the word in their overcrowded country.

In prison there was no concept of the word, either. A person didn't have use of a word that they couldn't put into practice. Alone.

But then sometimes, even with hundreds of people around, he had felt alone.

He rummaged through the cabinet, smiling when he pulled out the bag of Starbucks coffee. Miss Maggie Simmons had thought of everything. Bless her sweet soul. He filled the coffeepot with water, added a few scoops of coffee to the filter basket and set the power button.

While he waited for the coffee to brew he walked out the back door to the small deck that faced the woods. Springtime in the Ozarks. The air was cool, but hinted at a warm day, and the emerald-green grass was drenched with dew. Something moved. He watched, holding his breath to see what had darted through the trees. It appeared again, a small doe, ears twitching when she sensed his presence. A few minutes later she darted back into the woods.

The aroma of fresh-brewed coffee greeted him when he walked into the trailer. Real coffee, the kind a person wanted to enjoy, not gulp down with a few spoons of sugar added to kill the flavor. He poured a cup and walked back outside. An old lawn chair had been left behind. He sat and propped his feet up on the wood railing of the deck.

Now what? Think of the future, of life working for his dad as a paralegal? Or the past, and how it had changed everything, including where he should be now?

One stupid mistake, trying meth, had led to another mistake—dealing methamphetamines when his dad had cut off his money. He leaned back, closing his eyes when he remembered back to those days. He'd been angry then, mad at his dad for taking away his money, and mad at his brother Noah for telling his parents why he had lost weight and why his grades were failing.

Now he needed to thank them. His dad for taking away his money. His brother for noticing the signs of addiction. He also needed to make amends with the people he had hurt.

Michael's addiction had changed the course of his brother's life, as well. Noah had been set to take the bar and would have been a lawyer for their father's firm. Now he was an agent for the DEA.

Everything had changed.

A car rumbled down the road, coming closer. Michael walked back into the house. He reached the front door as his parents pulled up the drive. They had given him the night he needed to be on his own. He smiled as he glanced down at his watch. His mom was out of the car, carefully walking toward the trailer in high heels that weren't suited for the rutted, overgrown lawn.

He stepped onto the porch to wait.

"Michael, oh, honey, your hair is too long." She hurried up the stairs of the porch, her heels beating a rhythm on the wooden steps. She hugged him to her, holding him close. He held her tight.

"I love you, Mom."

She held him back, gave him a long look and then hugged him again. "Look at him, George. He doesn't look any worse for wear, does he?"

Michael made eye contact with his dad. Neither of them disagreed with Shelly Carson. They rarely did. And if she felt better thinking that he looked good, therefore he must *be* good, Michael was happy letting her believe it.

"He looks great, Shel. And it smells like coffee brewing. I could sure use a cup, since you dragged me out of bed before the sun came up."

"We have a lot to do today. Michael needs to get his driver's license. He'll need his car, clothes and a checking account."

Michael motioned his parents inside, as his mother continued to let them know what she had on her agenda for him. It would have been easy to tell her that he had other plans, things that he needed to do, but not today. He would give her this day.

He could handle it today, having his schedule planned for him. He had handled it for four years, but this time it felt different. This time it was being done by a person who loved him.

"I'd like for you to start work on Monday," his dad said as he poured himself a cup of coffee. "Why in the world do you want to live in this place?"

The conversation had been overdue. Michael knew his parents would want answers. Being a lawyer was out of the question. As a felon he could work as a paralegal for his dad's law office, but he would never be a lawyer. His job and his trust fund would pay the bills. Working at the church filled another need, one his parents wouldn't understand.

"This place sort of suits me. It's quiet out here, and this is a good starting place. I can be alone, spend time thinking about the future." Michael glanced around the sunny yellow kitchen with the avocado-green appliances.

"You could do all of that in town, in a nice apartment," his mother offered. He loved her optimism, her willingness to just sweep his past under a big rug.

His dad was more of a "this is just a bump in the road" sort of guy.

"I don't want the noise of an apartment in the city, or the crowds. Maybe later."

"Well, I do think you should call Katherine. Her mom said she was hurt that you never wrote. Michael, the two of you dated for three years. I think you owe her something."

Michael's mouth dropped and an explanation nearly escaped, one that couldn't escape. His mother didn't need to know, not yet. Katherine had been there during his meth years and she had been a part of that world. He hadn't answered her letters and he didn't plan on letting her in his life now.

His mom wouldn't understand. She would never understand that—what it meant to be an addict. To stay clean, he needed to stay clear of temptation. The phone rang. Michael shot his parents an apologetic look as he went to answer it.

He hadn't expected it so soon, but the caller identified

himself as a probation officer. Michael would need to set
up an appointment, and he would need to get in touch with
his sponsor at Narcotics Anonymous.

Reality hit home as he wrote the addresses and numbers
on a piece of paper. He had a lot to prove to a lot of people,
and he had no intention of letting any of them down. If he
let them down, he'd be letting himself down.

Thursday morning the door to Maggie's office opened
as she lifted a cookie to her mouth. She dropped it on the
desk and brushed crumbs from her chin as Michael Carson
walked in, hesitating just inside the door. He looked unsure,
slightly wary and sweet. She hadn't expected that the tough
guy, with the perpetual five o'clock shadow and hazel eyes
that challenged, had a sweet side.

"I didn't expect you so soon."

He lifted a box of doughnuts and smiled. If he wanted
friendship, that was a good first step.

"The receptionist told me where to find you." He took
another step into the room. "I brought doughnuts."

"That sounds good."

He offered the gesture, placing the box in front of her
on the desk. At close range she could see that his hair was
still damp and curled against his collar. The smell of soap
and aftershave lingered even after he moved away.

Maggie took a doughnut from the box.

"I wish I could offer you a good cup of coffee to go with
them, but Pastor Banks beat me here this morning. His is
barely drinkable."

And then more silence. What did she say after that? She
motioned to the chair on the opposite side of the desk. He
took the offer and sat.

"Have you enjoyed your first few days at ho
grimaced as the words slipped out. Too bad there w
an etiquette book on right things to say in tough situations.
"I'm sorry, that was a stupid thing to say."

His gaze connected with hers and one corner of his
mouth lifted in a smile. "I survived. And don't tiptoe
around, trying to say the right things. I'm a big boy."

"Good, because I'm notorious for saying the wrong thing."

"I'd rather you be honest, Maggie. And if you have
questions, I'll try to answer them."

"Honesty is always good."

"Fine, since we agree on that, I'd like to ask you a
question." He dusted powdered sugar off his hands before
looking up, his smile having disappeared. "Do you mind
having an ex-con here? Do I frighten you?"

Mouthful of doughnut, and total shock—not a good
combination.

Did she mind? Was she frightened? She stared at him,
trying to find the right answer, an answer that would have
told him too much. She had been frightened before. As a
child, listening to her mother partying with friends, and on
a cool night in September, the night Greg drove her to the
lake. Here, in this room with Michael, no, she wasn't
frightened.

His gaze remained unwavering, hazel-green pools in a
face with defined features, but that hard edge that said he
had lived through something difficult.

"I'm not afraid of you." Because of his eyes. The mirror
of the soul. And his were kind, belying the hardness of his
features. "There might be times when I mind that you're
here, but that's because it took me by surprise that you
would want to work here."

Another half smile. "That's definitely honest."

"You said…"

"I meant it. And thank you for the supplies you left behind. That first morning it was nice to wake up and find that you'd thought of the important stuff."

"The coffee was good?" Coffee, a subject she could deal with.

"Yes, and the toaster pastries." He looked away and she wondered what else had gone on in the last few days. "How did you guess?"

"About the pastries?" She shrugged and then smiled. "I didn't. Pastor Banks told me that you had mentioned missing Pop-Tarts. I thought it was a little strange, but hey, who am I to judge?"

"Yes, I guess it was a strange thing, but when you have four years to think about what you really miss, you can think of a lot. I've spent the last three days eating at every fast-food joint in town."

Too much, too soon. Maggie searched for a more neutral topic.

"How is your family?"

"We've had a good reunion. Mom even cooked."

"Sounds like a good homecoming."

His brows shot up at her comment and he half smiled. Okay, maybe not so great. Maybe he was just giving her the niceties, the details that would keep them on level footing as casual acquaintances. She was good with that.

"I can't undo what happened." He glanced toward the window as he made the statement that brought her front and center into his life. "My mom is always going to be afraid that I'll fall again. Dad is always going to think that life can go right back to the way it was."

"It might take time." She knew all about regret. She knew how it felt to live with choices she couldn't undo. Time would bring healing. Or so the saying went.

It was true, but she didn't think it would make him feel any better to hear those words now, not yet. He was a grown man and he'd figure it out on his own.

"This morning my mom called. She wanted to know where I'd be today and what I'd be doing. I'm almost twenty-eight years old and I'm still giving an account for every minute of my day."

"I'm sorry." Another platitude that wouldn't do him any good. The words had to mean something, or they were just words. Sorry. She thought it should be a verb, something a person put into action.

Her father had apologized to her mother twenty-seven years ago. He had followed the apology with the words that he didn't want to be a dad. He had other plans. Sorry.

Her mother had apologized for forgetting school programs, and not picking Maggie up after Girl Scouts. She had apologized the day before she took the overdose that claimed her life.

The police officer had apologized as she'd sat in the back seat of his car on her way to her grandmother's house. She had been fourteen and his apology hadn't really made sense.

Greg had apologized when he'd dropped her off at Faith's dorm the night he'd raped her. She could still see the accusations in his eyes and hear the callousness of his words. *I'm sorry, but this is all your fault. You let me think you wanted this.*

Michael stood. "I'm going to get a cup of that coffee. Do you need one?"

"No, I'm fine."

But she wasn't fine. She was anything but. Her heart was tugging at her, telling her to be the one to give him a chance. He needed a friend, someone he could count on, and she could be that person.

Or could she?

"Michael, good to see you here." The booming voice stopped Michael as he walked down the hall, seeking the kitchen.

He turned to face the bear of a man responsible for his being here. Robert Banks had started a prison ministry and from that ministry Michael had found faith, both in God and in himself.

"Pastor Banks, good morning."

"Did you find Maggie?"

Maggie. Yes, he'd found her. And she was another person in his life whose trust he might never gain. It seemed like there were plenty of those people, and they were all waiting for him to prove himself.

Or were they waiting for him to fail? And he had failed before. In the year before he'd gone to prison he had tried, really tried, to get his life together. He hadn't wanted to end up like people that he knew, the ones who lost everything to addiction.

"Yes, I found her in her office."

"Good. She's the one in charge of youth, and in a month or so, when you're settled and feel like working, she'll be the person to show you the ropes. Until then, get to know her, and let her show you what this after-school program is all about. It's quite a ministry."

"I'm looking forward to working with her. Dad wants

me at least four days a week. I can do the office work and legwork for him as a paralegal. But being here, well, you know how I feel about getting plugged in."

"That's the key, Michael, get plugged in. First to church, and then with the youth. You'll find that having people you can count on will make it easier when you face a struggle."

A few minutes later Michael returned to Maggie's closet-size office. The cluttered room held a conglomeration of gray metal furniture that looked like hand-me-downs from a government office, or even the prison. He felt at home here.

Maggie stood at the window. He stepped quietly, not wanting to disturb her. When he scooted the chair across the tile floor, she jumped slightly and turned.

"Sorry, I didn't mean to frighten you."

"You didn't."

She returned to her chair. The softness of her tone matched the soft look in her eyes. Her hands trembled. He wanted to tell her he understood.

He had a feeling he didn't understand. To give her space he got up, taking the place she'd vacated near the open window. No bars. He put his hand on the screen.

"You okay?" Her voice caught his attention and drew his gaze from the window to her face. His hand dropped to his side.

"Okay? Why?"

"You sighed."

"I'm fine. Sometimes I wonder how long it will take to get used to having my life back. I can eat when I want. I can take a shower when I please. It's more overwhelming than I had expected." He also hadn't planned on telling her all of that. Her soft look and the tenderness in her gaze—even if she looked unsure—that had been the lure, the reason for talking.

"You have your life back. That's a special gift."

"I do, but I don't have what I always planned to have at this stage of my life. I don't have the law degree, or a family of my own. I've never had a steady job."

He had never been in love. He couldn't share that with the timid blonde who stared up at him with a cup of coffee drawn to her lips and hesitation in her blue eyes.

"I think it will get better."

"I'm sure it will." He sat across from her, steadying himself when the gray folding chair started to buckle.

"Are you ready to get started, and to learn about our ministry?"

"I… Of course I am." What should he say now? Did she require an explanation for his reticence? Or would she understand?

"You can be a little more casual from now on. We don't normally dress up for this job."

He hadn't known, so he had worn slacks and a button-up shirt. It had seemed appropriate, even if it wasn't really comfortable.

His gaze settled on her pale blue T-shirt and capris. Her honey-blond hair was in a ponytail and a scarf was tied around her neck. Casual, but totally feminine. His throat felt a little dry. Probably from the day-old doughnuts.

"I wasn't sure about what to wear." He found himself suddenly unsure about quite a few things. "So, what do we do?"

She rested her chin on her hand, elbow propped on the desk. "We work with troubled teens from this neighborhood, and in the community. We mentor them, counsel them—generally step in for absentee parents. We provide after-school programs, summer activities—whatever it takes to keep them busy and off the streets. If they feel connected here, they're less likely to go out there looking for something to connect with."

"I think I can handle that."

"Do you have any questions or concerns?" She fingered one of the manila envelopes on her desk. Slowly her head came up, her gaze connecting with his.

"I can't think of any."

"Michael, you don't have to work here. This isn't required. You could go back to school, or get a job in Springfield." The words shot him down, making him wonder just how much she didn't want him around.

"I have a job. But I want to be here. I want to give back and make up for what I've done."

"You already have. You did your time. Working here isn't about a job or paying back. This is about having a call."

"I know that." Did she think that he didn't have a clue? "I'm here because I feel like God wants me here. I can help reach kids because of what I've been through."

"I didn't mean to sound like I don't want you here. Or like I'm judging you."

"Maggie, I never expected this to happen. It wasn't my goal when I was a kid...to end up addicted to drugs. But it did happen, and I am a different person now."

He brushed a hand through his hair, dismayed that he was the one shaking now.

"I'm sorry. You didn't ask for a lecture or an impromptu counseling session. It isn't really my place." She stood, looking for all the world like she didn't know what to do with him. Finally she continued. "But if you ever do need to talk, Pastor Banks is always available. And if you need a friend, I'm here."

"Thank you. And I don't mind your advice." But maybe he did. He wanted to be treated like he had something to offer this ministry, not like he needed to be ministered to.

"Okay then, it sounds as if we're on the same sheet of music. The kids come first. And we'll do this together, for them."

She paused, as if she meant to say more, but instead she shrugged and walked away. The empty cup in her hand suggested she might be on her way to the kitchen.

His gaze landed on the side of the gray-green desk. Kids had scratched their names in the rubber edging. Next to one name were the words "Jesus Saves." Another had carved, "I Hate My Life."

Funny how two kids in basically the same place could face life with such opposing points of view. He ran his finger over the torn edges of the words. *Jesus Saves... I Hate My Life.*

Chapter Three

Michael went from work to his brother's that evening. He smiled when his older brother opened the door and motioned him into his apartment. Noah was the other oddity in the Carson family. Noah, who had a heart of gold and a career that made their mother cringe. His work for the DEA kept him out of touch, sometimes for months at a time. And sometimes even at home he didn't seem reachable.

Stepping into the small one-bedroom apartment brought another smile to Michael's face. If an apartment could reflect the personality of the person that lived there, Noah's apartment did.

The place was practically bare, with a fold-out couch, a recliner that tilted dangerously to the left and a small card table shoved into the corner of the kitchenette. Thrown into the opposite corner was a collection of tattered, falling-apart suitcases.

"Nice place." Michael wondered if Noah got the same lectures from their mother about living somewhere a little nicer.

"It suits my needs."

"You need a wife." Michael pushed aside a stack of newspapers and sat on the couch.

"That's the last thing I need. What I want is a new case, so I can get back on the road."

"I'm not sure what the romance is between you and your job. You're on the road for months at a time. You live in rundown apartments and eat out of tin cans." Michael had received that information from their mother and from reading between the lines of the letters Noah had sent.

"You know why I do this." Noah shoved his glasses into his pocket and brushed a hand through hair that hung nearly to his shoulders but was usually pulled back in a ponytail. "So what's going on?"

Sometimes Noah was the greatest brother in the world. No, he was always the greatest. But sometimes "the job" took over. It bordered on obsession. Noah couldn't see that maybe Michael just wanted to visit. No, he had to suspect that something was going on.

"Nothing's going on. Life is great. I'm the family felon. My future career choices are limited. Oh, and I'm being followed."

"So, when were you going to tell me about this?"

"I'm here, aren't I?" Michael leaned back and closed his eyes. He wanted life to be simple again. He wanted easy decisions. He wanted to be a kid, deciding which camp to attend or what party—no, not a party—what friends to hang out with.

"Okay, so who do you think it is?" Noah pulled out a chair from the card table and straddled it, his arms resting on the metal frame of the back.

"It's Vince."

"Has he tried to contact you?"

"Not yet, but he will. He isn't going to forget a debt."

"With your help we can bring him in. He stayed out of sight after you got busted. I think he left the state. Since he's been back, he's been smart about moving his operation and using a lot of different people. His operation is a lot bigger than the average meth lab in a garage or shed."

"I know." He searched for the right words. "What I don't know is if I'm strong enough to fight him, or to go against him. I've been clean for four years. But I haven't really been put to the test."

"You have to believe in yourself. And you don't have to fight him. If you get in with him, you can get names, check out who is hanging out with him, and anything else usable."

Silence settled over the room. The dripping kitchen faucet beat out a steady rhythm in the stainless-steel sink and the *tick-tock* of the wind-up alarm clock grew louder with each passing second. Michael got up and walked into the kitchen. He searched the two drawers for tools to fix the sink. He found a hammer and considered smashing the clock. That would fix it.

"Michael, if this is too much, then don't worry about it. They'll get him."

"I want to help, but I don't want to get pulled back in. If I find out who he's using, I will let you know." Michael opened the fridge and pulled out a cola. "If I don't get to the house for dinner, Mom will be calling you to go look for me."

"I'll call you in a few days. We'll get together with the local P.D. and with your parole officer. You need to keep them all in the loop in case he does contact you. No reason to let them believe the wrong thing."

"Sure. Sounds good."

"It'll all work out." Noah's parting words as Michael walked to the door.

Michael turned, sharing a long look with his brother. Did Noah really think that it would all work out? Michael wasn't as sure. He definitely knew that it wouldn't be as easy as saying the words.

"I know it will. I'll be in touch."

"Why do we need to plant flowers?" Chance, always the most questioning of Maggie's teens, glanced over his shoulder to make eye contact with her. "I mean, really, Mrs. Ahrens never even comes outside. And I could be doing something else."

It was Saturday, which was why Maggie had only managed to lasso one kid for the project. She had thought it was such a good idea to plant flowers for an elderly neighbor.

"She looks out her windows, Chance. It would be nice if she had something to look at." Maggie glanced up and saw the curtain on the front window of the house move. "She's watching right now."

Chance looked up and waved. He flashed a brilliant smile, knowing his own charm. If he didn't learn to control that, she'd have serious problems with him and the girls in the group. It was definitely time for another abstinence class.

"So, when is the druggie going to start being a part of the group?"

Maggie sat back on her heels and pulled off her gardening gloves. "Druggie?"

She couldn't have heard him right.

"Yeah, the ex-con dealer."

"Chance, you're going to have to lose your attitude.

I'm not sure why you're here if everything we do is so absurd to you."

He shrugged. "I come for the food?"

"I don't think so."

"Sorry."

"He isn't a 'druggie.' He's a guy who made a mistake."

"Call it what you want." Chance dug another small hole and carefully tipped a flower from the plastic cup that held it. "You know, I really do like planting flowers."

"I won't tell."

Maggie's attention was caught by the red sports car that pulled into the driveway. Michael. She sighed, knowing this wouldn't be easy. Chance and Michael. Oil and water?

"Speak of the—"

She raised a hand to cut the words before Chance could say them. "Don't even say it."

Chance laughed as he patted dirt around the flower and then picked up the water can to give it a good start. Maggie watched for a second and then she stood to greet their visitor.

"Michael."

"Pastor Banks said I would find you here." He glanced in Chance's direction, offering the teen a smile that Chance wasn't keen on accepting. "I was looking for materials on the adult Bible study."

"Oh, I have an extra copy. Or you can get one from Don. He leads the group."

"Good. I tried the bookstores, but they're sold out."

And for this he needed to hunt her down? Maggie wasn't buying it.

"Michael, this is Chance. He's one of our kids." She hoped her smile would be contagious and Chance would give a little.

He did. He stood and held out a slightly dirty hand for Michael to shake. Michael took it in a hearty grip. So, he wasn't afraid of dirt.

"Nice to meet you, Chance."

"Same to you, man." Chance stood a few inches shorter than Michael. His body was gangly, like most teens, and his blond hair needed to be cut. Or at least that was Maggie's unasked-for opinion.

"Do you need help with the flowers?" Michael's attention turned to focus on the box of plants still waiting.

"No, we're fine, and you aren't really dressed for this."

"I don't mind getting dirty."

Chance laughed, but Maggie ignored him. "No need. Really. We're good."

He stood in front of her for several long seconds before he finally nodded. "I understand. Well, I have somewhere I have to be, anyway."

"See you Sunday at church?"

He nodded and walked away. Maggie felt like an idiot. He wanted to help. She could have let him. Instead he backed out of the drive and she let him go.

It didn't bother him. Michael told himself that as he drove away from Galloway, heading south on a paved farm road, toward his place. He didn't need Maggie Simmons's approval. She didn't have to like him. It would help, but it wasn't a requirement.

What bothered him was that she had made it pretty obvious his help wasn't needed. He wondered if she planned on continuing that theme when he did start working with the youth.

The whole world needed for him to prove something to

them. He had to prove he was clean. He had to prove that he could be depended on. Maggie Simmons seemed to *want* more than anyone, and for the life of him he couldn't figure out what it was that she wanted.

One thing he thought he knew for sure. She wanted him out of her life. He couldn't give her that. He had a few things to prove to himself. He could be trusted. He could stay clean.

Maybe it would be better if Maggie reserved some of her determined dislike for him until he had proven those things. He wasn't really the kind of person she needed to rely on, not when he wasn't even sure if he could be relied on.

A few miles from his house he changed his mind about going home. He had seen a motorcycle dealer a mile or so before his place. For a few days he had been thinking about buying one. He hit his turn signal and headed in that direction, the windows down, letting the breeze sweep through the car.

Flashing blue lights disrupted his plans. He glanced in his rearview mirror and groaned. A quick glance down at his speedometer and he realized he hadn't been speeding. As a matter of fact, he was going under the speed limit.

He pulled to the side of the road, hit the hazard lights button and waited. He had his license, registration and insurance card ready. The officer approached, his hand on his gun, looking prepared for anything. Michael rolled down his window.

"Officer."

"Mr. Carson."

Michael waited, knowing he didn't have a prayer if he got upset. He knew the drill and had been prepared for this. That didn't lessen the sting. Fresh out of the pen, of course he would be watched. And any wrong move could land him in trouble.

"Could you step out of the car, please? Keep your hands up so I can see them."

Michael pushed the door open and stepped out, hands up, palms out. He had been here before. The difference this time was that he hadn't done anything wrong. And that did make him mad.

"Could you tell me what I've done?"

"Routine traffic check. You swerved a little back there."

Michael shook his head. "You're going to have to do better than that."

"Turn around, put your hands on the hood of the car."

Michael obeyed, but his insides shook. Anger, some pretty self-righteous indignation and a healthy dose of humiliation were doing battle inside of him, and were ready to roll out in one overwhelming emotion.

He flicked his gaze to his right and watched as the officer did a cursory check through the windows of his car. Looking for drugs was Michael's guess.

"You won't find anything in there."

"And I'm supposed to take your word for that? Sorry, I'm not in the habit of trusting felons." The officer came back. "We're going to do a field sobriety test."

"Fine." Michael turned to face the man, who stood several inches shorter than he did. "I'll do whatever you say. But I'm clean. I've been clean for four years."

"You didn't have a choice."

Michael laughed at that. "Oh, yes, I did. Do you think drugs don't get through the doors of a prison?"

"Straight line, heel to toe."

Michael walked the line.

* * *

The steady thumping sound wasn't familiar. Maggie walked out the back door of the church, trying to figure out what she'd been hearing for the past thirty minutes. For a while she had ignored it, and then she'd thought that maybe Chance had stuck around after they'd finished planting flowers. Now it was starting to grate on her nerves, like the dripping of a leaking faucet.

The red sports car in the parking lot surprised her. Michael Carson. How long had he been here? And why hadn't he come inside? She walked around the corner of the building and spotted him. He wasn't alone. That surprised her more than his presence. Chance was with him.

They were playing racquetball off the retaining wall next to the church. Michael would hit, the muscles in his arms tightening and perspiration soaking the back of his shirt. Chance, not so sure of this sport, would come back, making a solid effort.

They were talking. Maggie couldn't hear them, not from her vantage point. But they seemed to be having a real heart-to-heart. Not wanting to disturb them, she stayed near the building, happy to observe without getting involved. Even if a corner of her heart felt a little envy. Chance wasn't always the most trusting kid. He didn't take easily to people outside his social circle. And he wasn't given to smiles like the one he wore at the moment.

Maybe Chance found it easier to trust than Maggie did. She would like to think so. It would be good if he could connect with a man, someone who could be a role model.

She wasn't quite prepared to put Michael Carson into that position. Not yet. He needed to show them that he could be that person.

"Hey, look who came out to join us." Chance waved his racquet. "I told him you were still here."

Michael nodded. He didn't smile. That had to be because of her earlier dismissal of his offer to help. She crossed the parking lot to where the two now stood, racquets held loosely at their sides. Michael held the ball, bouncing it lightly in his hand. His gaze came up, connected with hers, making her doubt that it had been a good idea to come out here.

Broad daylight and she didn't feel safe. Not that she felt in danger. Not really.

Chance cleared his throat, his eyes narrowed. He shot a look at Michael and then back to her. A casual shrug and he handed the racquet he held to Michael.

"I need to go. I, uh, have homework."

Maggie came out of her daze. "Don't lie, Chance."

"I should have homework," he hedged.

"See you tomorrow." Tomorrow was Sunday, and church. Chance hadn't worked up to that, not yet. She didn't pressure him, just casually asked from time to time.

"Maybe tomorrow." He darted away, and she knew he wouldn't be there.

Michael started to move away. Maggie couldn't let him go, not yet. She had to apologize. He didn't deserve to have her push him away. She could let him work with her without letting him into her life.

She really had to work on that trust issue. Or so Faith kept telling her. She had to trust herself to make the right choices, and trust the people in her life not to let her down.

"I have some cola in the fridge inside, or bottled water. Do you want one?"

He stopped, turning with eyes widened in surprise. He pointed to himself and smiled. "Are you talking to me?"

"I'm talking to you."

He held up the racquets and the ball. "Do you play?"

"No, I don't play." Well, that came out totally wrong. She managed a tight smile. "Racquetball. I don't play racquetball."

"That's what I thought we were talking about." He laughed, the sound sort of carefree and delicious, better than coffee with cream.

And just the fact that she had that thought meant that Faith had been a very bad influence on her.

"It's nice out here." She nodded toward the picnic table under the shade of a huge oak tree. "We could sit in the shade."

Not inside, confined in her office. She glanced toward the parking lot where her car was parked and so was his. People could drive by and get the wrong idea.

Michael nodded his understanding. "Not ready to face what people will think if it gets around that we were here together?"

Forget the delicious coffee-and-cream laugh. "That isn't it at all. I don't want to give people room to speculate."

"Ah, speculation. Yeah, I know what you mean. People do like to assume the worst."

The way his eyes shifted away from her, she thought that there was more to that comment, something he didn't feel like sharing. Probably the same something that had brought him back here with a racquet.

Speculation. Now she was doing it. Maybe he liked racquetball and didn't want to go to the club to play. "I'll get the colas and meet you back here."

When she walked out of the church carrying a couple cans of soda, he was sitting on top of the picnic table. His long legs, clad in shorts, were stretched out in front of him. She felt a moment of envy, seeing his tan, and guessing that it came easily for him.

He smiled, an easy smile that lifted one side of his mouth and flashed straight white teeth.

"I'm afraid we only have diet." She handed him a can and he took it.

"It'll work."

Maggie stood in front of the bench, not really sure what her next move should be. Her indecision caught his attention and he patted the spot next to him. That left her in a predicament. Sit next to him, or look further jerky and emotionally unstable.

She sat next to him on top of the table. At least she could drink the soda and not concentrate on finding a topic of conversation they would both be comfortable with.

"I like it here in Galloway. It's quiet and sometimes I forget that Springfield is just a traffic light away." Michael ended the silence. "And I really like living outside of town."

"I've always lived here."

"Really? Do you have your own place or do you live with your parents?"

"I live with my grandmother." And she didn't want him to ask more than that. She knew he would. A quick glance in his direction and she saw the questions forming. "My mother passed away when I was in my early teens."

"I see." But the tone, soft and a little distant, said that he didn't see. "And your dad?"

She never had an answer for that question. Her dad, not in the real sense of the word, didn't exist. He didn't exist, had never wanted to be a part of her life, but yet he did inhabit her mind a lot. She thought of him, wondered about him and sometimes resented him.

"Maggie?"

"Sorry, I got lost in thought. No, I don't have a dad." She hated the word illegitimate, so she wouldn't use it. It made it sound like her life didn't count. And her life did count.

"I'm sorry, I shouldn't have pushed you to talk." He leaned back, looking up at the tree that spread like a leafy green umbrella over top of them. "I wanted to talk about something other than myself."

"That's understandable. What happened?"

He sat up, his eyes making direct contact with hers. He hadn't expected that question. She could see it in the widening of his eyes, that she'd taken him by surprise.

"What do you mean?"

She shrugged. "You left earlier, but now you're back, and I think that racquetball game was more than an exercise routine. It looked a lot like a guy trying to clear his mind by pounding the tar out of a poor defenseless ball."

He smiled and glanced sideways at her.

"I got pulled over." He brushed a hand through his hair. "The cop did it to mess with me. He checked my car, made me take a sobriety test. And then he let me go with the casual warning that he'd be seeing me around."

"Nice." Maggie sat for a minute, sipping on the diet soda and trying to decide what else needed to be said.

"I never expected it to be easy." Michael sighed. "But I didn't expect it to be this difficult. I know that I have to prove myself, but I'm not sure if I can ever measure up to what everyone seems to be expecting."

"I'm sorry if I've been one of the people pushing you to measure up. That isn't what I intended."

"Really?" He hopped down from the table. "So what did you intend to do?"

Maggie shook her head. "I don't know, Michael. I don't think I planned on making you feel anything. If it makes you feel better, this is more about me than you."

"Because you don't want me here, in your life and in your ministry?"

"Not for the reasons you think." She gave him that, knowing he needed some kind of explanation. The reasons were too varied to go into detail. She didn't trust herself to be a good judge of character. She felt territorial and protective of her kids. And she didn't want to be let down. Multiple choice, with no wrong answers.

"Are you going to share the reasons?"

"No, I'm not." She stepped down from the table and stood a short distance from him. "I think it's enough that you know that I'm really trying. And I want you to succeed."

"That's something, I guess." He tossed his soda can into a nearby recycling bin. "See you tomorrow, Maggie."

She watched him walk away wondering if she could have said more. Of course she could have, she just didn't know what it would have been.

Chapter Four

Michael left church on Sunday afternoon without being caught by any well-meaning parishioners or Maggie. He needed to get away, to escape the prying eyes that watched with open curiosity. And after the way their conversation had ended yesterday, he didn't want to talk to Maggie.

What he didn't need was company. The car parked in his driveway came as a surprise and a letdown. He felt his insides tighten at the thought of company, another person wanting to see how he was doing.

The door of the convertible opened and a man stepped out. Michael pulled up next to the car, finding a smile for Jimmy Grey, a longtime friend, and someone he hadn't seen in four long years. Jimmy had been one of the few friends who had written letters.

"About time you got home." Jimmy flashed his big smile. His curly blond hair was cut short, keeping the curls in control to some degree.

"I was at church."

"Oh, yes, the newly reformed Michael Carson. I like it."

Jimmy's hand extended. "It looks good on you, man. I guess a little religion never hurt anyone."

"It sure wouldn't hurt you." Michael moved back and leaned against the side of Jimmy's convertible.

"No, it wouldn't hurt. So, tell me, how are you and were you ever going to call me?"

Michael fished his keys out of his pocket. "Let's go inside. I'm starving, and I could use a cup of coffee."

"You're actually living here?" Jimmy nodded toward the sixty-foot-long, single-wide mobile home with its small front porch and metal siding.

"I like it. I might see if the church will sell it to me. I wouldn't mind building a house out here someday."

"Funny, ten years ago I wouldn't have seen us here with me as the good one."

Michael laughed, knowing that Jimmy didn't mean anything by that. If anything, he agreed. Jimmy had always been the rebellious one. Michael, unfortunately, had been the one who'd made the wrong choice. No excuses. He'd messed up. He'd paid. He didn't have anyone to blame but himself.

"I'm glad you came out, even if you weren't invited." Michael unlocked the front door and motioned Jimmy inside.

"Good grief, is that a rat?" Jimmy stepped to the side in time for Michael to see the mouse run under the couch.

"Just a mouse, but he's pretty good company. He doesn't eat much, he never talks and he doesn't hog the bathroom."

Jimmy glanced back, shaking his head. "You're a strange dude. So, have you seen Katherine?"

It had to come up. "No, and I don't plan on seeing her. That part of my life is in the past. We were never in love. We were just cohorts, hiding our drug use from our parents. I can't let myself get pulled back into that codependency."

"I guess that's probably true. And she is seriously in trouble. She's down to about a hundred pounds. Her parents are finally starting to get that she has a problem."

"My mom still thinks she's just thin, and I should give her a call."

"I'm not sure if you should."

Michael nodded as he pulled lunch meat and cheese out of the fridge. "Do you want mayo or mustard?"

"Neither. Do you have a tomato in there?"

"Do you think this is a restaurant?"

They were sitting on the back deck eating their sandwiches when Michael worked up the courage to do what he had been putting off. He could have said it in a letter. That didn't seem right.

"Jimmy, I need to apologize to you."

Jimmy dropped his feet from the railing to the floor of the deck and tossed the last corner of his bread into the yard. "Why do you think you need to apologize to me?"

"It's time for me to make amends to the people I hurt. When we were roommates in college, I stole quite a bit of money from you. Dad had cut me off. I needed a fix, and I didn't care who I had to hurt to get it."

"Shoot, Michael, I knew you did that. I forgave you a long time ago."

"Yes, but I need to apologize, because I need to start forgiving myself. I probably owe you about five hundred dollars."

"Forget it."

"No." Michael stood and leaned against the deck so that he could face his friend. "I have to do this. Tomorrow I'm going to get the cash and bring it to you."

"If it'll make you feel better, why don't you put the

money in the offering plate? I don't need it and I don't want it. Don't soothe your conscience by doing something that I don't want you to do. I'm not mad, and I'll only be mad if you try to pay me back."

"I have to do this."

"You have to make amends? Yeah, okay, so make amends. Is that why you're working at the church? Are you making amends to God, too?"

"No, that's something else. I know that people are going to think that, but it isn't about making amends. I really feel like this is something I'm supposed to do."

Jimmy stood, patted Michael on the back and headed for the door. "I'm glad to hear that. I don't want to think you're brainwashed."

"It's church, Jim, not a cult."

"Yeah, yeah, I know. But you know church has never been my thing."

"I know it hasn't. But if it hadn't been for God, I wouldn't have survived the last four years. I probably wouldn't have survived the four years before that, either."

"Probably not." Jimmy stopped in the center of the kitchen, looking distinctly uncomfortable with the "God" talk. "I need to go. Dad needs some help with things around the house."

"How's he doing?"

"Fine. The Alzheimer's is in the early stages, so he's still Dad. I know that will change in the next few years."

"Jimmy, if you need anything, I'm here."

He smiled. "You know, Mike, it's good to hear that. I've missed you. Not just for the last four years, but before that. You were gone for a long time."

Eight years of his life, gone. Four years to meth and

four to prison. But it wasn't just about the lost years. It was more about lost friendships, lost experiences and lost trust. He couldn't get back what was lost, including those eight years, but he could definitely make the next eight years count.

Or he could mess up. Maybe being aware of that fact would help him to be stronger.

May fifteenth. Only two more weeks of school. Maggie relished the thought, knowing it meant no more homework for the kids or for her. Algebra was *so* not her thing. Which explained why she had escaped for a few minutes of fresh air while the kids played darts or went out back for a game of basketball.

She absently rubbed the soft ears of the black Labrador sitting next to her. The animal looked up with sad brown eyes. He belonged to one of the neighbors, but he liked the attention and the leftovers the kids gave him.

A flash of red pulled her attention away from the dog and to the intersection a block away. Michael Carson. She hadn't expected him today. He had stopped by a couple of times a week, slowly introducing himself to the kids and getting to know the routine. He had been distant, sharing little of his new life with her. But on Sunday night the elders had given him permission to become a real part of the team.

Michael stepped out of the car and waved. His boyish grin flashed brightly on his tanned face. Maggie's gaze traveled down, taking in the T-shirt that stretched across athletic shoulders and the faded jeans that looked worn and comfortable. She pulled on a cloak of detachment that would make it easier to deal with him. The dog pushed against her leg, snarling softly at the new arrival.

"Are you out here waiting for me?" He held his hand out to the dog, who sniffed and then licked, having decided the stranger could be a friend.

Stupid mutt. Who said dogs were a good judge of character?

"No, I wasn't waiting, just getting fresh air. I hadn't really expected you today."

"Yes, well, I had to leave work early, so I thought I might as well swing by here."

"Had to leave work early?" She grimaced as the question came out. "Sorry, none of my business."

The lines of his mouth tightened into what wasn't exactly the carefree smile she had noticed when he'd first stepped out of the car. He sat next to her on the steps. The dog switched sides and nudged into his arm.

"You know, my life is a continuous learning experience, with a lot of lovely surprises thrown in along the way."

"Really."

He stroked the dog's head and in turn the animal licked his hand. "You don't really want to hear this, do you?"

"I do, but I don't know how much you want to share."

"Thanks, because this isn't something that my parents want to hear. They would like to think that everything is perfect."

"That's understandable."

"I got called in for a random drug test by my probation officer." He looked up, his eyes connecting with hers, seeking something. Understanding maybe? Or compassion? She breathed in, not sure which response to give.

"Is that standard?"

"Or do they suspect me of something?" He shook his head. "I'm sorry, it isn't your fault. Yes, it is standard.

Somehow I pushed it to the back of my mind. But today it happened."

"How did it go?" She covered her face with her hands. "I'm sorry, but I can't seem to ask the right question or give the correct response for this."

"Join the crowd. This isn't exactly something I planned for my life. And I doubt that you thought you'd be thrown into the role of supporting someone who is going through this."

"So, we'll get through it together." The words slipped out and once again she knew she'd said the wrong thing. But this time for a different reason. She couldn't be the one getting him through this. She had already tried that. She had been the supporting one, trying to help her mother.

"Don't worry, I won't hold you to that. But I appreciate you listening to me." He stood and reached for her hand to pull her to her feet. "And in case you're wondering and you're too polite to ask—I'm clean."

"I know that."

"So, let's go tell the kids the truth about my life."

She stood and turned to walk up the stairs. On the last step she stopped and waited for him to join her. He hadn't moved. "Are you ready for this?"

"I'm ready."

The shuttered look that fell over his expression closed her out. That was fine. She didn't mind being closed out. It meant she didn't have to get involved. Of course, it felt as though she was already pretty involved.

"If you're sure."

"Of course I'm sure. Just a moment of doubt."

"We all have those."

"You're right." He took the steps two at a time and

passed her. When he reached the door he opened it, motioning for her to enter first. "After you."

End of conversation, just like that. Maggie let it go. She had a group of kids waiting for her. They were her ministry—not Michael.

The kids were behind the church playing basketball. Michael followed Maggie out the back door. As they stepped outside, she turned, offering him a smile that she probably meant to be encouraging. He didn't feel encouraged. He had dropped by to visit the kids from time to time; he and Chance had connected, but this time it felt different. This was a step forward. This meant really immersing himself in this ministry.

It also meant that he now had to be up front with the kids. They needed to know the truth, the whole truth, before they heard rumors and invented their own stories about his life.

"Hey, guys, let's all sit down on the picnic tables." Maggie's voice grabbed the attention of the kids. The ball dropped to the court, to be picked up by Chance. The huddle of kids climbed on the tables, watching expectantly.

They were looking at him.

Maggie reached behind her, grabbing his hand to pull him forward. "Michael Carson is going to start joining us on a regular basis next week. He'll be here at least three afternoons a week, and he'll help us on different weekend activities."

The enormity of his commitment hit home. Doubts whirled around inside him, calling him a fraud and making him question if he had the ability. What if he let them all down?

"Hi, guys." He stepped forward. Maggie's hand dropped

from his arm. He hadn't realized until it was no longer there how much that touch had meant to him. "I guess I've met most of you, so today isn't as much about introductions as it is about getting real."

Maggie moved from his side. She took a seat at the picnic table, next to one of the girls, and nodded for him to continue. His gaze remained locked with hers.

"Most of you probably know that I've been in prison for the past four years." He grinned and Maggie responded with a smile that settled in her blue eyes. "I guess I can start by saying that I'm an addict. I'm also a Christian. I've been clean for four years, and I plan to stay that way."

The kids remained quiet. There were nine of them today. They were an odd assortment. One girl looked to be fourteen. She had wire-framed glasses and a soft expression. Timid. But she looked happy. Another girl had dyed her hair black, and her gaze seemed to dare him. The boys—most were sweaty teens who wanted to play basketball and chase girls. One boy looked wary and angry with the world.

They wore expressions that ranged from contented to hopeless to lost and angry. From *Jesus Saves* to *I Hate My Life,* like the carvings on the desk in Maggie's office.

He understood those feelings. He had gone from one extreme to the other. Maggie's encouraging smile brought him back to the present. He smiled down at her, ignoring the array of questions flashing through her eyes.

"If any of you have questions, I'm willing to give you the answers that I can. If I can't answer, I'll tell you why. If you don't have questions today, then maybe tomorrow. Or next week. But I'm always here if you need to talk, if you need anything."

Always here. He realized the importance of those

words. Other people were counting on him. Maggie. She was counting on him, too.

The boy with the lost look shook his head. Michael waited, wondering what he would say, if he would say anything.

"Whatever, man," the kid whispered. He glared at the table, his jaw muscles clenching.

"Whatever?" Michael took a step forward, stopping when he saw the worried look on Maggie's face. "What does that mean?"

"It means that adults always say they're going to 'be there for you.' But most of them aren't."

"I'm sorry." Michael was. He was more sorry than he could say that this kid felt that people weren't there for him. What had happened to create cynicism in someone so young, with so much life ahead of him? "I can't help what other people have done. But I can tell you that I'm going to be here. And I think that you already know that Maggie is here. She's always here."

The kid glanced in Maggie's direction. He sort of smiled. "Yeah, she's here."

Michael didn't know what that meant, but it frightened him for Maggie's sake.

The last kid left at six o'clock. Maggie did a final check of the building and walked back to the kitchen where Michael waited for her. She held up her keys.

"Are you ready to go?"

"More than ready. That was more exhausting than I ever imagined. And those guys can really play ball."

"You'll get used to it. And don't forget about Friday night."

"Friday night?" The puzzled look told her he'd already forgotten.

"Bowling. We try to have a regular activity at least twice a month on Fridays. This Friday is bowling, and I thought you might like to go. Look, if you have something else to do…"

"No, I'll be here."

She shrugged and he followed her out the back door. His cell phone rang as she was locking up. As hard as she tried to ignore him, his conversation carried.

"I don't think I can see you. But if you need help, I'm here." He looked away, his brow furrowing. "No, I don't think so. Katherine, it isn't too late."

Maggie walked on to her car.

"Wait." Michael jogged up to her as she was digging through her purse, looking for her keys. "Sorry, I had to take that call. It was an old friend. One that I can't help."

"You don't have to explain to me."

"I wasn't explaining, I was just talking. I grew up with Katherine. Now she's in a place where I don't know how to help her." He looked away, but when he turned, his smile was back in place. "Are you going home, or do you want to grab something to eat?"

"I'm going home. I have to help my grandmother with the yard."

"I see. Yes, I guess I should head home, too. I keep forgetting that I have a lawn to mow."

"See you Friday, then." She reached for her door handle, but his hand shot out, circling her wrist. When she glanced over her shoulder, his hand dropped to his side. "What?"

"Maggie, the boy with the glasses, the one who doesn't think he can count on anyone. Be careful of him, okay?"

"What?"

"Be careful. I don't know, maybe I'm just being overly cautious."

"You are. And don't worry, I am careful." She opened the door and slid behind the wheel. "Friday, Michael. Don't forget."

He was still standing in the parking lot when she pulled onto the street. His cell phone was to his ear. She couldn't help but wonder who he was talking to and if he was falling back into old habits.

"Vince called again." Michael opened the front door for his brother. It was Thursday and he'd just had his second meeting with his probation officer. That should have been enough stress for one day. If only that could be the end of it. "I'm not sure if I can take this."

"You have to decide." Noah pulled off his black-framed glasses and slipped them into the collar of his shirt. "Nobody is going to force you. If you want to call Officer Conway and talk to him, do. If you don't, then hang up when Vince calls. Get your number switched to unlisted."

All good points. Michael tossed a crumb of bread into the corner of the room and avoided Noah's questioning look. "It's for the mouse."

"I don't think I want to hear this."

"Probably not."

"Why don't you get a dog? Normal people have dogs."

"The mouse doesn't eat as much."

Noah walked to the kitchen and poured himself a glass of tea. "Michael, make a decision."

"I have an NA meeting tonight." Michael had survived the kids. Narcotics Anonymous, his first meeting, sounded simple after a dozen or so teenagers.

"Michael, you can't discuss this at NA."

"I know that." He brushed a hand across his face. When

he looked up, Noah was at the door. He never stayed for long. "I think I can do it. The next time Vince calls, I'll talk to him. He says I owe him money. He's trying to use that on me."

"So let him. Use it as a way to get in. As an informant, the police want one thing from you. They want names. You're the only one who can decide what you want to do about this."

"What I want to do?" He sat in the sideways-tilting recliner. "I want to move past this. I want for this to not be my life."

For a minute Noah's expression softened. "I know. Remember, someday this will be the past. Right now you have to concentrate on what has to be done. Get it over with so that you can move on. Make the move into Vince's life, Michael."

Noah made it sound so easy, like something that people did on a daily basis. But who really went out of their way to make a deal with the devil?

Chapter Five

Michael pulled over when Vince drove up behind him a few hours later. The call that Noah had suggested he make had been made. There would be no turning back. He parked in a well-lit parking lot, not wanting this first meeting, one that he wasn't really sure about, to be in a dark alley somewhere.

He let Vince approach him. In his rearview mirror Michael watched as the man he once considered a friend stepped out of his Corvette. Four years had aged Vince. He was thin, his skin was sallow and he looked ten years older than he should have.

A person couldn't put drain cleaner in their body without doing serious damage.

"Michael Carson, long time no see." Vince leaned in the window. "How's church life?"

"Fine, it's working for me."

"Is it, Mike, or are you just making a good show of recovery?"

Michael stared straight ahead, finding the answer that he needed. "Draw your own conclusions, Vince."

Vince laughed. "You were always a hard one to figure. I'm not sure yet if I even want to talk to you. But I do know one thing. You owe me."

"That's your opinion." Michael reached to turn off the radio. "I have to go."

"See you soon?" Vince put a hand on Michael's shoulder. "You know, Mike, I don't like to play games. If I find out that you're playin' me, you'll be sorry."

"I'm not playin' you, Vince. I'm trying to stay out of jail." He moved his shoulder, shaking Vince's hand free. "I might see you around."

Vince stepped back from the car and Michael pulled away. His heart raced in his chest, needing a way out. He needed a way out. This time, though, he wasn't alone. If God was for him, who could be against him?

He had something else to keep him moving forward. He had Maggie and the kids at church. For the first time in a long time he felt needed, and like he could be of use to someone.

Michael's first outing with the kids, and Maggie almost felt sorry for him. She had watched him climb into the driver's seat of the van full of teens, looking slightly on edge. Were the tight lines around his mouth due to the kids or had something else happened? Probably the kids. They could be an overwhelming bunch. Especially when ten of them showed up, like tonight.

Ten teenagers, two adults and one twelve-passenger van, on their way to the bowling alley. Maggie wondered if this would fit her grandmother's idea of a promising date.

She glanced sideways at Michael, who had insisted on driving. His concentration was on the road, but from time to time he glanced into the rearview mirror to check on the kids. From beneath half-closed eyes she studied his profile, strong with a generous mouth that smiled often, and hazel eyes flecked with green. Even though she couldn't see his eyes, she knew the color. His steady gaze often connected with hers, startling her with the intensity of his attention.

He glanced her way and caught her staring.

"Something on my face?" He grinned and then flicked his attention back to the road.

"No." She forced a smile. "I'm sorry, I didn't mean to stare." And she couldn't finish, because she wouldn't lie. The truth would have sounded ridiculous. *I'm staring at you because you're so stinking gorgeous you don't look real.* Or maybe, *It scares me to be here in the dark with you and I'm glad we have ten teenagers to keep us honest.*

Both thoughts were so out of character that she quickly pushed them aside. These were "Faith" thoughts. Faith was the quirky one. Maggie had always been pegged as the serious one. Her entire life she had been the kid the teachers labeled as "shy" and often keeping to herself. Her mother would read the notes on the back of the grade card and ask her why she didn't play with the other kids.

The list had been long. She felt silly in her yard-sale clothing, the other kids teased her for being shy and they asked why she didn't have a dad.

Faith hadn't come along until later in her life to drag her out of her shell. And Maggie had been there for Faith when she'd struggled with cancer treatments.

"I should probably warn you that I've never been bowling." He slowed to make the turn into the parking lot of the bowling alley.

"You've never bowled?" Now he tells her.

"Don't act so surprised, millions of people haven't. It

wasn't on my mother's list of lessons we took." He shot her a grin and winked. "But I can speak two languages and waltz…if that would help."

"Probably not. Don't worry, we can teach you to bowl."

"That's what I was afraid of." He continued to smile as he pulled into a parking place. "Is there any way that I could claim a wrist injury and get out of this?"

"No way at all." Turning to face the kids in the back of the van, Maggie aimed a warning look in their direction. "Okay, guys, remember the rules. Chance, rule number one?"

Chance sighed, playing the part of the injured teen.

"Don't leave the group without permission."

Maggie nodded her head and then focused on another boy. "Brad, rule number two?"

"Show respect to the other bowlers. No bad words, no fighting."

"I think you covered rules two and three." Maggie smiled at all of the kids. "Rule number four—have fun."

In unison they groaned, as if being told to have fun was the worst rule of all.

Inside the darkened interior of the bowling alley a rush of activity surrounded them. First, everyone had to get shoes and then find the right bowling ball. Maggie scurried from one teen to another, trying to get them all taken care of.

When she finally had a free moment, she turned to look for Michael. He stood off to the side, looking like a lost child at the mall. She wanted to ignore him, but she couldn't.

"Did you get shoes?"

He shook his head, the lost-child look again. His long lashes framed his hazel eyes and a shy, out-of-place smile lurked on the firm lines of his mouth. Maggie hooked her arm

through his, a gesture that should have been one of camaraderie, but when he pulled her close it changed. She pulled
away and led him to the counter where shoes could be rented.

"What size do you wear?"

"Eleven, I guess."

She narrowed her eyes as she looked down at his feet.
"You don't know what size shoe you wear?"

"I know what size shoe I wear, but I don't know about
bowling shoes."

The man behind the counter handed Michael a pair of
boat-size shoes. He stared at the red, blue and tan shoes like
they were a contagious disease.

"They won't bite."

"I'm not sure about that."

Maggie propelled him toward the benches behind
their lanes.

Michael pulled off his tennis shoes and slipped his feet
into the bowling shoes, making only a slight frown.

"You've really never bowled?" She tied the laces of her
shoes and then straightened in the chair.

"Not once that I can remember, but I'm sure I'll be fine.
How hard can it be? Roll the ball down the lane and watch
it knock down the pins."

Maggie stood and he followed. "Oh, of course. You
make it sound so simple. How hard can it be?"

For Michael it wasn't too difficult. Maggie watched as
he hit his second strike and then she went in search of a
snack. When she returned he was sitting on a bench waiting
for her. He inclined his head to the seat next to his.

Maggie handed him the soda she'd bought for him and
sat. She held out a bag of chips as she watched Chance
prepare to stomp the competition.

"Are you surviving?" She swallowed a bite of chips that had far too much sour cream and onion flavoring.

"Yes, I'm surviving." He nodded toward Chance. "That kid has something special. He has a lot of anger, but he also has potential."

"A lot of these kids have potential, Michael. The problem is, nobody expects that from them and they don't expect it from themselves."

"You really take this personally, don't you?"

She didn't know how to answer that. She did take it personally, not only because she cared, but because she had been one of these kids, the ones that were pushed aside and unwanted. She had been the dirty, hungry kid in second-hand clothing. If it hadn't been for her grandmother, and a Sunday school teacher named Irene, she might not have survived.

For Michael she formed an easy answer. "Yes, I take it personally."

His eyes narrowed. He had more questions. "You're doing a great job with them."

"We try. If we can teach these kids to respect themselves, to believe in who they are and in whom God created them to be, we might change the entire course of their lives."

He stared at her as if she had four eyes.

"Is that too optimistic?"

"No, not at all. I just wonder if the kids realize how lucky they are to have someone like you believing in them."

"We all need someone to believe in us, Michael. God always believes, but that isn't easy for a kid to grasp. Sometimes it just takes the belief of one person to make the difference."

"Do you believe…" He looked away, shaking his head but not finishing.

"Believe what?"

He laughed. "It sounds ridiculous for a grown man to say this."

"I've heard ridiculous before."

"Do you believe in *me?*" His gaze flitted away from hers, breaking the connection between them.

Maggie's heart paused, as if it, too, wanted to hear her answer. It had to take a leap of trust, one she hadn't taken in a long time. She trusted her grandmother. She trusted Faith and Pastor Banks. She could count dozens of people she trusted. But did she trust Michael?

She wanted to. She wanted to believe he wouldn't let them down. He wouldn't hurt her.

"You're really having to think about this, aren't you?" His eyes reflected pain, but he smiled.

"I want to believe in you."

"You're painfully honest, Maggie. I like that about you."

He stood and walked away, leaving her to deal with her painfully honest self. Yes, she believed in him. That didn't mean she had false expectations. She had believed in people before.

Michael glanced at his watch again. Only five minutes past nine. He hit the left turn signal and slowed the van to make the turn into the church parking lot. In the seat next to him Maggie laughed. After the conversation at the bowling alley, she had withdrawn. The laughter meant she was back with him. He shot her a look that asked for an explanation.

"You've looked at that watch every two minutes for the last twenty minutes." She reached out to pat his arm. "I hope we haven't kept you from something."

"My mom is hosting a fund-raiser. She expects me to be there."

"You don't want to go?"

"I'm not exactly the poster child of social acceptance at the moment. I'll go, people will stare, politely whisper behind their hands about where I've been and how embarrassed my parents are, and a few of them will ask me how I'm doing or if I have plans for the future."

"It sounds horrible." She cringed and shot him a sideways look that he caught in the dim interior of the van. "I'm sorry. I should have come up with something more optimistic."

"I'd rather hear that than platitudes about how it is all going to work out."

"But it is going…" She smiled. "Sorry again. But next time you have something going on, let me know. I could have dragged Faith along tonight, and you could have gone to the fund-raiser."

"I wanted to go with you tonight." He parked the van and cut the engine. "I'm not here just to kill some time. I want to be a part of this ministry."

The back door of the van opened and the kids piled out, leaving them alone. He wondered about their actions, which seemed suspicious.

Did teenagers play at matchmaking?

He turned to face Maggie and caught her watching him, an intent look in eyes that sparkled like sapphires in the dim light of the van. Her lips parted slightly, as though she meant to say something. But for some reason that gesture drew him to her. Mesmerized, he leaned, his breath catching in his lungs at the thought of Maggie in his arms.

The wary look that crossed her features stopped him.

For a second it looked like panic. He leaned back into his seat, letting the moment pass. That was the smartest move. Neither of them needed strings. At least he didn't. He needed to get his life together, and to find out where he was going.

And better this way than to find out the moment was his, not hers. Maybe she hadn't felt it.

"I'm sorry." In the dim glow of the streetlight he saw her confusion. "I shouldn't push my way into your life." He tried to explain, reaching to tug at the tendril of hair that had fallen loose from her ponytail. The silky strand slipped through his fingers and what he meant as a playful gesture became something stronger and more intimate.

"I need to go." She reached for the door handle. "Thank you for helping tonight. We couldn't have done this without you."

"Maggie, wait."

She shook her head. "No, Michael. It isn't you. It's me."

With that, she slipped out of the van, leaving him alone to ponder what he had learned about himself and about Maggie. The panic in her eyes said it all, and yet he felt like it created more questions.

Maggie sat behind her desk for thirty minutes, contemplating what had happened in the van. In her limited experience, that had definitely been a "moment." And she didn't need that, not now, and not with Michael. She was focused on the youth group, which didn't leave room for "moments." Michael obviously had his own issues to deal with.

She called Faith, doodling on paper as she waited for her friend to answer.

"Hey," Faith answered, sounding distracted.

"Hey, to you, too. What are you doing?"

"Writing."

"Oh."

"Sweetie, what's the matter?"

Maggie threw a wadded-up piece of paper at the trash can. That didn't help. She wadded up another and tossed it harder, the force making it bounce off the side of the can. "I'm such an idiot."

"What does that mean?"

She opened the drawer of her desk and pulled out the giant-size Reese's that she'd bought the day before. "I'm an idiot because I'm going to believe in this guy and then he's going to walk away."

"He'd better not hurt you." Faith, always ready to fight when a fight wasn't needed.

"That isn't what I mean. I mean, I'm going to end up letting him into my life and then he's going to leave. He'll get tired of working here with the kids. Or he'll get tired of this life and realize there are other things he can do. This really isn't his world. I think he's just a temporary visitor." She contemplated the peanut-butter cup and how good it would taste before she shoved it back in the drawer. "And he might fall back into his old habits."

Her biggest fear.

She couldn't admit to Faith that she had been tempted, just for a moment, to let him invade her personal space. How long had it been since that had happened?

"Maybe you should see him as a man and not a project. Remember, projects are my hobby. He isn't one of your kids. He probably isn't looking for a glass of milk and chocolate-chip cookies."

She rubbed a hand over her eyes. "I've already made that mistake once, or maybe twice, trying to change someone who didn't really want to be changed."

"Maggie, he isn't your mom. And he isn't Greg."

"Well, I'm not going to be the victim again."

"There you go, that's my friend Maggie talking. You're strong, you're a hero to so many people. Look at the lives you've changed at church with your milk and cookies."

Maggie laughed and the tightness around her heart eased. "Aren't you the encouraging optimist?"

"No, I'm very jaded. That's why we're such good friends. I see black and white. You see lovely shades of rose. And I love you for that. I love that you believe in all those kids. I'm not so sure that I love that you're starting to see Michael Carson as one of them. He isn't."

No, Michael definitely wasn't one of the kids. Maggie started to tell Faith how very aware of that fact she was, but she didn't. She could expect the best for her kids, they were easy. She saw possibilities for a better future in each one of them. Michael only raised questions.

"Why don't you come over for coffee and we'll do some nice, safe online shopping?"

Maggie nodded, but something outside the window caught her attention. She froze as a shiver of fear slid up her spine and lingered in her scalp.

"Maggie?"

She couldn't answer, not when a shadow flitted across the window. Instead she gasped and slid beneath her desk.

"Maggie?"

"There's someone out there."

"I'm calling the police. I'll use my cell phone and you stay on this line with me."

"No, I don't want the police. What if it's a neighbor looking for a cat?"

"Maggie, respectfully shut up."

Not a problem. Besides that, she was shaking too hard to argue. Someone was out there. She could hear them at the window, shoving against the screen. With the phone held to her ear she reached around on the top of her desk for her purse, and her mace. Faith was there, talking to the police, and then saying reassuring things about help being on the way.

And then she heard the sirens.

Chapter Six

Michael answered his cell phone, easing away from the crowd with an apologetic look for his mother. She sighed and whispered something to the woman at her side about his "church work."

"Noah?" Why would Noah be calling?

"There's a problem at the church."

Michael threaded his way through the crowded art museum and walked out of the building. "What's up?"

"A prowler call. I had my scanner on and I thought you'd want to know."

"I'm at the gallery, and I left Maggie at the church. I should have made sure she left or got home safe." He closed his eyes. "Do you think it's Vince?"

"I don't think he would do that. The police are on the scene now."

Michael rubbed the back of his neck, wishing the gesture would be a magic cure for stress. It didn't help. He kept picturing Maggie at the church, afraid. And that thought got replaced by the look of panic in her eyes when she'd hurried from the van.

"Michael, do you want me to drive down there and check on her? I think they were going to escort her home, but I can make a few calls."

"If I leave…" But then, how could he stay?

"Mom forgave you for skipping out on her dinner party the other night. This time she won't go easy on you."

"She'll get over it. Make calls, see if she's okay. Get a message to her that I'm going to be there in five minutes."

"It isn't too late to call this whole thing off."

"Yes, it is." He had committed to getting information on Vince. He was already in the game and he couldn't back out now. He also wouldn't let Maggie be hurt.

His mom took the announcement that he was leaving as well as he thought she would. Her eyes reflected hurt and her pursed lips meant that he would hear about it later. He kissed her cheek and told her he loved her. That softened her a little.

"I love you, too. I just worry. Michael, I don't want you to do anything that will get you hurt again."

"Mom, I'm not going to get hurt. I have to check on a friend. On Maggie."

"Maggie, the girl from church?"

"Yes, Maggie."

He hurried from the gallery, glad that nobody tried to detain him to talk. And then he had to drive the speed limit to Galloway, for fear of being pulled over again. He couldn't risk that.

When he pulled up to the church, the police were still there. Maggie was sitting on the front steps. Faith was with her. He hadn't been needed after all.

More often than not, Maggie let him know that his presence wasn't even wanted. They had settled into an uneasy truce that sometimes felt like friendship.

She looked up when he approached. Her eyes were luminous, but there were no tears. Of course there weren't. She looked like she didn't need anyone, not him or Faith. Not surprisingly, Pastor Banks was at the corner of the building, talking to the police. He lived in the house next to the church, he would have seen the lights.

"Michael, what are you doing here?" Maggie didn't seem at all like a damsel in distress who needed his rescuing.

"My brother called. He heard the address on the scanner and thought I'd want to know." And he wanted to be someone who could be counted on. He didn't know if he needed to prove that to her or to himself.

"You didn't have to come over. We're fine."

"I can see that."

Faith stood, casting a look at him before leaning to kiss Maggie on the top of the head. "I'm going now. Looks as if the big, strong man is here to take care of you."

"I don't need a big, strong man to take care of me. I can take care of myself." Maggie smiled though, at Faith, not at him.

"Of course you can." Faith shook her head and then gave Michael a conspiratorial wink. "Make sure she gets home okay."

Michael nodded at Faith, and then he tensed. What now? What did he say when his presence wasn't wanted. And worse than that, when his presence was probably the reason for the entire situation?

"I'm going to talk to the police." He started to walk off.

"Michael, would you ask them if I can leave? Gran is going to be worried."

"I'll ask."

The officer that he approached recognized him, but not

in a way that looked welcoming. "Michael Carson, I didn't expect to see you here."

"This has something to do with me, I just don't know what."

Officer Wayne nodded. "Gotcha, we'll keep that in mind. But now I'm going to have to ask you to leave. We don't need you at a crime scene. We've got enough civilian bystanders lurking around."

"Fine." He tried to let that slide off. "She wants to know if she can leave."

"Sure, take her home. She a friend of yours?"

"I help out here, working with the teens."

"Strange, I never figured that one." He looked cynical. "She can go. Tell her we might need to talk to her again."

"I'll let her know."

Pastor Banks was sitting next to Maggie when Michael walked back to join her. They both glanced his way. He didn't want to know what they were thinking or how many doubts they were having about him. He could imagine.

"The cop told me to take you home."

"I can drive myself."

"Okay, drive yourself and I'll follow you." He tensed, ready for a fight and unwilling to lose.

"Let him follow you, Maggie." Pastor Banks stood. "Someone saw a guy running away from the church. They said it looked like a kid."

Michael shot Maggie a look. She glanced away, but not before he saw that flash in her eyes. They were both thinking the same thing. The boy, Curt, from the youth group. He was new, Maggie had revealed, and had only been in the area for a few weeks.

"Fine, follow me." She took the hug that Pastor Banks gave when she stood. "I'll see you at church on Sunday."

"If you need to stay home…" he offered.

"I don't need to stay home, but thank you."

Michael followed her to the parking lot. At her car they stopped. "Maggie, I'm sorry about…us, earlier. We have to work together. I really don't want there to be a problem between us."

"There isn't a problem."

But he thought maybe there was. Maybe that was for the best, for both of them.

Saturday, a week after the prowler and the fiasco of his leaving the art gallery, Michael was summoned to his parents' house for a welcome home party. They had waited several weeks for this, his mother had said, and it couldn't be put off any longer. She wanted the community to know that she was proud of her son.

Proud? Or maybe ignoring the obvious, that he was no longer welcome in their circle of acquaintances? He wouldn't be the one to tell his parents. He had already broken their hearts once.

He pulled up in front of the house on the motorcycle he'd bought a few days ago. The driveway and street were lined with cars. Dozens of people had turned out to welcome him. Or maybe they just wanted to see the golden boy gone bad. Didn't they have enough memories of him as the bad Carson? He knew that at least half of these people had witnessed his addiction in action, barging into dinner parties high on meth and other inappropriate party tricks.

He had apologized to his parents for those days, but that

didn't lessen his grief for the pain he had caused them and for the years he had lost that couldn't be regained.

As much as he didn't want to hurt his mother, he knew he couldn't go in and face those people. Not yet. He didn't want to spend an evening avoiding their curious looks. He didn't want to overhear their whispered conversations.

He wanted to escape. He wanted to go somewhere quiet, without crowds of people who had no interest in his life or who he was now. These people didn't care about the changes he'd made or what God had done for him.

He started to pull away and then he saw his brother walk out the side door of the garage. Noah waved and then pushed his too long hair back from his face as he trotted down the sidewalk to Michael.

Michael pulled off his helmet and brushed a hand through his hair. Noah smiled, an envious gleam in his eyes.

"You bought a bike." He shook his head. "Interesting way to spend some trust-fund money."

"It's used, and it saves on gas money."

"You got me there." Noah glanced back at the house. "Are you ready for this?"

"Not at all. I'm thinking about not going in."

"They'll understand if you escape."

"I don't want to hurt them." It was a little too late for that.

"Dad knows that it's too soon. He'll explain to Mom." Noah pulled a package of spearmint gum out of his pocket and offered Michael a piece. "Go for a ride, Michael, and clear your head. You might decide to come back."

"I think I will take that drive. I'll probably be back."

Before he pulled away, Michael dialed his cell phone and tested his Bluetooth after putting on his helmet. He didn't stop to consider his actions. If he thought about it, he would question his sanity, and his reason.

"Hello?"

Michael didn't respond until her second hello. He had pulled out of River Oaks onto the highway. He needed those extra seconds as he shifted gears to adjust to what he'd just done. Common sense told him this was a mistake. It was too late now.

"Maggie, I'm glad you're still there."

He listened and thought he heard the shuffle of papers and the soft exhale of a breath. In the background he heard music; a gospel station.

"Of course I'm still here. I'm overworked, overdedicated, and I think someone called me overzealous. But I'm actually just relaxing, reading a book and drinking a cup of coffee."

Relaxing. He couldn't have imagined that hearing her voice would have that effect on him, but it did. She sounded as though his call hadn't bothered her. For the time being he didn't hear hesitation or caution in her tone.

"So, what do you want?" she asked. "And why do you sound so muffled?"

"I'm on my cell phone, and what I want is a friend I can count on."

She remained quiet and he wondered what might be going through her mind.

"Shocked into silence, aren't you?" He laughed into his end of the phone and heard her soft chuckle. She should laugh more often. For some reason she calmed him, made him feel grounded. That didn't really make sense, considering that half the time she acted like she didn't even like him.

"Yes, you shocked me. Don't tell my grandmother I

can be silent. Not that she would believe it." She paused. "So, what do you really want?"

She hadn't bought it, that he wanted her friendship. But he did. Since he even found it hard to believe, he shouldn't be shocked that she felt the same way. He looked down at the speedometer.

"There's a party going on in my honor."

"And so you're driving around in your car? That makes a lot of sense."

"I couldn't go in." He shifted and slowed to make the next turn.

"You've lost me."

"I wanted to know if you would go with me. I know that sounds crazy, and I'll understand if you don't want to go. Why would *you* want to go when *I* don't want to go? Right?"

She didn't answer. He wondered what thoughts were going through her mind. Was she considering her reputation? How it would look to be seen with him, with an ex-con. Or did she care?

"I don't know..." she started.

"Is it because—"

This time she cut him off. "No, Michael, that has nothing to do with it. I just don't understand why you would call *me*. You have friends."

"All of my friends have moved on with their lives. They have families now, or activities that keep them busy. The people at my mom's house aren't there to be friends. They're there because they like to gossip, and maybe because they're curious. Or they showed up to support my parents. It isn't about me."

"So you thought you'd invite me? Why? To give them something to talk about besides you?"

He wondered at that comment, but knew she wouldn't explain.

"I'm inviting you because I know where you stand. One thing about you, Maggie Simmons, is you're honest."

"I'm not sure if you meant that as a compliment, but I'll take it that way."

"Will you go?"

She paused. He could hear her steady breathing and her nails clicking on the desk. "I don't know. I'm not really dressed for a party."

"You look fine."

Maggie looked up, her eyes widening as he walked into the room. The smile that sneaked up on him took him by surprise, especially when it accompanied a strange tightening in his stomach. He paused midstride, not at all sure if he should have made this call or followed that action by walking into the church.

"You know, sneaking up on me could get you hurt." She stood, small and diminutive in a floral skirt and a pink T-shirt. Her blond hair was pulled back in a clip and fine strands had come free to frame her face.

He agreed, she could definitely hurt a person.

"So, about the party. You'll go? You don't even have to pretend to like me."

"Is taking me some kind of rebellious 'who cares what they think' plan?"

"No, inviting you is a moment of weakness. I wanted to be abused by someone I could trust not to stab me in the back." He tossed her the spare helmet that he had carried in with him.

"What's this?"

"It's commonly referred to as a helmet."

"I mean, why did you just throw it at me?"

"To put on your head so that in case of an accident, you don't hurt that sweet brain of yours."

"You're telling me that you not only want me to go to a party that I haven't been invited to, you also want me to ride on a motorcycle?"

"You got it, babe." He took the helmet from her hand and pulled the clip from her hair. Silky blond hair released in a sweet strawberry-scented wave. He put the helmet on her head and tugged the strap tight.

"I'm not sure about this."

"You'll be fine. I won't let anything happen to you. Promise."

She sighed, crossing her arms in front of her as she did. "I'm not sure why I'm saying yes, but okay, I'll go."

He remained in front of her. At that distance the air around him seemed to evaporate. Her blue eyes were searching his face, asking questions. He knew the answers, vaguely, but they were hidden somewhere in the far corners of his mind and he couldn't get a grasp on them.

"Thanks, Maggie." He lifted her hand and kissed her palm. Her eyes met his. "Let's not go there, okay."

"I'm sorry. You're right, that was totally inappropriate."

She nodded. "Yes, totally inappropriate."

"And now you're thinking about not going?" He sighed, overwhelmed by the amount of mistakes he seemed to be making.

"Maybe it isn't a good idea."

"You could be right."

Her fingers were on the buckle of the chin strap. Michael waited, unsure of his own response. At that moment he didn't know if he wanted her to go. Drawing her into his life would make him responsible for her, for what could happen if something went wrong in his deal with Vince.

Did he really want that?

Chapter Seven

❧

Maggie's stomach tied itself into knots during the ride to Michael's parents' house in the gated community of River Oaks. It was her first time on a motorcycle. She shifted from exhilaration to panic, back and forth like a Ping-Pong ball. Her arms were around Michael's waist and her chin rested on his shoulder. She hadn't planned it that way, but the motion, the curves—all worked against her to create a force that pushed them together.

For some crazy reason she trusted him. He had promised he wouldn't let her get hurt and she knew he meant it.

As they rode through the gates of the community, motioned forward by a guard, the tension inside her doubled. She had never been here, never walked inside these homes with their lavish brick-and-stone facades, and professionally developed landscaping.

She had a push mower and a Weed Eater. Dandelions grew along the petunias in the flower beds outside the home she shared with her grandmother. And she was wearing flip-flops. She couldn't forget that.

They stopped. Michael looked over his shoulder and smiled. "Here we are."

"Yes, here we are." He got off the bike and reached for her hand. She had to let him help her. If she didn't, she'd fall. Her legs were cramped and had turned to rubber, all in one. It didn't seem possible.

"Stop wringing your hands."

"I'm not wringing my hands." She reached up to undo the buckle on the chin strap of the helmet. Her fingers trembled.

Michael reached up and undid it for her, his fingers brushing across her throat. She closed her eyes, trying to forget that his face was less than a foot from hers. She couldn't ignore the Oriental spice scent of his cologne and the sweet scent of bubblegum.

"We're going to have fun."

She opened her eyes. "Is that a promise or wishful thinking?" Humor, always a good thing to fall back on, didn't help this time. It came out flat, not at all funny.

"Probably wishful thinking." He took hold of her hand and together they walked toward the home that looked like an English manor house plopped down in the middle of the Ozarks.

"Do we have to go in?"

"Well, since that's my dad on the front porch, waving, I would say we don't have a choice."

"I'm going to be sick."

"You'll be fine."

"Remember that I did this for you, okay? If you doubt my sincerity when I say that I'm behind you, and I want you to make it, remember this."

"I'll remember."

A few minutes later they were walking through the front

door. Michael's grip on her hand tightened. If they held a contest between them to guess who was the most nervous, she figured it would have been a tie.

And neither of them seemed to fit this place. Michael, dressed in dark slacks and a dark sweater seemed to fit, but he didn't really. Instead he seemed as uncomfortable and out of place as she was in her casual clothing and flip-flops. They were both misfits. For some reason that made her feel better.

"Michael, you made it." The woman with the hazel-green eyes had to be his mother. She hugged him tight, took a step back and then her gaze fell on Maggie. "And you brought a friend."

Maggie swallowed against the lump that lodged in her throat and held out a hand. "I'm Maggie Simmons."

"Nice to meet you, dear, I'm Shelly Carson." Mrs. Carson cast a disparaging look on her son. "Take your guest to the bar, Michael."

"Mom, no bar." His smile tightened. "We'll find a soda in the kitchen."

"They have sodas at the bar, and bottled water," Shelly Carson continued.

Maggie contained herself, but disbelief trembled inside her. An open bar for a son who was honest about his problems. And Maggie had her own problems with drinking. It had controlled her life for several years after her mother's death. It had been a coping mechanism that had almost destroyed her.

"Mom, we'll go to the kitchen." Michael's hand was back on hers. He led her through the crowd, exchanging pleasantries with people who smiled politely and didn't seem to notice that Maggie didn't belong.

They walked down the tall, arching hallway to a kitchen

that Maggie could have fit half her grandmother's house into. "Mom doesn't get it. She tries, but this is her life, and she can't comprehend that it isn't mine."

"I understand." She didn't know what she meant by the words. She understood his addiction. She understood the problem with his mother. And now she understood why he needed a friend.

He glanced sideways. "Yes, I think you do."

He opened the double doors of the restaurant-size refrigerator. "Diet? Water? What do you prefer?"

"Water, please." She took the bottle he offered. "Michael, I don't drink, either. I understand more than you think."

He closed the doors and turned, his eyes widening. "Maggie has secrets?"

"Not really, just past struggles and a story of my own."

"And you're not ready to share."

"No, I'm not."

"Let me show you around. This place is so big we can get lost and not see life for hours. Maybe they'll all be gone by the time we get back."

The house took some navigating. Maggie could see how a person could get lost. They ended up in a television room, a plasma screen hanging on the wall and a circular sectional in the center of the room.

"We could watch a movie?"

"No, thank you." Maggie walked around the room, stopping when she came to a family photo album on a table. "Did you grow up in this house?"

"My parents have lived here since my senior year of high school. I spent that year in Massachusetts. My mom insisted that I attend the school my dad attended." He stopped next to her. "Family memories."

"Didn't you have a happy childhood?"

He shrugged and picked up the photo album. She followed him to the leather sectional. "I guess. We had a lot of fun together. We traveled. We spent weekends at the lake house. But there was a lot of pressure."

"Pressure?"

"You don't get to be a Carson without pressure. There's a certain amount of achievement expected. Top grades, top schools and all the right friends. I managed most of that, but I didn't always make the right friends."

He opened the album. Maggie looked at pictures of a toddler with large eyes and long lashes, dressed in cowboy boots and a hat, with tiny Wranglers and a Western shirt. A two-year-old Michael, before life had added shadows to his expression and age had added the angular dimensions to the structure of his face.

"Wasn't I cute?"

Yes, he was cute. She turned the page and saw more pictures of a charmed life and a boy who always looked like he belonged. She wondered how that would feel.

Toward the end of the book it all changed. The pictures became less frequent and the appearance of the young man in them altered. He grew thinner, his face took on a gray tinge, and his eyes no longer sparkled. Maggie glanced at him, the way he looked now, and saw that the light was back in his eyes. She tried to imagine him as the person in those pictures, the one who looked like a lost soul.

"Well, I think this trip down memory lane has gone far enough." He pulled out an old photo of himself and a group of friends and stuck it in his pocket before closing the photo album. "That was disastrous."

"Not really. I think it shows someone who made mistakes, but who has recaptured his life."

He set the book down on the table in front of them. "Sweet Maggie, you're very sweet."

His eyes sparked, a dangerous fire that made her wonder if that other person was completely gone. She didn't really want to know. "We should get back to the party. Your mother will be hurt."

"You're right. She's been hurt enough."

He took her hand and led her back through the maze of rooms and hallways to the main living area. The crowds had grown. Michael tensed at her side.

"Something wrong?"

"No, nothing."

She thought that something was definitely wrong. His gaze had transfixed on another man, a guy a little older than them, and a thin brunette at his side. The man, in his sport jacket and dress slacks, seemed to fit. The woman didn't.

"Friend of yours?"

"Old friend. I really didn't think they'd be here."

Maggie glanced around them, taking in the assortment of people. Her calm dissolved when she saw a face from her past. A man she had known in college. That had been several years ago, and she prayed he wouldn't remember. She didn't need that, not tonight.

Michael's dad joined them at the edge of the room. Maggie liked George Carson. There was an openness about him, and his smile seemed to be the real thing. Another man, a little older than Michael, crossed the room. He had the same hazel eyes, but his were more amber than green.

"Maggie, you've met my dad. This is my brother Noah."

"Nice to meet you, Noah." She needed to escape, to give them time alone. "I think I'll get a soda, if the three of you don't mind."

Michael nodded toward the bar that had been set up in the tiled family room. "Tell him what you want."

Maggie managed to get her drink and was circulating through the crowd, making her way back to Michael, when someone grabbed her arm.

"How did you manage to get an invitation to a party like this, Maggie Simmons?"

"Blake." She pulled loose from his hand, fighting the small wave of panic that ensued from that trapped feeling. "I'm a guest of Michael's."

"Figures, he always did have a thing for slumming."

Maggie opened her mouth to comment but words wouldn't come. And then Blake was yanked backward. His eyes widened in surprise as he fell back against the wall. Michael stood in front of him, his body tensed.

"Michael." She stepped forward, touching his back, feeling the tightening of the muscles. "He isn't worth it."

Michael raised his hands and stepped away. "You're right, he isn't. But you are."

His gaze followed the retreating Blake, who had hurried away from them. Maggie took a shaky breath as she watched the other man walk out the front door. She turned her attention back to Michael.

"I'm not worth you getting into trouble."

"You are." He turned, Blake forgotten. Michael cupped her cheeks in his hands and leaned forward. "You are worth something."

He stepped closer and for a moment, just briefly, Maggie forgot where they were. She forgot her fear, just for a moment, but long enough to notice its absence. How had that happened?

She didn't have to think because Michael was leaning closer, his gaze connecting with hers. His hands, warm and strong, still cupped her cheeks and his fingers slid into her hair. He whispered something about her being sweet and then his lips touched hers. The kiss was brief, sweetly chaste, but Maggie's heart melted at the touch.

"We should go." Michael pulled away from her. "I think we've made a great floor show, but I've had all the fun I can handle for one night."

"I'm sorry. If I hadn't been here…"

"I would have been miserable." He took her by the hand and led her from the room. They made brief apologies to his parents. He told them he would be by in a few days for a real visit, and then he led her outside into the falling dusk of early evening.

In the quiet, gated community of River Oaks, life seemed idyllic and strangely at odds with the tumultuous emotions that Maggie hadn't expected. Nothing seemed real in that place with lush, emerald-green lawns, pristine flower beds and tinkling fountains.

"Maggie, here." Michael handed her the helmet as she stood in awe, listening to the songbirds and drifting on the scent of wisteria.

"I'm sorry, thank you." She slid the helmet over her head. This time her fingers managed the buckle. Michael was on the bike and the engine purred quietly. She climbed on behind him.

They rode back to the church as twilight turned to night. The sky changed from pink and lavender to midnight blue as the sun set behind a thin curtain of clouds. Unwillingly, Maggie's mind took her back to another drive in the dark and to a time when she had felt unloved and unwanted.

She shook herself free from the memory. This wasn't a dark road outside of town. Michael wasn't Greg. She was older and wiser. She knew who she was and what she wanted out of life. She wasn't trying to find someone to love her.

"We didn't eat. Are you hungry?" His voice reached her over the low hum of the motorcycle as they cruised into the parking lot.

Maggie leaned forward, so that he could hear. "I'm not hungry, and stop beating yourself up."

"I didn't really plan to beat myself up. But I would have enjoyed teaching Blake a lesson. What he said was inexcusable."

He stopped the bike next to her car. Neither of them made a move to get off.

"I have cookies in the church. Do you want some?" She knew that Faith would have accused her of trying to fix him with milk and cookies.

"You wouldn't have liked me a few years ago." His jaw clenched. He had pulled off his helmet and he brushed his fingers through his flattened hair, bringing the wavy curls at his collar back to life. "I'm not sure that I even liked myself."

"You probably weren't that bad."

"I was." He shook his head, snorting softly before continuing. "Maggie, you're incredibly naive."

"I'm not. I've lived through more than you think."

"But you managed to maintain your innocence."

She shook her head as she slid off the bike. "Explain it to me, Michael. Tell me just how bad you were."

She pulled off the helmet and he took it from her.

"No, I don't think so. You don't need to hear what I've done or where I've been. Just remember, I'm not the kid who went to prep school. I've seen a lot and I've been through a lot. I've done things that I'm not proud of."

"I believe you." But she no longer wanted to take the conversation further. She didn't need a show-and-tell, comparing their lives and sad stories. That would bring them too far into each other's lives.

Maybe it was too late, though.

"I think I've misjudged you." Michael's eyes sought hers, seeking answers. "What have you been through, Maggie Simmons?"

"The usual teenage rebellion." She wouldn't tell him more.

"I don't think so."

"Let's agree not to talk about the past. You have your secrets, and I have things I'd rather not delve into. As far as the east is from the west, that's where I want to leave my mistakes. They're in the past, where they belong."

"I guess you're right." He put the kickstand in place and got off the bike. "Why don't you call me when you get home? So I know that you made it."

She nodded. "I can do that."

"Okay."

He should go now, she thought. He should turn around and leave. Instead he reached for her hands. "Do you know how good it feels to touch another person? I didn't realize that until back at the party."

"I'm not sure what you mean."

"Human contact. In prison this kind of human contact doesn't exist. Four years of not being held, of not holding. That can drive a person nearly as crazy as always being surrounded by gates, fences and walls."

Her heart clenched. She didn't know what her next move should be. His hands were on hers. She wanted to hold him.

As fast as the thought came, she tried to fight it back. Michael didn't need a moment with her. She didn't need one with him. They both had things to work through and neither of them needed casual moments just to feel good.

Her heart was in disagreement.

When Michael's hands moved to her hair and then slid down to cup the back of her neck, she didn't argue, didn't try to pull free. The past no longer held her in a fearful grip.

A car horn honked and a group of teens driving by yelled her name. Michael groaned as she pulled away.

"That was embarrassing." She bit down on her bottom lip, carefully avoiding eye contact with the man standing in front of her.

"No, not really." He lifted her chin. "It felt too nice to be embarrassing."

"Yes, but I'm the one who has to answer questions." She lifted her purse, holding it so that the light from the street-lamp shined in on the contents. "And I need to find my keys."

"Nothing happened, Maggie."

"You're right, I know that, but I do have to think of the kids."

She dug through the contents of her purse, her hands shaking. The dark made it difficult to see anything. The orange glow of the streetlamp wasn't a lot of help.

"Problem?"

"Hold this." She handed him lipstick, old grocery receipts, a package of gum and her small can of mace.

"In your ignition, maybe?" He cleared his throat. "Is this mace?"

"Yes."

"Why?"

She looked up, her mouth dropping open as she searched for an answer. What did she say about mace and fear of the dark? She sighed. "I'm single. I spend a lot of time on the road and I like to know that I can protect myself."

The mace had been a gift from Faith.

She looked through the window for her keys. "No, not there."

Whispering a silent prayer for help, she searched again and found them buried in a side pocket. Michael held out the lipstick, mace and wadded-up receipts, but he took her keys. He unlocked the door and handed them back to her as he opened it for her to get in.

"I'm glad you have mace. It pays to be safe."

"A friend thought I needed it." Sliding into the worn seat of her aging sedan, Maggie smiled up at him. "I'll see you tomorrow at church."

"Yes, of course you will."

His cell phone rang. He flipped it open, frowned and then offered an apologetic smile. "I have to take this."

He walked away. She didn't purposely try to hear the conversation, but a few words drifted her way. "I don't know if I can…maybe I could do it" and "I'll meet you."

"I have to meet someone," he explained when he rejoined her.

"This late at night?"

He looked away, but not before she saw a flash of something that looked like guilt. "Yeah, this late at night."

"Michael, do you need help?"

His eyes flashed dangerously and he slipped his cell phone into his pocket. "Of course I don't need help. There's absolutely no reason for you to worry about me, Maggie."

She didn't need to worry. He made it sound like the most reasonable thing in the world. She did worry, though. She worried that he would get hurt. She worried that *she* would get hurt. The only one she could really protect was herself.

The only way to do that was to put distance, emotional distance, between herself and Michael Carson.

Chapter Eight

"Maggie, is that you?"

Maggie kicked off her shoes and turned to lock the front door before answering her grandmother. "Yep, it's me."

She walked into the living room, knowing what she would find. Her grandmother looked up from the pieces of quilting she held in her lap. Another masterpiece for the shop her grandmother consigned to. Betty Gordon had managed for years to supplement her income by selling the handmade creations.

Maggie bent to inspect the beautiful pieces of antique rose and pale yellow cloth interspersed with cream-colored lace. The wedding-ring pattern in the quilt was one of her favorites.

Grandma smiled and looked over the top of her glasses. "Do you like it?"

"It's beautiful. I would say it's one of the best you've done, but I think you get tired of hearing that."

"This one is special, though. It's for you. I thought you would like it for your hope chest."

"Grandma, I don't have a hope chest and you know it. Now why would you make me a wedding-ring quilt when I'm not even dating?"

Grandma shrugged and managed to look slightly guilty. Maggie sat in the recliner next to her grandmother's rocking chair. She watched as the needle began to work through the fabric, guided by aging hands that weren't always steady.

Her grandmother was getting older, and that sometimes frightened Maggie. The two of them were a family and had been since Maggie's mother died thirteen years ago. That had been a strange turning point for her, to lose her mother and then to come here, to constant stability, to someone who was always there.

"What brought that frown?" Grandma looked up from the quilt, the threaded needle held just above the cloth.

Maggie looked up and smiled. She didn't want to discuss where her memories had taken her. If she closed her eyes she could still remember being a frightened child, wanting to be rescued. She could remember her mother, lucid and loving, and then manic, searching for a fix.

"Maggie?" Her grandma was still looking at her, waiting for an answer.

"Just trying to decide what you're up to. Is there a new single guy at church that I haven't met?"

Grandma focused her eyes on the needle as she once again guided it through the material. She remained silent, feeding Maggie's belief that she was up to something.

"Come clean. What's up? You haven't entered my résumé in some single's group, have you?"

"I would never interfere, not with God's plan or His timing."

"You're wasting your time, Grandma. I'm not even thinking about marriage. I'm happy here with you."

"Of course you are, you're settled and you're comfortable. That doesn't mean this is God's will forever. Our plans aren't always the same as His."

The words stung. She would never dream of trying to live outside of God's will. She was single because she wanted to be single. Greg had been her last real relationship. He had taken what wasn't his to take. He had taken her sense of self. He stole from her, and now when she taught the kids about abstinence, she thought about that night and about how sometimes the choice is taken from a person.

And she also thought about second chances. Forgiveness did that for a person. It meant new opportunities. What had happened with Greg had not been her fault.

"Maggie?"

"Yes, Gran?"

"Just checking to see if you're still with me."

"I am. But, Gran, you have to understand. I really think that being single is the right thing for me. At least for now. I love working at the church, with the kids. But they keep me busy, and that doesn't really leave time for dating."

"Maggie, you keep yourself busy. You could go out, but you spend your nights over there, doing whatever you do."

"I work." She smiled at her grandmother. "And you're right, I kill time over there when I know you're not at home."

Her grandmother let the quilt rest on her lap and pulled off her glasses. Understanding shone from her gray eyes and she smiled.

"You haven't made a mistake, Maggie. You thought Greg was worth investing in." She pointed with her glasses. "He didn't deserve you. He didn't deserve for you to believe in him. But someday you'll find a young man that you can count on, someone who will always be there for you."

Maggie looked away, unable to face her grandmother for fear she would read something into a look. Maggie had never told her what Greg had done, and how much he had taken. "You're right, Gran, there are some really good men out there. I just haven't found the right one. It obviously wasn't Greg."

"Greg Lawrence was never the right one for you. I was so glad when you broke things off with him. I never trusted that boy."

Maggie wished she had listened to those warnings when she'd first started dating Greg. In her innocence, and her desperate need to feel loved, she had believed that she could change him. Now she knew better. Instead, she had been the one to change.

Grandma reached across the end table and touched her hand. "I just want you to have the kind of love I shared with your grandfather. You deserve that kind of love."

"I would love to have that, Grandma. I'm not sure if it will happen. The older I get, the more I wonder."

Maggie could have mentioned her mother and the choices she had made, but she wouldn't do that to her grandmother. Maggie's mom had taken a turn during her college years, falling in love with Maggie's dad, only to be left behind when he went back home to Chicago, to a family that expected something of him, something more than a girl from a poor, working-class family.

Tonight Maggie had felt more like her mother than ever before. She had walked through the doors of Michael's home and into a world where she knew she didn't belong.

"It will all work out, Maggie." Grandma said it like it was an indisputable fact.

Maggie turned away from her grandmother's probing gaze and focused on the wall across from the chair. Focusing on a twenty-year-old photo of her mother, her eyes burned and she told herself that tears were silly.

Tears wouldn't bring her mother back and she would never be her daddy's little girl. Childhood dreams faded, leaving pain-filled memories of a child who spent too much time alone and too many nights afraid.

"Honey?"

"I'm fine, Gran, really I am. I have forgiven Jacob Simmons." She paused there, not even sure how she meant to end that statement. She had even forgiven Greg. She had forgiven her mother. Words were difficult to find and she ended by shrugging her shoulders, hoping to let the conversation die.

"We have to keep praying for your father." Grandma's answer seemed too simple.

"Of course, we'll keep praying."

"Don't say it like you don't believe." The warning, spoken in a subtly soft voice, couldn't be ignored.

"You're right, but I guess sometimes I don't believe it. Sometimes I don't want to pray for him." She smiled at her grandmother, who had resumed her sewing. "It really is a beautiful piece, Gran. I'll treasure it forever."

The needle continued to work through the fabric. Her grandmother kept her head bent over the scraps of fabric, illuminated by a circle of light from the table lamp. "I only want you to be happy."

"Thank you." Maggie rose from her chair and leaned to kiss her grandmother's cheek. "I really need to get to sleep."

"Good night, honey."

When she walked into her room she paused to look out

the window. The sky was dark, covered with a thick blanket of clouds that blocked the moon and the stars. Michael was out there somewhere.

She didn't want to think about him, but she couldn't help wondering what he was up to and if he was okay.

Two hours after leaving Maggie at the church, Michael pulled up to Jimmy Grey's apartment. He glanced up at the darkened windows of the second-floor apartment as he got off the bike, and for a second he reconsidered. He even felt a little bit guilty as he knocked on the door. Not too guilty, though, or he wouldn't have knocked.

He could have gone somewhere else. Maybe to Noah's. But if he went to Noah's he would have to explain his reason for not wanting to go home. Would Noah, who seemed to like his loner existence, understand that Michael needed someone to talk to? Not that he wanted to talk about Vince and how it felt to pretend that he was being drawn back into that life. Instead he wanted to talk about the real world that other people lived in, the one with families and careers.

And he didn't want to tell his brother that he didn't think he was strong enough for what he'd gotten himself into. He wanted to be strong enough. If he backed out now, he would never know.

The door opened, the chain grabbing and keeping it from opening more than a few inches. A dim light from inside spilled out, lighting the step. Michael shrugged. Jimmy didn't speak, just opened the door and motioned him inside.

"You look like a man who could use a…"

"Don't say it and don't offer." Michael brushed a hand through his hair and plopped down, uninvited, onto the leather sofa.

"What's going on?" Jimmy lowered himself onto a stool at the bar that separated the living area of the condo from the kitchen.

"Not much."

"You show up at my house in the middle of the night because nothing is wrong? Not buying it, my friend."

"I'm not trying to sell anything, so there's nothing for you to buy." He leaned back, closing his eyes and wishing he hadn't done what he had that night. "Look, Jimmy, I'd really like to talk, but I can't."

"Okay, you can't talk. Does this have anything to do with Katherine?"

"A little, but she's just a small part of it."

"So…"

"I just wanted to hang out, maybe talk about something other than what is going on."

Jimmy smiled at that. "Oh, sure, of course. We could talk about the price of gas or maybe about politics."

"Aren't those the things that other people talk about?"

"Sure, other people do. We could talk about church. People talk about that, too."

"Jimmy, when did you become a cynic?"

"When my mother took off and left me to take care of my dad. That wasn't supposed to happen to my family. We weren't perfect, but I never thought we'd fall apart."

Michael let go of his own concerns. Maybe he wasn't here for himself. Jimmy needed a friend, too. Something normal, maybe that meant just being a friend for the night.

"I'm not very interested in going home tonight,"

Michael admitted. "And we haven't really had a chance to talk. Have you heard from your mom?"

"She's in Florida. She calls, but we haven't seen each other."

Michael leaned against the back of the couch and Jimmy talked. It felt good to be the listener, the one giving support. When Jimmy finally ran out of words, he stood.

"We should get some sleep. Let me get a blanket and pillow. I'd let you use the spare bedroom, but I'm using it for an office. I don't even have a bed in there."

"I don't mind sleeping on the couch."

"I'll be right back."

Michael walked to the window and looked out. The gray car, Vince's car, cruised past. They were following him. They probably suspected he was an informant. Weren't they smart?

"I did see Katherine tonight, twice." He turned. Jimmy had dropped blankets and a pillow on the couch. "You were right, she's at rock bottom. I wouldn't have suspected it before, and she even looked like she was functioning at the party tonight. But she's in pretty bad shape."

"You're going to try to help her?" Jimmy sat, lacing his fingers behind his head. "Don't let it drag you back…"

"I'm not going to do that."

"I'm just saying…"

"I can do it. I just don't want to give Vince a reason to come after the people I care about." He arranged the blanket and the pillows on the couch. "At this point, in the condition Katherine's in, I definitely don't trust her."

"People you care about?"

Jimmy would latch on to that. Michael shrugged, because he didn't have a real answer, at least not one he wanted to think about. He could have said something about his family, or the kids at church. Instead his mind took another route, thinking about Maggie.

He would see her at church the next morning and he would see her each day that they worked together. Keeping his distance from Maggie Simmons wasn't going to be an easy thing to accomplish.

"What do you want for breakfast?" Maggie poured water into the coffeemaker and turned to smile at her grandmother. "I can't believe I managed to get up before you."

"I stayed up late, working on your quilt." Grandma pulled orange juice out of the fridge and poured a glass. "You never told me where you were last night. Is everything okay?"

Maggie turned so that her grandmother couldn't see her face or read her expression.

"Maggie?"

"I went with Michael. His family threw a welcome home party for him, and he didn't want to go alone."

"That's very sweet of you, dear. And he's a nice boy. I just keep thinking back to all of those prayers for him over the last few years, and look what God did with those prayers."

"Yes, God has done a lot."

"Well, there are still a few doubting Thomases in the church. They'll see, though. Michael just has to keep moving forward, and he'll show them that he is a changed person."

"Yes, he's a changed man." She took the glass of orange juice her grandmother pushed across the counter to her.

"There are people blaming him for the prowler the other night."

Maggie made eye contact over the top of her glass. She

took a sip and set it down. "He didn't have anything to do with that. We think we know who it was."

"One of the kids?"

"Maybe."

"Maggie, honey, please be careful. I don't like that you spend so much time over there alone."

"I know, Gran, but during the day there are a lot of visitors, or people needing help."

"I just don't like it."

Maggie kissed her grandmother's powdery-soft cheek. "I love you, Gran. I promise I'll be careful. Now sit down and let me make breakfast."

Sunshine streamed through the kitchen window. Maggie reached to pull the miniblind closed, leaving the room in shadows. Her grandmother flipped on the light before opening the fridge to pull out bacon and eggs.

"You sit down, and I'll cook."

"But I wanted to cook for you today." Maggie pulled out a chair to sit. After years of the same argument, she knew who would win.

"I want to spend my day without indigestion," Grandma informed her—the same old reason. "Sit down, dear, let me cook."

Maggie did as her grandmother ordered, accepting the fact that she really wasn't the best cook in the world. The Sunday paper was on the table. She opened it thinking she would read, but then she couldn't.

The shrill ringing of the telephone shattered the stillness of the room. Maggie slid out of her chair and hurried to answer it. "Hello."

"Maggie. Good, you're still there." Michael paused. "I wanted to catch you before you left for church."

"I'm still here."

Michael didn't speak again, not right away. That gave Maggie time to escape her grandmother's prying eyes and ears. She walked outside, the cordless phone held against her ear with her shoulder and a cup of coffee in her hand.

"Michael?"

"I wanted to check on you. You didn't call last night."

She set her coffee on the table so she could pull out a chair, dusting it off with her hand before she sat. Some might have called it stalling. She preferred to think of it as gathering her thoughts. She hadn't called him. Why?

"Maggie?"

"I'm here." She should have said something more than that, but couldn't. Michael had called to check on her. A slender thread tugged on her heart, telling her that he was different. He didn't need to be fixed, like her kids, and he wasn't going to use her.

But then, she had made mistakes in the past. As a child she had even believed her dad would ride in on a white horse to rescue her. When he didn't show up after her mother's death, she put that dream away.

"You're okay?"

"Why wouldn't I be?"

"Last night. I shouldn't have done that. I put you in a bad position, and I don't want to do that. You're right to keep your distance, and I need to remember that I have issues of my own to work on."

"We're fine, Michael. I think we both know that we have priorities."

"Good, I wanted to make sure. I really appreciated you going with me."

She didn't have an answer, not right away.

Michael laughed. "You don't have to tell me you had a good time."

"It wasn't so bad."

The call ended with him telling her he'd see her at church. She walked back into the kitchen where she met her grandmother's questioning looks. Maggie poured herself another cup of coffee.

"Michael Carson?" Her grandmother pulled the Crock-Pot out of the cabinet as she asked the question.

"Yes."

"How is he doing?" Grandma turned to the refrigerator and pulled out a roast.

Maggie watched, wondering about the roast and the carrots that followed. Her grandmother only thawed out a roast for Sunday lunch if they were expecting company.

"Grandma, why are you making a roast?"

"Because I thought it would be nice if we invited that young man over for lunch."

"Gran, I love you, but please don't do this."

"I just thought it would be good to show him that he has friends, people who are supporting him and believing in him."

"And I'm trying to be one of those people. But I can do that without letting him take over every aspect of my life. He's in my office, working with my kids and going to my church. Isn't that enough?"

Maggie heard a barely audible *tsk-tsk* from her grandmother. She leaned against the counter, the warmth of the giant mug of coffee seeping into her hands as she lifted it to her lips.

"Maggie, honey, I don't think God ever said, 'Be merciful and compassionate only when and where it makes sense or feels safe.'"

It seemed as if it was a day without easy answers.

"Gran, I love you."

"I love you, too, honey." Her grandmother patted her cheek. "And I'm praying for you, because I know this isn't easy, letting Michael in and allowing him to be such a big part of your life. I know that you have memories…" Grandma looked away, but not before Maggie saw tears. "Memories of your mother. Don't forget, she was my daughter. It hurt me, too. But I think it would be good for us both to realize that sometimes people get help and they recover. Life isn't hopeless, not when God is involved."

Maggie thought back to a lifetime of unanswered prayers. She had prayed, wondering if God was real. And then she had prayed for her mom, and for her dad to come and rescue them. She had watched her mom slip further and further away, until the day she left for good.

Remembering, Maggie heard the whispered pleadings of a child, begging God to help her mom. Asking Him why it had to be the parent who loved her and not the father that hadn't married her mother.

"Maggie, honey?" Grandma's gentle voice broke into the haunting memories of the past, drawing her back to a sunlit kitchen and a new day.

"I'm sorry, Gran, I just got lost in thought." She looked down at the cup she still held between her palms. "Michael Carson is just a man who needs friends. Maybe a prayer has been answered. Maybe he has a praying grandmother and we're an answer to her prayers for her grandson. He needs people he can depend on right now."

"And he's blessed to have you."

Maggie wanted that to be a good thing. Michael needed

friends. She could be that for him. It sounded so easy. But then, every time she bought something that promised to be "easy to assemble," it never was, not really.

Chapter Nine

Michael knew where to find Maggie. He went in the side door of the church, effectively avoiding crowds of people, many of whom seemed to have opinions about his life. It had been several weeks. He hoped that eventually the talk and the speculation would end. When people saw that he had truly changed and that he could be counted on, maybe then.

The classroom where she taught was empty.

"Looking for someone?"

He turned, smiling at the woman walking toward him with an insulated mug of coffee. He knew that she had just refilled it and that she would take it into church with her. He smiled, finding it amusing that he had learned her personal habits so quickly.

"I thought I'd walk in with you." He lifted his empty mug. "And I'm going armed with coffee. I hope you didn't empty the pot."

"I didn't." She turned back toward the kitchen and he followed her.

"Maggie, about last night."

"Hold out your cup." She lifted the glass carafe and he held out his mug. "Michael, we discussed it. Let's not ruminate over it."

"Ignoring this won't make it go away."

"So, what do you think we should do? Do you think you should leave?"

"Is that what you want?"

She rolled her eyes toward the ceiling and shook her head. "No, that isn't what I want. You're starting to grow on me. We can't get rid of you now."

He sighed, relieved to hear that. The words were on his lips, to promise that he wouldn't do it again, but he held back, not sure if he wanted to make that promise.

"Good, because I'd like to stick around. And I don't want there to be problems between us."

"That's good to know. And now we need to go. I hear 'Blessed Assurance' playing."

Echoes of mercy, whispers of love—Michael knew the words by heart. It had been his favorite song during the sermons at the prison. He had memorized the words, finding strength in the knowledge that he had received mercy and a new beginning.

"Join us for lunch, Michael." Her grandmother's request as they walked out of the church, even though expected, still took Maggie by surprise. She looked to Michael, half hoping he would turn the invitation down.

"I'd love to."

Of course he would. If it had to do with food, Michael was there. He glanced her way and she put on a quick smile.

He continued the conversation with her grandmother. Maggie smiled at people walking past them on the way to their cars, to their lunches. Michael and her grandmother were in deep conversation. He towered over her tiny grandmother. They looked like quite a pair. Gran in her cotton dress, Michael in black pants and black shirt, his dark hair brushing his collar.

He looked past her grandmother to where Maggie stood. His gaze captured hers with a questioning look and she felt her stomach curl in response. Expected or not, she resented that response.

"Do you mind me coming over for lunch?"

Mind, of course she wouldn't mind.

Michael in her home, seeing the need for repairs. Michael sitting next to her at the small table in the kitchen.

Michael, not Greg, she reminded herself.

"No, I don't mind."

She opened her purse and started to rummage for her keys. Michael stood next to her, his smile tipping the right side of his mouth. At least he knew not to comment.

Somewhere in there, maybe at the bottom, those keys were there. She knew they were in there. She didn't have pockets. She hadn't left her keys in the car. Or had she? She groaned at that thought, because she did clearly remember locking the car doors.

"God, why are you doing this to me?" She mumbled the words into the bottomless pit of her purse, still seeing no keys.

"What?" Michael leaned closer. "Is God in your purse?"

"Oh, be quiet." She considered dumping the purse and its contents on the ground for a more thorough search. That would be more embarrassing than having locked her keys in her car.

"You can't find your keys." Michael chuckled...big mistake.

"Oh, like you've never lost your keys." She shoved her hand into her purse and pushed aside six months' worth of shopping lists, two bank deposit forms and half a dozen gum wrappers. Eww, and something sticky. "I know my keys are somewhere."

"That's a given." Michael remained serious this time. "Could the somewhere be your ignition?"

"In my locked car?" She mimicked what she knew he wanted to say. Having lost control and now facing a definite bad mood, she didn't try to tone her words down. Humiliation did that to a person.

He touched her shoulder and then his hand slid down, resting on the small of her back. An innocent touch, comforting, supportive. She tensed and Michael withdrew his hand.

"Maggie?"

"You're probably right. I think they are in my car."

"That isn't what I meant."

She looked up, refusing to answer his unspoken question. He would ask what was wrong. She didn't want to answer.

"Let's go look." He moved in the direction of her car. The keys were there, hanging in the ignition. Michael cast a questioning look in her direction, complete with raised brows and a quirky grin. His hand went to the door and he pulled on the handle, locked of course. He tried the back door and then moved to the passenger side.

All locked, she could have told him. She never locked her doors, but today she had. Of course she had, bad luck always went in threes.

Bad luck number one: Michael called, ruining her Sunday. Number two: she locked her keys in her car. What would number three be? The ideas that popped into her mind were less than pleasant.

"An extra key wouldn't be a possibility, would it?" Michael broke into her reverie, his tone crackling with humor.

"Yes, on the key chain." And locked in the car. She closed her eyes as he groaned. Her day was going from one bad blond joke to another.

In her mind she pictured the flurry of e-mail forwards with the subject heading, "Did you hear about the blonde who locked the keys in her car?" She really hated blond jokes.

"So, we all ride home together in Michael's car. Later the two of you can figure out how to get that door open." Grandma had arrived on the scene after saying goodbye to her friend, and her suggestion sounded like a perfectly reasonable solution.

Pulling up in front of their home a few minutes later, Maggie glanced sideways to gauge Michael's reaction. She tried to see the small home as he saw it. Okay, it didn't look so bad. Small but well-maintained, the square house was encircled by a picket fence. The tiny yard needed mowing, but rosebushes bloomed profusely along the front, offsetting the neglect of the overgrown lawn.

Of course in her mind she could still picture the home where Michael's parents lived. And she knew he had to see the comparison, as well.

Her gaze locked on the roof. He would never know how it leaked. Roofs were really expensive to replace. She would get it done eventually. And so what if the carpet was a little threadbare? Filled with love, her home grew in dimension.

Splat. The first drop of rain hit the windshield as they stepped out of the car. More followed. So much for "partly cloudy and a slight chance of precipitation."

Running for cover, Maggie looked up at the sky, now knowing what the third in the series of bad luck would be...the leaking roof. The three of them rushed through the rain and into the house. They were greeted by the tantalizing aroma of roast beef simmering in the Crock-Pot. Maggie forgot the leaking roof, but only for a minute.

"Maggie, you get a bowl for the living room, I'll get one for the bedroom. Michael, sit down and relax, we'll have dinner on the table in a jiffy."

Grandma's orders shot through the room. Maggie shook her head, wondering how her sweet little grandmother ever dredged up such a powerful voice. Michael stood in the living room looking just as surprised. She shrugged and offered him a smile.

"Go ahead and sit down." She nodded toward her favorite chair, the recliner, and handed him the remote. "I'm sure you can find a game to watch."

"No, let me do something. Can I set the table?"

"Set the table?" Her brows rose. "You know how to set a table?"

"I haven't been at a country club for the last four years."

Maggie rubbed a hand over her face. "I'm sorry, Michael."

"You've seen where my parents live, and you're having a hard time separating me from that place. That isn't who I am now. You can't go through what I've been through and then blithely go back. Even if I wanted that, people wouldn't let it happen."

"Well, I like who you are now."

"So, let me set the table."

"Okay, maybe, but I have to get bowls."

She rummaged through the kitchen cabinets, finding a couple of large bowls. "Here, you can go stick these under the leaks."

"Ah, a job I can do." He took the bowls and she watched

him walk away. A sigh heaved out of her. This hadn't been her plan, to let him into her personal life, to allow him space in her world.

Why not? The thought nudged at her. She pushed it back where it came from. She had answers, very reasonable ones. She didn't have to explain them to herself. But the biggest—she didn't want to be let down—kept returning as a reminder.

Grandma smiled when she walked into the kitchen. With effort Maggie returned the gesture. Plates. She needed plates. Michael was back. As she pulled the plates down, he rummaged in the cabinet next to her, pulling out glasses. He didn't ask her for help, but opened the freezer and started emptying ice-cube trays.

"Turn the radio on." Grandma's quiet voice had returned.

Maggie set the plates down and reached for the small radio they kept on the counter. She found a country station and turned the volume on low.

"I like that song." Michael smiled over his shoulder as he set glasses down on the table.

She didn't need to know that he liked country songs about finding true love, the kind that lasts forever. She could have gone her entire life without knowing that. Rather than comment, she picked up the pile of plates and scooted past him to the table.

As she set the plates on the white-painted table that she'd bought her grandmother for Christmas, Michael appeared at her side holding a basket of rolls her grandmother had baked the night before. The yeasty, fresh-baked aroma wafted up, reminding her that breakfast had been more than four hours ago.

Other mouth-watering aromas filled the room, drawing the three of them to the table. Maggie moved to her chair.

As she reached for it Michael pulled it out and gestured for her to sit down. When she hesitated, he nodded and motioned to the seat. What was she going to do, push it in and pull it out for herself?

She sat and he took the seat opposite hers.

"Michael, why don't you ask the blessing?" Grandma reached for Michael's hand, he in turn took hold of Maggie's. She closed her eyes, making it easier to accept his touch, the strength of his hand on hers.

When he said, "Amen," she pulled her hand from his and reached for her fork.

Outside, the rain continued with spring fierceness. Thunder crashing blended with the songs on the radio, occasional static, the clank of silverware and ice jiggling in cups.

The void of conversation grew louder.

Maggie tried to think of something to say, but she really didn't know what, not to Michael. The weather topic was out. They all knew it was raining. Politics, that conversation would only ruin their appetites.

Silence continued until a drop of rain fell on the center of the table.

"Not another one!" Grandma jumped up, moving plates of food as she did. "Get a bowl, Maggie."

Heat burning her cheeks, Maggie hurried to do as Grandma asked. Michael helped by moving food. This day would never end, not soon enough for her liking. She returned to the table with a plastic bowl and set it down to catch the drops of rain.

They all sat back down and resumed their meal. Grandma mentioned something about church. Michael told them how much he was enjoying the trailer and living in the country. Maggie pretended interest in both topics.

Out of the corner of her eye, she saw Michael move his empty plate to the side. She raised her head, her gaze locking with his. He winked and looked away.

"I'll help do the dishes." Michael aimed that comment at her grandmother.

Maggie shook her head slightly and sliced her hand across her throat to silence him. Typical male, he didn't notice. Or chose not to. A smart guy like him, it wouldn't take him long to catch on. As his hand reached to gather plates, Grandma slapped it away.

"You'll do no such thing, Michael Carson. Dishes are my job." Grandma's gaze flitted to the window and she smiled. Maggie followed her gaze. Sunshine, golden and warm, filtered in through the kitchen window. No more rain.

"I should help," he insisted, obviously not getting it.

"You can help." Grandma stood, gathering plates as she did. "You can help Maggie get the keys out of her car."

"I'd love to."

"Good boy," Grandma put the dishes on the counter and turned on the faucet.

"Grandma, I can manage to get my own keys. Michael probably has somewhere he needs to be." She gave him a pointed look. "Don't you, Michael?"

"No, actually, I don't. Come on, Maggie, this will be fun. Get a hanger and we'll go break into your car."

"This cannot be my life."

But it was her life. A few minutes later she couldn't deny that fact. She was in Michael's car and they were pulling away from her house. Out of the corner of her eye, Maggie saw Michael move and she knew that he was watching her.

In the close confines of his car she couldn't miss the small details. The scent of his cologne, the way it drifted through the air when he moved, and the subtle scent of the leather upholstery. He shifted gears as he pulled out onto the road, brushing his arm against hers.

It was that touch, his arm against hers, that brought back a flash of memory. Night time, a deserted park, Greg, his voice soft, seductive and then angry. The memories shouldn't be so strong, not after so many years. It had been several years since it had really bothered her.

But in the last few weeks she had been put to the test. Michael had done that. For whatever reason, or maybe for many reasons, he brought back a past she had left behind. He made her think about her mom, about the dad she didn't know and about Greg. She was surviving, though. At least she had that—the knowledge that she was moving past the fear.

"Maggie?"

"Yes?"

"Your grandmother is great. But I guess you know that."

"She practically raised me, and I wasn't always an easy kid to love."

"I can't believe that."

His quiet statement caught her attention. She turned and smiled at him. "You have no idea."

And she wasn't about to tell him.

"Here we are." His unnecessary statement came at the perfect moment. He pulled his car in next to hers. Maggie reached for the door but his hand on her arm stopped her from escaping.

He had no way of knowing what that did to her, to have her hand on the door, wanting to open it but not being able to. He didn't know about her nightmares or the memories that touch evoked.

Moments ago she had convinced herself that the fear had been put in the past. A simple touch brought it back. But it wasn't a simple touch, a kiss or a word, it was his hand on hers, keeping her from getting out of the car.

"Michael, I have to get out of the car." She pushed the door open, pulling free from his restraining hand.

Eyes closed, she leaned against the car, waiting for peace to return. Obviously the old fears weren't completely gone. Michael had joined her. The woodsy scent of his cologne hinted at his presence. He didn't touch her. She opened her eyes and tried to smile.

"What happened?"

"Happened?" She blinked a few times, clearing her eyes of unshed tears.

"Maggie, I don't know what happened to you, but I do know fear. Whatever this is, keeping it inside doesn't help. If you keep it buried, and hidden, it's going to turn into something larger."

"I'm not hiding anything."

"You are. And the only way to heal is to open the wound."

"I know that." She slid past him and walked toward her car.

"Can I help?"

"Yes, you can get the keys out of my car."

"That isn't what I meant."

"I know." She handed him the hanger she'd brought from the house. "I know you mean well, Michael, but this is something I have to deal with."

"If you change your mind…"

The sweetness in his expression curled around her heart. She wanted to touch him, to let him in. She reached up, resting her palm on his cheek, but only briefly.

"Maggie, Maggie, I don't think you have any idea what you're doing." He sucked in a breath and walked away.

No, she didn't know what she was doing, and that was the problem. She hadn't known what she was doing with Greg. She'd gotten in over her head and then she hadn't been able to get away. With Michael she was already floundering.

She watched as he worked at the wire hanger. He straightened it into a hook and held it up for her to inspect.

"Have you done this before?"

"You remember that I haven't always been a good guy, right?" He grinned as he felt around the edge of the window. "Couldn't you have made this a little easier, though? If you had just left the window open an inch..."

"That wouldn't have been any fun." Maggie smiled, relaxing as the banter between them eased the tension of a few minutes ago.

Michael held the piece of wire at different angles and then pulled it back. Maggie leaned against the door and watched.

The hanger slid between the door frame and the window. Michael twisted it and tried to turn it toward the lock. The fixed concentration gave him a cute, boyish look as he bit down on his bottom lip and narrowed his eyes to study the job at hand.

As if making that face would help the process.

"Maybe we should pray," he suggested after another unsuccessful attempt.

"For God to help us unlock my car door?"

"Hey, we have not because we ask not. Isn't that what Pastor Banks said in his message this morning? Didn't he say that God is the God of small problems and big alike? I fully believe He is also the God of small miracles, and getting into this car will be one."

"So pray."

"I have." He stepped away from the window, giving it the evil eye. Like that would make a difference.

"And?"

"I don't think I can do it."

"You tried."

"I wanted to do more than try. It's like this car is defying me to gain entrance."

"I doubt if the car has thought through its motivation."

Michael tried again, slipping the hanger expertly between the window and door, this time hitting the lock. He turned and grinned as he opened the door. Maggie applauded his talent.

"Thank you. I really couldn't have done it without you."

"I enjoyed today." He smiled with the words, convincing her of his sincerity. "Your grandmother is quite a cook."

"Yes, she is." What else could she say? She jiggled her key chain and focused on a butterfly that flitted through the air.

"I should be going."

"Why did you call this morning, Michael?" Not what she had meant, but the words tumbled out.

"I felt like we ended things on the wrong note last night. But maybe there's more to it than my fumbling attempts at friendship. Whose mistakes am I paying for?"

Words failed her, and that didn't happen often. What should she say…that they were her own mistakes?

"Well?" He shrugged. "No comments?"

"It's just…" She looked up, wishing she could read his heart and know his intentions. "After going to your home, meeting your parents, I wonder how long you'll be here to help us."

"That's a snobby thing to say."

She shook her head. "What?"

"You saw where my parents live, and so now you think I'm too good to be here? That I don't belong? The problem is, I don't know if I belong anywhere. Contrary to your opinion, I don't belong in my parents' world. I visit there, but I don't fit, and I haven't fit for a very long time." He lowered his gaze to meet hers. "And from what you've just said, I don't belong here, either."

"No, that isn't it."

"Really? To me, it feels like the way it is."

"I don't want the kids hurt. They're starting to trust you. If you leave, you'll become another person in their lives who has let them down."

"Is this about them, Maggie, or is it about you?"

She couldn't answer that question, but he smiled as though he knew the answer and then he walked away.

Chapter Ten

Michael rolled out of his bed on Monday morning at a few minutes until six. Four years of early rising had made it almost impossible to sleep late. He stood up, stretched and took a moment to enjoy the fact that his back didn't ache from sleeping on a four-inch mattress.

When he came out of the shower the telephone next to his bed was ringing. He picked it up as he reached for his shoes.

"I haven't seen you in a few days. I thought you realized that you still owe me?" The voice caught Michael off guard.

"Why are you calling me?"

"Mike, I'm hurt. We have a lot of catching up to do."

"It's too early in the morning for this, and I don't really have anything to say to you." He started to hang up but Vince stopped him.

"Oh, I think you do." He laughed. "Maybe your lady friend will make the payment you never did. That's a good idea. I should stop by and visit her."

"Stay away from her." Stay cool, Michael. He closed his

eyes and tried to follow that advice. "Stay away from her. Stay away from the church. This is between us."

"Then remember to keep it between us. And keep Katherine out of it. You know she isn't good at keeping quiet. Don't make me have to do something that you'll regret."

Michael hung up. His dad expected him at the office, but he couldn't go until he knew that Maggie was safe. And he had to check on Katherine. As much as he hadn't wanted to renew that friendship, he couldn't leave her hanging.

The knock on Maggie's office door caught her by surprise. She looked up from the book on her desk as Michael walked into the room carrying a cup of coffee. She glanced at the clock on the wall. Not even eight and he hadn't shaved. What was she supposed to say to him? He wasn't supposed to be here on Monday.

"You look as if you didn't expect me to come back." He sat in the chair across from her desk. "You know, if we're going to be hanging out in here, we really need to get more comfortable furniture."

Maggie closed her book. "If there was money in the budget for furniture, we would probably spend it on something more important."

"I see." He set his coffee down on her desk. Hers. So what was he doing here and why did he think "they" needed more comfortable furniture?

And what should she say to him?

"Maggie? I asked if you would like a cup of coffee. It's fresh, I just made it."

As much as she hadn't wanted to be bothered, she really needed that cup of coffee. She nodded and pushed her empty cup across the desk. "Please."

Michael's eyebrows shot up, but he didn't say anything as he took her cup. She watched him walk from the room, taking a deep breath as soon as he was gone.

When he returned he had a cup of coffee. He set it down in front of her with a packet of cream and several packets of sugar. The subtle fragrance of soap and cologne mixed with the stronger aroma of fresh coffee. Maggie smiled up at him, determined to make this work. He had surprised her, showing up this early.

Her reaction to seeing him had come as a bigger surprise.

"Thank you. I needed that." She smiled, feeling more at ease as she adjusted to his presence.

He started to speak but stopped. Maggie set her cup down.

"I'm sorry, Michael, I guess you just took me by surprise this morning."

"You expected me to just show up for a few hours a week. Oh, no, wait, I remember. You expected me to show up for a while, and then get tired of playing church."

"No, not really. I shouldn't have said that. You know, the tongue can really get a person into a lot of trouble. Especially if said person is grasping, trying to explain something she doesn't understand." She tossed him a freezer bag of chocolate-chip cookies. "Could this be a peace offering?"

"Yes, sure. Why not?"

"Breakfast of champions," she murmured as she dunked a cookie into her coffee. It was good coffee, not the cheap stuff they normally bought for the church kitchen. She took a big drink and savored the flavor.

"Where did you find this?" she asked.

Michael shrugged off her question. "I bought it downtown."

"It's really good."

"Maggie, I want to be a real part of this ministry."

She finished her cookie before answering.

"You know, you're ruining the cookie-and-coffee ritual with all of this jabbering."

His eyebrows shot up. "I didn't realize this was a special moment in your day."

"It is, and since you insist on talking, the moment is blown." She smiled, amazed by her own ability to tease him and seeing that he was just as amazed. His eyes widened as she continued. "I know you've been gone for a few years, but you might need to read a textbook on being 'male' in the modern age. Maybe buy one of those 'Men are Martians' books or something. You're supposed to hide your emotions, not lay them out on the table." While she talked he reached for a pen and paper. "Excuse me, what are you doing?"

"Taking notes. Obviously, I missed this class in college. Okay, repeat that part about hiding feelings."

Maggie lifted the cup of coffee and took a long sip to hide her smile. She set the cup back on the desk and leaned forward, resting her arms on the desktop.

"Okay, here it is. To be male in this day and age you're supposed to keep your emotions on the inside, not talk them to death. When the woman starts talking emotions, long-term commitment or feelings, you're supposed to smile, nod and stare into space as you think about your next meal or what kind of car you want to buy."

He circled the words "buying car" on the piece of paper and added a few exclamation marks after "hide feelings." Maggie watched him take notes and felt her tension slip completely away. It was replaced by some other emotion, one that she wasn't really able to define.

"Got it?" She allowed her smile to sneak out. How could she not smile when he was sitting across from her, chewing on the eraser of the pencil as he studied his notes?

"Got it. Be cold. Be unfeeling. Play it cool. Do these things and women will love me." He dipped a cookie in coffee and took a bite. "Does it help that I'm dangerous, a guy with a past and a known bad boy?"

"Of course, the danger element is always good. That makes you unattainable, and some beautiful woman will set her sights on you."

"Very interesting." He stared off into space.

"Michael?"

He ignored her.

"Michael, are you listening to me?"

"Oh, I'm sorry, I was thinking about cheeseburgers. Were you talking to me?"

Maggie picked up a piece of paper, crumpled it into a ball and tossed it. The missile made contact with his forehead. He picked it up off the floor, tossed it in the air a couple of times and then aimed it at the trash can in the corner of the room.

"I think you have it down pat." She emptied the coffee in her cup. "And now I have work to do."

"Is that my cue to leave?"

"It should be. You have a job to go to, right?"

He leaned back in his chair, taking the front two legs off the ground. His hands were behind his head and he didn't seem to be with her on the leaving part.

"Maggie, do me a favor."

"If I can."

"Be careful, okay? When you're out, watch who is around. Keep your car doors locked."

"Are you trying to scare me?"

He shook his head, but she didn't buy it.

"No, I'm not. And I debated with myself about not telling you this. But there are people from my past who are dangerous. They really don't like that I'm clean."

Fear sneaked in, even though she told herself to not fear.

"I'll be careful, but you be careful, too."

"I will. See you this afternoon." He grabbed another cookie from the bag and walked out the door.

"I would really like to see the neighborhood and learn more about the people here." Michael smiled at the widening of Maggie's eyes when he brought up what had been on his mind since he'd showed up at the church that afternoon.

He had been here since four o'clock, after having spent a day at the office worrying about her and thinking through his next step with Vince.

"Okay, I think we can manage a tour of the neighborhood before the kids show up. I have a photographer coming today to give them lessons. I need to be back before he shows up." She reached for her purse and dropped it into an open filing cabinet. With her foot she closed the drawer. "We could take a walk around the block. That's probably the best way to see the people and get to know them."

"Sounds good to me."

Cool spring air and a strong breeze whipped against Michael's face when they walked out the back door of the church. He hadn't expected the sudden drop in temperature, not after a week of eighty-degree days. Next to him, Maggie shivered. He pulled off his jacket and handed it to her. A smile of appreciation lifted the corners of her mouth as she took it.

"What kind of homes do most of these kids come from?" he asked as they walked down the path toward the street.

"It varies. Working-class families aren't always dysfunctional."

"I realize that. I know quite a few wealthy, dysfunctional families."

His hadn't been one of the dysfunctional families, and so his spiral into drug addiction had really rocked the foundation of his home. What had happened? His parents had dealt with their own feelings of guilt, and they had all realized that sometimes the world creeps in and people take the wrong path.

At his side, Maggie nodded toward a small house with a neat yard and a newer sedan parked in the drive. "Cathy lives there. She's fifteen. Her mom is a nurse. Her dad died in a car accident four years ago. Cathy's mom works hard, but she makes time for her kids. Cathy has always been in church. We just try to pick up some of the slack for her mom."

He didn't have a comment, and Maggie seemed to be in her own world as she shared the stories with him.

"Chance lives there."

The house she motioned to was surrounded by an overgrown lawn. Several broken-down cars littered the drive. A new sports car was parked in the carport. That didn't fit the picture. Michael felt a shudder of apprehension as he looked at that home.

"Do you know anything about his family?" Michael took hold of Maggie's hand and they crossed the street.

"Enough. Chance hasn't had the best time of it. His mom is in and out of the home. It's a long story."

"I'm willing to listen."

"We'll be late. Remember, the kids will be at the church."

Michael glanced back over his shoulder at the house on the corner. He didn't know much about Chance, but he knew that it would take a strong kid to survive that life.

"Maggie, I wish you wouldn't stay at the church alone at night."

"I'm not afraid." She looked up at him, her bright blue eyes softening. "Stop worrying. I've been doing this for a few years now, and I really am careful."

Of course she was. He knew that, but it didn't take away the uneasy feeling that continued to grow.

The kids gathered around the photographer. He'd brought them all disposable cameras to practice with. Maggie sat next to Michael because sitting somewhere else would have been rude. Chance smiled their way and snapped a picture.

"I got a shot of the lovebirds." He sat back in his chair and laughed at the joke.

"Not cool, Chance." Michael shook his head at the teenager.

No, definitely not cool. Maggie started to get up, to put distance between them and end the thoughts zooming through the minds of the curious teenagers.

"Kids can come up with some strange ideas," Michael said as he leaned over and whispered, "Insane ideas."

The photographer, the father of a church member, invited them all to go outside. The kids rushed after him, leaving chairs scattered everywhere. Maggie went behind him, straightening the chairs.

"You really love these kids, don't you?" Michael was next to her, helping to straighten the room.

"I do love them." Because she looked at them through

Faith's rose-colored glasses, seeing potential. "I was one of them."

Michael stepped back, eyeing her with disbelief reflecting in his hazel eyes. "I don't see that."

"That's because I had potential." She managed a smile. "People look at the kids, at the way they're acting and not at the reason they act that way. What's going on in their lives that makes them behave the way they do."

"You're skirting the subject. We were talking about you."

She headed toward the door with Michael behind her. As she reached for the knob, he touched her hand, stopping her. Maggie turned, carefully avoiding eye contact. His shoes were very nice.

"I'm not talking about my life. The past is the past."

"But somehow still strangely with us." His hand was still on hers, his fingers brushed her knuckles.

Maggie pulled her hand out from under his. "I was one of these kids. My only anchor was my grandmother and a Sunday school teacher who taught me that Jesus loves me."

"And someday maybe you'll tell me the rest of the story?"

"Maybe someday."

They walked outside. The kids were snapping pictures, laughing, pretending to be great photographers and models. They were dreaming of what they could be. That's what Maggie wanted for them. She wanted them to dream big and to realize their potential.

John, a studious boy with short, dark hair and wire-framed glasses was aiming at a squirrel perched in the oak tree next to the church. Michael left the group and wandered up to the boy. Maggie could hear their conversation, and she smiled.

"Newspapers need photographers, John." Michael

pointed to a bird's nest and John aimed. "No one would think you're crazy for wanting that. You could take classes at the community college."

"I never thought of that." John held the camera up and focused. "I just know we can't afford the university."

"You could try for a scholarship." He patted the boy on the back. "Don't sell yourself short."

John nodded and moved away, intent on another shot. Michael walked away, his phone ringing. Maggie watched as he moved farther away from the group. A small moment of doubt flicked through her mind. Would he fall? She hoped not. But she couldn't give complete trust, not yet.

Her mother had promised too many times that she was going to go straight and get clean. It had never happened. But her mother had never had an anchor. Michael walked back to where she stood, leaning against a tree. Michael had an anchor. He had something to believe in, to find strength in.

"I need to go."

"I don't understand."

"I have something to take care of. Will you be okay without me?"

"Sure, we'll be fine."

"I'll be back later." He pulled his keys from his pocket.

"We'll be done later."

"Maggie, I know you don't understand this." He looked over her shoulder. She knew the kids were back there, probably overhearing. He took her arm and led her away from the group.

She waited until they were far enough away before responding. "I'm trying to understand. I don't want to be unreasonable if you have something else going on. But you made a commitment to the kids, to be here and to be a part of this. That isn't a 'sometimes, when I feel like it and don't have something better to do' thing."

He shrugged back into his jacket. "I understand my commitment to the kids. I didn't mean for this to happen, but I can't let down someone who needs help."

"No, I know that you can't."

"I don't want to let you down, either." He sighed and then he backed away. "I have to go."

She nodded, recovering enough to offer him a smile. "I understand."

"I really hope you mean that."

So did she. As he walked away she said a prayer that he would be strong. And then she prayed for herself, because she suddenly realized that maybe she was the one who needed strength.

Michael walked along the brick sidewalk of the downtown shopping area. He hadn't been here in years. The changes took him by surprise. Loft apartments, restaurants and upscale shops lined the streets. There were people everywhere, all kinds of people.

The coffee shop was on the corner. He walked through the door, not at all charmed by the ringing bells that announced his arrival. Katherine sat in a corner of the nearly empty establishment. Her face was on the table and her arms covered her head. She didn't look up, not even when he sat down.

"Kath, you okay, baby?" He touched her arm and she jumped. The flesh was hanging on her and her skin had yellowed. The high school beauty queen who had worried about carrying a few extra pounds was gone. He felt hollow on the inside, knowing she had taken a good friend of his with her.

"What are you doing here?" she mumbled.

"You called."

"I didn't. I wouldn't call you. And shouldn't you be playing with the preacher girl?"

"Leave Maggie out of this."

She nodded and buried her face in her folded arms on the table. "Go away, Michael."

"I can't. I'm going to get you some help." He waved to the cashier and asked her for coffee and a few pastries, he didn't care what kind.

"Michael, you can't help me."

"I can, and I will."

"You think you can help everyone because you think you've found the answers."

"Maybe I have." He touched her hand. "Please, Kath. Have you had a hepatitis C test? We need to get you somewhere so you can get some medical help."

"No." She looked up, for a moment lucid. "Michael, Vince isn't happy that the cops are everywhere. He blames it on you."

"I can take care of myself."

"Can you take care of your friend?"

"You mean, Maggie?" He couldn't give in to anger, not with Katherine.

"Yeah, Maggie."

"She's a good friend."

Katherine looked up, a wistful expression on her face. "I want to be me again."

"Then let's get you into a treatment program. Katherine,

I'll be here to help you." He could do that. He hadn't believed it at first, but now he knew. He was strong enough.

"But…" She jumped up, nearly tripping over her chair that fell backward in her attempt at running. "Vince."

Michael followed her glance toward the front of the building and saw the gray car cruise past. Vince had followed one of them. Vince, who had a vested interest in Katherine, and maybe even loved her in some odd form of the word.

Michael grabbed her arm, hurting inside when he realized his hand went completely around her forearm. "Come on, we're going out the back."

She stumbled again. This time he picked her up and ran.

Chapter Eleven

Michael looked up when his dad's secretary, Janet, knocked on his open door. "Your dad wants you to do some research on the Forester case."

Michael nodded, but his head ached and the thought of more research didn't sound like the antidote to relieving stress. It had been two days since he'd helped Katherine check into a rehab facility. Her family was crushed. They had thought it was an eating disorder.

He still didn't get that. Did that mean they thought an eating disorder should go untreated? Either way, their desire to keep up the front of having the perfect family had almost killed their daughter.

"Do you want me to bring you the file?" Janet still stood in the doorway.

"Please." He smiled up at her. "And you wouldn't have a couple of aspirin and a big jug of coffee, would you?"

She laughed as she walked out of the room. "I just happen to have them both. I'll be back in a few."

Janet returned carrying a tray laden with coffee, a bottle

of aspirin and a sandwich. Janet always thought of everything. Sometimes he felt as if he had two mothers.

"Don't take aspirin on an empty stomach," she warned.

"Oh, so that would be the reason for the sandwich?"

"Precisely." She started to walk away but stopped. "Don't let things get to you."

He nodded in reply. "Thanks, Janet. I'm okay."

As the door closed behind her, Michael slumped forward, resting his head in his hands. He really was okay. Except for the pounding in his head and the way his heart sometimes raced at breakneck speed. Like right now.

His cell phone rang, the musical tone jangling his nerves. He pulled it from the clip and answered.

"Hey, Mikey, just checking in again." The voice was too friendly, too chummy. Michael closed his eyes, remembering that for a time he had bought the "let's be friends" routine.

But that had been a long time ago. He was older now and wiser.

"Hi, Vince." He took a deep breath to strengthen his resolve. *Resist the devil and he will flee.*

"Got something down here, if you want to come and get it."

"No, I don't think so." He had to play the game a little longer. The noose was tightening. Vince would soon be gone. Michael would get the names, find out the connections, the police would finally have what they needed to make a conviction work.

Lead us not into temptation but deliver us from evil.

He could almost hear Pastor Banks's voice as the two of them worked on memorizing scripture.

Vince laughed, the sound cold and carrying not even a

hint of amusement. "You don't think you're interested. But I think you do want it."

"I'm not interested, Vince."

"Really? Is that little blonde you're hanging with making things difficult for you?" Vince laughed again. "Let's play church, Mikey. That'll make your life better. Then you won't want drugs."

"I'm not interested."

"You owe me. And I'm going to make you pay for taking Katherine away."

Michael pushed the off button on the phone. And then he turned it back on. The first number he dialed had been disconnected. Something had obviously happened to his NA sponsor. He searched for another and dialed.

"Hello?"

Her voice was like an instant antidote. "Hi."

"Michael?"

"I'm going to play racquetball. Do you want to join me?"

Maggie watched his car pull into the parking lot. She grabbed the two bottles of water she had pulled out of the fridge when he'd called and headed for the back door.

"I'm sorry, I shouldn't have called you." His first words to her when she approached him were spoken in a rush.

"You don't have to be sorry."

"Yes, I do. You have a life and you're busy. Playing baby-sitter to a grown man shouldn't be your responsibility."

"I didn't think you were calling me for a babysitter."

"You're right."

He handed her a racquet and a ball. "You can go first."

"You know I can't play, right?"

"I'll teach you."

"What happened?" She waited until they were at the wall before asking.

"I needed to get out of the office." He nodded toward the wall. "Serve. Don't you have days like that? Days when you just need to be outside in the fresh air?"

"And what do you mean, 'serve'?"

"Hit the ball at the wall."

"I can hit the ball at the wall. I can even trip and fall."

"Very cute." He nudged her shoulder with his and then stepped away from her. "I couldn't reach my sponsor."

The rush of honesty came out, hurried, like he didn't really want her to catch it. She didn't serve. "I'm not the person for this."

"I didn't ask you to be." He took the ball from her hand. "I came to play racquetball. But I thought since you were good enough to meet me out here, you deserved honesty. I think that one of my steps is being honest. Maybe that's my own personal step, but it's something I have to do. I spent several years living a double life, trying to be the Michael Carson that my parents expected me to be and then being someone else when I wasn't around them."

"How did that work out for you?"

He grinned and served the ball. "Not so great."

The ball came bouncing back and Maggie was pretty sure that she was supposed to hit it at the wall. She did. Michael laughed, but he didn't correct her. The next time he hit the ball she caught it in her hand.

"So, if we're here, and we're being honest, maybe you should tell me what happened."

"Serve."

"No."

He shook his head and walked off. "Maggie, I need to

do this. I can't talk yet. But if you'll give me five or ten minutes without talking, without you asking me questions, I'll talk."

She hit the ball and he somehow managed to get back in time to hit it. It wasn't a perfect game by any stretch of the imagination. Maggie knew that she messed up quite a few times. Michael never said a word.

He chased her wild shots, running until his hair hung damply on his forehead and perspiration glistened on his face. After fifteen minutes he stopped.

"Whew, you can't play, but you can definitely run me ragged."

"You have no one to blame but yourself." She nodded toward the picnic table. "I brought water."

"Thanks." He took the racquet and ball from her hand and followed her to the table.

"My old dealer called me today."

She sat back on the picnic table, sipping at the water and unsure of the proper response for his revelation.

"I..."

"You have to understand the statistics, Maggie. Addictions can stay buried within us, rearing their ugly heads the minute we drop our guard."

"I know about addictions." She fiddled with the cap of her water bottle. "And today, what did that do to you?" She bit down on her bottom lip, looking for better words. "I mean, you're here, so obviously you did the right thing."

"I did the right thing. Or at least I finally did the right thing. I called my sponsor, didn't get an answer, started to panic, and then I realized that I needed to pray first." He shrugged. "I prayed, and then I called you."

"I'm glad you did."

"You know, some days I'm stronger than others. There are times when the sound of his voice wouldn't bother me at all. Today it hit me at the wrong time. But I didn't have a desire to rush out and score some meth. I just knew that I had to get my mind off the call."

She hugged him, which hadn't been her plan. He didn't hug her back, a big sign that she'd made a mistake.

"I'm sorry I got carried away, but I'm proud of you."

He recapped his empty bottle of water. "Yes, well, I'm trying not to be too proud. I can't afford to get carried away. I can't afford to lose focus."

"You're taking my talk about not wearing your emotions on your sleeve a little to the extreme, don't you think?" Her attempt at humor didn't work. He shook his head and hopped down from the picnic table.

"Yes, that's it exactly." He backed away from her, hitting the trash can with the empty bottle in the process. "You're sweet, Maggie, and I appreciate that you were here for me today."

She let him walk away. She had gone far enough into his life for one day. Time to slowly back out and keep her defenses in place.

Michael handed the Weed Eater to a kid who looked like he could handle it. He glanced across the church lawn to the corner where Maggie planted flowers with a couple of the girls. Three days had passed since their racquetball game and in that time their conversations had been stilted, just touching on the weather and how the kids were doing. Maybe he had shared too much and been too honest about his struggle?

He glanced her way again, and this time their gazes

connected. She looked away first, leaving him with unanswered questions. He didn't want to lose her friendship.

"Can you handle it, Zack?" He pointed to the Weed Eater the kid held.

"Sure, I guess. But why are we doing this again?"

"Because it saves the church a lot of money if we do the yard work. And because it's good to give of our time."

"Okay, that's cool with me."

Chance walked up, his smile tight and a tinge of blue on his cheek. He had showed up for church on Wednesday night. It had been the first time, and obviously it hadn't gone over too great at home. He had said it wouldn't.

"Can I talk to you?" Chance didn't give him time to answer. The kid grabbed him by the arm and pulled him away. "Did you know that Curt is a weirdo, and he's been spying on Miss Simmons?"

"Okay."

"Did you know?"

"Calm down, Chance. Is Curt here?"

"Shoot, no. I told him not to come back here again."

Michael almost laughed. "Chance, that might not be the best way to handle the situation. I could talk to him."

"I had to do something. But maybe it won't matter. They might be moving him to a new foster home."

Michael shook his head. Another foster home. He couldn't imagine being these kids and being bounced around this way. If it wasn't foster care, it was from parent to parent.

"You're a good kid, Chance."

"Sure, okay."

"I mean it. And thanks for worrying about Maggie."

Chance shrugged and walked off. "I've got to mow,"

A blast of water hit Michael in the back. He jumped and turned around. It was Maggie. She laughed so hard she lost her footing and fell back, the hose still in her hands. Two of the girls were helping her. Five minutes ago she'd been avoiding him. What had happened to change that?

"I think this is war." He ran for the hose, pulling it and Maggie toward him, both at the same time. The more hose he gathered to his side, the closer she got to him. "You are so going to drown for this."

Three feet away from him, she shrieked and ran, taking her two mighty soldiers with her. Michael grabbed the hose and sprayed, hitting all three of them across the backs of their legs.

"Do you give?" he yelled. "You know I'm going to win."

Maggie turned just as he sprayed, taking a face full of water. She sputtered and choked, wiping at her face with her hands. Michael dropped the hose and ran to her side.

They were both laughing. He offered her the end of his shirt to wipe her face. "I'm sorry, Mag, I didn't mean to do that."

She opened her eyes, mascara running down her cheeks. "Mag?"

"Sorry. *Maggie*."

"I don't mind. It's just a first. And thank you for the use of your shirt." She blinked a few times. "Michael, how did you get the scar on your side?"

"An accident." One that he hadn't planned on talking about.

"A car accident?"

"Maggie, not right now."

She shrugged and her gaze flew to something behind him.

"What in the world is Chance doing?"

He turned, falling for it, and got a face full of water.

"Gotcha!"

Yes, she had gotten him. Before he could get his face wiped, she was gone.

Maggie changed into a pair of sweats and a T-shirt that she kept in her office and then she went in search of something high calorie to make up for the yard work they had done. She glanced out the window as she poured herself a glass of milk. The kids were leaving. Except Chance. He stood under the basketball net, shooting one shot after another. Michael slapped him on the back in a gesture of camaraderie and walked off.

He would be coming inside now. She took a sip of milk and wiped her mouth with the back of her hand. He would want to talk. After she had carefully avoided him since their racquetball game, now he was going to ruin it for her. Or maybe she had ruined it. After all, she had been the one to spray the hose. Why had she done that?

Oh, she remembered why. Because she had caught him glancing her way and she had seen the questions in his hazel eyes. He hadn't understood her silence. He probably thought his struggle offended her. Instead it was her fear of getting hurt that forced her to build walls.

She cared about him—as a friend. She had tried to tell herself that it was okay to care.

The side of her that feared getting hurt didn't agree. Michael had something to prove to himself, and she knew that he needed space to do that. She really wanted to give him that space. She needed it, too.

She had just sat behind her desk when he walked into

the room. Actually he stopped and leaned against the door frame. She ignored the confidence that was such a part of his bearing. There he stood in white leather tennis shoes, faded jeans and a T-shirt, and he looked as though he had it all in control. The world was his for the taking.

Or at least it appeared that way on the surface, probably more to people who didn't know him. But she had seen the pain in his eyes, the hardness that sometimes sneaked in. She had seen the scar on his stomach that was evidence of a life that hadn't been spent in church.

"So, how about that dinner you wouldn't let me buy you the other night?"

"I don't think so. I have work to get done, and I thought I'd order a pizza to take home."

His cell phone rang as she finished talking. He shot her an apologetic look as he answered. Maggie tried to pretend she couldn't hear the conversation. She could, and it stung.

"I'm sorry, I did forget dinner. I'll be there in fifteen minutes."

She waited for him to end the call before she flashed him her best "It's really okay" smile.

"Sorry." To his credit he looked it.

"You have to leave?" She tried to sound unaffected by that. So why in the world did she feel hurt and let down? Because this always happened when she got attached or let herself start to care. It had even happened when she was six years old and Davy Parker had asked her to be his girlfriend. She had circled "yes" on his note. He smiled, and the next day he passed a note to Cindy Johnson asking her the same thing.

"I forgot a dinner engagement and I'm late."

"Of course, I understand." At her age she shouldn't have gotten her hopes up about dinner. She should have remembered Davy Parker.

"I don't want to leave, Maggie. I wouldn't go if I didn't have to."

Or her dad. He could have been there for her during a childhood that had been anything·but stable. She stood, planning to escape, to get herself a cup of coffee and another dozen cookies. "You don't have to explain your actions to me, Michael."

Okay, that didn't sound at all like the voice of someone who didn't care. She would have to work on that, on getting down a certain degree of neutrality.

"I'm not walking out on you. I forgot a prior commitment, that's all." He stood and moved closer. Maggie felt him invading her imaginary circle of personal space and backed away.

Age twenty, Greg in a car, wanting more than she had ever considered giving, and taking it when she said no.

She slid past him, heading for the door. He reached for her arm and she moved from his grasp. Michael, not Greg, she reminded herself, and Michael wouldn't hurt her. She knew that without doubting.

But he could hurt her. Somewhere along the way her heart had become entangled, forgetting that she didn't want to form attachments. The sincerity in his hazel eyes and his love for the kids made her want to believe in him.

More than that, sometimes when he looked at her, the way he was looking at her at this very moment, she felt like he honestly cared about her.

"Maggie, I'm not sure what's going on."

She nearly laughed. The poor guy probably didn't get

it. If anyone could have less experience with male/female relationships than she did, it would have to be Michael Carson. He wouldn't notice a girl getting attached if she used Super Glue.

Okay, so not his fault. Give him a break.

"I need a glass of water to wash down my milk. I poured that huge glass. Silly me, I forgot that I don't like milk."

"I promised you dinner, and I'm going to keep that promise." His cell phone rang again. "But maybe not tonight."

"Big plans?" she asked when he hung up.

"I'm supposed to have dinner with my parents and an old college buddy of my dad's…and like the evil twin I am, I forgot."

"Oh." That one pathetically lacking word slipped from her lips. What else could she say? "You have a twin?"

He laughed. "You know I don't have a twin. Hey, I have an idea. Why don't you come with me?"

"I don't think so." She reached for her coffee cup and slid past him.

"Why not?"

"I'm wearing sweats and a T-shirt. And because my last visit with your parents was a little bit of a disaster."

"It wasn't."

"Michael, you might not have noticed, but I don't belong in your world."

"You belong wherever you want to be, Maggie."

He had her there. "Okay, I don't want to be in that world."

It was the world of her father and her grandparents. And they had never thought she belonged.

"I don't get you, Maggie."

"It isn't a requirement for working here. We can work with the kids and not completely understand each other.

You`should probably go now. You don't want to be any later than you already are."

"Fine, I'm going. But, Maggie, eat something other than cookies. You need to take care of yourself."

She smiled at that. She had been taking care of herself for a long time, long before he showed up.

"Have a good time, Michael."

He shot a smile over his shoulder as he walked out.

An hour later the ringing of the telephone interrupted her work. Maggie glanced at the object, wishing it could understand that she didn't want to be bothered. It rang again and she knew she would answer, it might be her grandmother.

"There's going to be a young man at the door in about five minutes." Michael's voice, and he sounded very pleased. "It's safe to let him in."

"Oh, are *you* matchmaking now?" She smiled, shifting her shoulder to hold the phone against her cheek.

"Not on your life. I just wanted to warn you, so you wouldn't be afraid to open the door."

"So what does the young man want?" She shoved aside a pile of papers. It was never easy to get everything in order for vacation Bible school. "Is he here to clean?"

"It's a surprise. I just wanted to do something nice for you." He was smiling, she could hear it in his voice. "I have to go, so hurry and answer the front door."

As if on cue, a banging on the front door of the church ended their conversation.

The surprise at the door brought a mist of tears to her eyes. The young man held out a tray and as she took it, he bowed and handed her a note. Maggie thanked him, offered a tip that he wouldn't accept and then stepped back into the building to lock the door.

The aroma that wafted out from under the coverings on the tray made her mouth water. Maggie didn't make it to her office. She sat at the front desk and lifted one of the coverings. Chicken with a creamy—she leaned to sniff—mustard sauce, asparagus, rice, a roll and even cheesecake for dessert.

Her hand still clutched the note. Lifting the flap, she pulled out the piece of paper and held it up. "Someone has to take care of you. Eat this before it gets cold and forgive me for running out on you. Michael."

Of course she would forgive him, how could she not forgive him when her heart had just melted into a huge puddle on the floor?

Chapter Twelve

Friday afternoon, after brief spring showers, the sun came out and so did the kids. A large group gathered in the rec room to play pool or Ping-Pong. Most of them, but not all. Maggie peeked through the miniblinds in the church kitchen and watched Michael playing basketball with Chance.

He pulled down the bandanna that was wrapped around his forehead, wiped his face, then he pushed the red cloth back into place. Glistening with sweat, he held the basketball over his head and jumped, making the shot with ease. Chance shook his head and walked off.

"Spying?"

Maggie jumped, spinning to face Pastor Banks. "Just watching them play," she hedged as she brushed past him, reaching for a glass. "I came in to get a glass of water."

"Maggie, you're nearly twenty-seven years old. It's okay for you to be attracted to a man." Pastor Banks followed her to the sink. Sometimes she regretted that he had filled the role of father figure in her life. It made him incredibly opinionated at times.

"Who said I'm attracted to anybody?" She ran the glass under the water, emptied it and refilled it. "I was watching their silly game. Chance is really doing great. Don't you think?"

"We're not talking about Chance, we're talking about you and the fact that you won't let yourself have a relationship, other than friendships."

"I'm not that needy." She smiled, hoping to get a similar response from her pastor. He didn't smile. "Pastor Banks, I'm happy doing what I do. This is the commitment that I've made, to serve God by working with teens. I don't have room in my life for relationships that might take my time and attention away from what I do."

"Not true. You're trying to protect your heart. You have to stop punishing yourself for mistakes that your parents made." Pastor Banks pointed to a chair and she didn't dare tell him no. She plopped down, concentrating on the glass of water and hoping the sermon wouldn't last the usual hour.

"Go ahead, I'm listening."

"No, you're not. You're closing your ears to everything I say." He pulled the glass out of her hand. The fatherly look in place on his face, telling her he *would* be heard. "Maggie, you have to forgive your dad and stop living your life in this shadow of guilt. You did not make a mistake, your parents did. I know that isn't what you want to hear, but you have to stop punishing yourself as if your very existence is the sin."

The words sank in, even when she tried to shrug them off. This was a new sermon, not the old one about forgiving her dad. Or even the one about letting someone in. This one would take some time to digest.

"I'm illegitimate." She looked up, blinking back the tears that burned her eyes. "Do you know how that hurts? All of my life I've been asked, 'Where is your dad?' and I didn't have an answer. How could I tell kids that I don't have a father? Not a real father, the kind who shows up at school programs or holds your hand when you cross the street."

"But you do have a Father, a Heavenly Father, and He wants you to give this pain to Him. If you don't, then you're carrying the burden alone."

She knew that, but it didn't make it any easier. She reached for her glass of water and Pastor Banks slid it across the table to her. After taking a drink she lifted her eyes to meet his.

"You're right. I can't paint everyone guilty because of what a couple of people have done. I know that's wrong, but I have a hard time opening up, knowing that I could be hurt again." She slid her hand down the side of the glass.

"What if you keep yourself closed off and you miss out?"

"Good point."

"Maggie, are you doing okay, having Michael here? Is it bringing up too much of the past, and too many memories about Greg and what he did? You told me when we started this with Michael that you'd be honest with me if it was a problem. I promised you I'd move him out of the youth ministry if it didn't work."

"I'm fine with Michael. To be honest, having him here has proven one thing to me. I'm healing. Michael isn't like my mom. He's going to make it. And what Greg did is in the past. Sometimes it comes back to haunt me, but it doesn't have a hold over my life."

"I'm glad to hear that. So what is the problem between you and Michael?"

"I want to know that we can count on him. I don't want to start relying on him, or have the kids attach themselves to him, only to have him decide he doesn't need this anymore."

Or worse, what if he slipped? What if the past pulled him back into the life he had escaped? She shouldn't doubt, but the phone calls and times that he left without giving an explanation worried her.

She didn't want to lose him. And that thought frightened her more than anything, because she didn't know exactly what it meant.

"I don't think that's going to happen."

Pastor Banks's statement brought her head up and for a moment she wondered if he knew what she was thinking. "I'm sorry, what isn't going to happen?"

"He isn't going to change his mind about being here." His eyes softened with compassion. "You're like a daughter to me, Maggie. If I could take this pain from you, I would. I can pray for you, though. I want you to pray about it. Let God take the burden. Don't keep holding on to it, pretending it's gone when it isn't."

She promised to pray. But she didn't tell him that the burden had changed and had become something completely different. The new fear was that if she didn't keep her distance from Michael Carson, her heart would end up broken.

Michael wiped his face with the bandanna he had tied around his neck. Chance shouted to get his attention, but Michael's mind was still on the conversation he'd overheard when he went inside for a drink of water.

Maggie's words, tight with pain, had buried themselves in his heart. He tried to force them from his mind and the role he played in that pain.

He didn't want to be another person who hurt her, but he couldn't be the person she leaned on. He didn't know yet if he could even be strong enough for himself.

"Are we going to play?" Chance rushed forward, hands out for the pass.

Michael tossed the basketball to the teenager, who made the shot with ease. The kid had talent, surprisingly good talent, maybe even exceptional. Michael relayed that information verbally and Chance turned several shades of red. Compliments were something the boy never seemed to understand.

"You're good, Chance. Keep this up and maybe you'll get a college scholarship."

Chance shook his head and lifted the basketball to let it fly through the hoop again. "I'm not even on the team at school."

"Not on the team? Why not?" Michael grabbed the ball as it bounced across the pavement of the driveway.

"I just never make the cut. And my grades didn't used to be so great. It doesn't matter." The lanky kid, all legs and arms, blond hair falling into his eyes, shrugged his shoulders.

"Next year you have to try. Think about it, Chance, you might be able to get a college scholarship."

Chance shook his head. "My dad would just say we can't afford it."

Visions of a shiny new sports car parked in Chance's front yard flashed before Michael's eyes. He tossed the basketball toward the hoop and watched as it circled the rim and dropped through the net. He took a deep breath, releasing his anger with Chance's dad.

"Where does your dad work, Chance?"

Chance trotted across the pavement and grabbed the ball. "He doesn't."

Michael nodded and jumped forward to grab the basketball. Chance slid past him. As he did, Michael caught sight of another bruise. This time the dark swelling was on his arm. Maybe it wasn't a fist mark, maybe the kid ran into something.

Michael doubted it. He wanted to ask questions, but the timing wasn't right. In the last couple of weeks, Chance had started to come out of his shell, to drop some of his anger.

A car honked. Michael glanced toward the road and saw the car from Chance's driveway. He turned his attention back to the kid at his side. Chance stood frozen in the parking lot, the basketball in his hands.

Michael looked back in the direction of the car that had slowed to a crawl as it passed. Chance's dad. Obviously the guy was a "businessman." Michael felt a sickening knot in his stomach.

"My dad." Chance spoke softly as he dropped the ball on the pavement. "I should go."

"Chance, are you okay?" Michael grabbed the ball, which had rolled a few feet from where Chance dropped it. "Do you need to talk?"

The kid shook his head, blond hair falling into his eyes. "No, why would I need to talk? I just need to go."

They walked back to the church.

"I'm here, if you change your mind." Michael put a hand out and stopped Chance from going inside.

Chance jerked away from Michael's hand. "I don't need your help, so back off."

Michael watched him walk away, but in his mind he replayed all of the times in his own life when he had pushed away the people who wanted to help him. He was still rebuilding those relationships, but he had pushed some people so far away, he thought he might never repair the damage. And now, if he pushed Maggie away to keep her safe, what would happen to the friendship that was growing between them?

Maggie looked up when Michael walked into her office. He didn't return her smile. He crossed the room, peeked out the window and then sat in the chair across from her desk.

"What's wrong with you, did you lose the game?" The kids had been gone for almost an hour. In that time, Michael had been missing in action.

"No...well, yeah, but that isn't it." He folded his hands on the desk and leaned forward. "Chance's dad is beating him."

"Yeah, I know."

He looked up, his eyes widening. "What do you mean, you know?"

"Chance has been in and out of foster care for years," she explained.

"But his dad is beating him."

Maggie felt sorry for him. He had grown up in a different world, one that had protected him from the harsh realities of life...for a while.

How could she explain a system that was overworked and limited on funds? "Michael, the system isn't perfect. We hotline his dad, Family Services comes in and investigates. Sometimes they can pull Chance from the home and put him in a foster home, or a group home, sometimes there isn't enough evidence. And the biggest problem is that there aren't enough homes for teenagers. They end up shipping them all over the area and sometimes out of state."

"I didn't know." He looked down at the desk. "I wonder if I'm cut out for this."

"For what? For ministry?" She reached across the desk

and covered his hand with hers. "The fact that you care says a lot, Michael. If you didn't care about these kids and what happens to them, I would tell you to take a hike."

He looked up then and smiled. "I know.

"God has a way of leading us into unknown territory."

"But I'm not qualified to minister to these kids." He leaned back in his chair and laced his fingers behind his head. "Ministers minister. I'm an ex-con with no experience, not even in life. I can handle teaching them some math, or even some Spanish, but I don't know how to handle situations like the one with Chance."

"Listen to your heart. You're doing a better job than you think."

"I'm an ex-con, Maggie. I'm an addict." He stood and lifted his shirt. "You saw this the other day?"

She nodded as he pointed to a jagged scar on his stomach. He sat back down, lowering his shirt and lifting his head so that she could look into his eyes.

"What happened?"

"That's what happens when a drug deal goes bad. That's from a broken bottle." He looked up, meeting her gaze head-on this time. "That is a reminder of where I've been."

"Which is exactly why you need to be here. Because you can relate to what some of these kids are facing."

"I don't want to let you down."

Good, because she didn't want to be let down. More and more she found herself believing in him. That scared her more than the idea of always being alone.

Michael pounded on Noah's door. His brother finally opened, holding the phone to his ear as he motioned

Michael inside. He turned the phone off and tossed it on a table as he pointed to the couch.

Michael sat. "Why isn't Vince in jail?"

"You're asking the wrong guy. I'm not on the local team. I know a few people. I was willing to help. Now it's up to them, and I'm afraid I'll be leaving in a couple of weeks. Why?"

"Because I just left an apartment where some very nice people were socializing, and Vince is getting suspicious. He isn't very happy about me getting help for Katherine. Maybe I shouldn't have stepped in, but I couldn't leave her like that, and I didn't realize that they'd developed a relationship."

"I doubt if it had anything to do with love. She just needed a way to get hooked up with her fix." Noah walked to the fridge and pulled out a couple of colas. He tossed one to Michael. "How is Katherine doing?"

"I think she's going to be out in a few weeks. She's doing great, I guess. Or at least she is as long as she's locked up."

"You did a good thing, going to bat for her. I know it wasn't easy."

"No, it wasn't. But now I have to figure out the best way to keep Maggie safe."

Noah shrugged as if the answer was easy. "Keep your distance."

"You make it sound easy."

Noah set his can of soda on the table. "I guess I'm just used to it."

Michael digested that statement and realized that he had just been given an important look into his brother's heart and life. He kept his distance. From everyone.

"I'm not sure if I can keep my distance. Remember, I'm helping with the youth at the church."

"I know that. But I'm telling you, if she doesn't matter to you, she won't matter to Vince." His eyebrows shot up. "Does she matter to you?"

"She's a friend. She's had enough tough times in her life. She doesn't need for me to add to them with my personal drama."

"This is almost over, Michael. Start creating a normal life for yourself. Don't let these things control you. Your life is much bigger than a few incidents with Vince."

"Or the harassment of a few cops who don't believe I'm clean."

"They can't help themselves. If they think you're going to give them a break, they're going to keep their eyes on you."

"I've given them the only break I can. I'm getting the names of people that Vince is using." He stood up and walked to the door. "I've done what I could to make amends."

"Take care of yourself." Noah's words followed him out the door.

Michael would take care of himself. And he had something else he wanted to take care of. Maggie had gone shopping in Branson. He had the day to get this job done.

Two hours after leaving Noah's, Michael pulled up in front of Maggie's house. After parking, he eyed the roof. He felt a moment, or longer, of doubt. How in the world could he do this job?

"Michael, what are you doing here?" Betty stood in the open front door, staring at him over the rim of her glasses as he walked up to the house.

"I..." He held up the tools he'd bought. "I'm going to fix your roof."

"Now aren't you a sweet thing." She stepped out the door onto the front stoop. "Michael, do you know anything about roofing a house?"

He held up the book on roofing. Betty looked at the thin publication. Her eyes narrowed and then widened as her mouth formed an O. "I see."

At least she didn't laugh. He felt a little comforted by that. But then, people who were frightened generally didn't laugh.

"I guess I don't really know how—" he looked up at the roof again "—but I think I can do it."

"Of course you can." Her smile reassured him. "Maggie isn't here."

"I know. That's why I'm here." He took a step toward the house. "Would you mind showing me the areas where the roof leaks?"

"Of course, come on in. We can have a glass of cold lemonade while I show you around."

An hour later the supplies were delivered and Michael found himself on the roof, ready to begin the job of roofing.

Sort of. Well, he was ready. He just didn't know where to start. Or how.

He squatted precariously, holding the how-to magazine in one hand and a hammer in the other. The magazine pages flipped in the wind and he tried to push them down so that he could read the page on "first steps to roofing."

A car honked and his foot slipped. He scrambled to steady himself and lifted his hand to wave at Pastor Banks. The magazine slipped down the roof, the wind tossing the pages. Michael watched as his guide to roofing fluttered to the ground. He sighed and shook his head. It would have been easier to hire someone.

Somewhere he had heard that gifts were more special if they were made by hand, not store-bought.

Pastor Banks parked his car and stepped out onto the sidewalk. He glanced from the pile of roofing materials, to Michael. A broad grin spread across his face.

"Are you moonlighting as a roofer?"

"Something like that."

Pastor Banks grabbed the magazine and an extra hammer before reaching for the ladder. He shifted the heavy aluminum contraption and then jiggled it before putting his foot on the first rung. Michael could have told him that climbing the ladder took a lot of faith.

"I know you can probably do this on your own," he started with that statement as he sat, "but I've been meaning to get something done about this roof for several months. The two of us should be able to get it patched up, and then later maybe some of the men from the church can finish the job. If you don't mind the help, of course? And maybe you could stop calling me 'Pastor' and call me 'Robert'?"

Michael sat back on the slope of the roof and laughed. Raising his shirt, he wiped the sweat from his brow and then shook his head.

"I think Betty would prefer for me to have help," he admitted. "She looked a little worried when she left. And I think I can manage to call you Robert, at least while we're facing death together."

"I can't think why Betty would be worried." Robert Banks chuckled as he started to work.

"If she was praying when she left, it was probably for the safety of her house."

"She's definitely a praying woman," Pastor Banks agreed.

Michael watched the other man's actions and began to mimic his movements. Pastor Banks had definitely done this job before. As the two of them worked, they discussed the church and then Michael's job. The topic of conversation switched to Maggie, a topic Michael had wanted to avoid.

"Maggie is a special young woman," Pastor Banks started. "I've watched her grow up, and she's done remarkably well, all things considering."

"To be honest, I don't know that much about her life." Michael turned to face the other man. "But I admire what I do know about her."

"Michael, I have to ask. Is there something going on between you and Maggie?"

Michael sat back on his heels. "Why would you think that?"

"People talk, Michael. The church is abuzz with gossip. Nice how they forget that gossip is one of the top ten— 'Thou shalt not bear false witness.'" Pastor Banks sort of laughed. "I think they think that gossip is a gray area, not really a sin, and great entertainment."

"Yeah, well, I definitely don't need for people to gossip about my life. I've given them enough real information to work with."

"So, about Maggie?"

"We're not involved. I think of her as a friend. But as for involvements of the romantic kind, I don't have that in mind. I have a lot to learn about life and about myself before I can undertake relationships."

"That's understandable. And don't worry, Michael, I

think you have more of a grasp on life, and yourself, than you think."

"Sometimes I think that, too. Sometimes I doubt it. Depends on the day and the circumstances."

"Would it help you if you knew that we all doubted ourselves?"

Michael grabbed a few nails from the pouch around his waist and picked the hammer back up. "Yeah, that helps."

"The work won't get done on its own," Pastor Banks reminded.

"What about Maggie's dad?" Michael pounded nails into the shingles he had placed on the roof.

"You'll have to wait for her to tell you what she wants you to know."

"I don't know if that day will ever come. I'm not high on her list of people to trust."

"Don't push her. She'll open up in time."

Michael lifted his shirt again, wiping the perspiration from his forehead and neck. "I can't pay for the mistakes other people in her life have made."

"True, very true. Be her friend and let her make the decision to let you into her life." Pastor Banks reached for more shingles and went back to work.

"I'm not like her father."

Robert sat back on his heels. "She told you?"

"I overheard."

"I see." He placed a section of shingles on the roof. "Jacob Simmons isn't her favorite topic."

"I'm sure he's not."

Michael let the conversation drop. The sun turned up the heat and the roof grew warmer. Pastor Banks pulled a handkerchief from his pocket and mopped at his face.

"Phew, it is hot up here. What do you think—let's finish this last bad spot and get down before we both suffer from heatstroke?"

"Sounds good to me."

Michael sighed with relief when he stepped down off the ladder. It took a minute for his legs to adjust to terra firma. Pastor Banks took the final step and joined him.

Michael pulled two bottles of water out of his cooler. "Here you go."

"Thank you." Pastor Banks took the bottle Michael offered him. He unscrewed the lid and downed half the contents in one gulp. "Let's sit down."

Michael nodded and dropped to the ground under the shade of a pretty ancient walnut tree. He finished his water and screwed the cap back on. Pastor Banks was staring at the empty bottle in his hands.

"I'm going to give you some advice, Michael."

Michael looked up, ready for any kind of advice he might hear.

"About relationships."

"Something I haven't had a lot of opportunity for." Michael laughed. "And something I'm not sure I'm ready for."

"You'll be ready. Probably sooner than you think. And when it happens, remember this, relationships are hard work. Building the relationship is work. Maintaining it is work. Keeping it fresh, also work."

Michael laughed. "That's the advice? I thought you were going to tell me something magical that would make it work. You've blown me away. I thought when love happened it would be her feeling it, me feeling it and, *tah-dah!* Love."

"Boy, are you naive." Pastor Banks stood. "I should get

home. I have a relationship of my own that is feeling neglected and would like to go out to dinner tonight."

"I couldn't have done this without you."

"No, but I admire that you would have tried."

Michael hoped that the other project he had undertaken would be as well received as the roofing job. Maggie needed healing, bridges built that would connect her to people who would shelter and care about her. It wasn't his place to build those bridges, but he had taken the steps anyway.

If something should happen to him... He briefly closed his eyes, pushing away thoughts that couldn't bring him peace.

Chapter Thirteen

"**Y**ou let him fix the roof?" Maggie blinked a few times, thinking her grandmother had obviously lost her mind. She dropped the bags she'd carried in from her shopping trip and turned to give Faith a look that would stop the giggles.

"He looked so earnest about it, dear. He wanted to do something good, and I let him."

"He's taking over my life."

"Taking over your life?" Faith laughed. "For someone who is normally pretty serious, that's a little on the dramatic side. Unless, of course, there's more to this than you're telling us?"

Faith smiled at Maggie's grandmother and added a conspiratorial wink. Maggie walked down the hall to the kitchen. The sinkful of dirty dishes looked like a good distraction and a way to work off her anger or whatever the emotion was that tumbled around inside her.

"I've been saving money to get that roof fixed." Maggie turned on the hot water to wash dishes. She squeezed a good squirt of lavender-scented liquid into the water and inhaled when the aroma drifted up. She had always thought that lavender was supposed to be soothing. Obviously not.

"Well, now you can thank God for answered prayers and use the money for new carpet." Faith set the plates into the sink and grabbed a dishrag. "And thank God for sending Michael Carson."

"Yes, of course." Maggie scooted Faith out of the way and grabbed the rag from her hand. "Go play the piano for us."

"You're using me. Play the piano yourself."

"Gran gets sick of 'Mary Had a Little Lamb.'" She shot a smile at her grandmother. "Right?"

"And 'Twinkle Twinkle.'" Grandma joined Maggie at the sink. "Go play for us, Faith. We've missed hearing you."

"Yes, I'm such an amazing talent," Faith commented as she walked out of the room.

Maggie ignored that comment. Faith had a gift, whether she wanted to admit it or not. Someday…someday she would not only recognize it, but hopefully use it.

Faith yelled from the living room, accompanied by the sound of her fingers running over the piano keys. "I'm going to play, but you're going to stop fighting with Michael. Give the guy a chance. He needs to prove himself, so let him."

"I'm trying." Maggie smiled at her grandmother who was watching her. "But the two of you have to remember that this is about helping him as he gets involved in ministry, not about giving him carte blanche to my life."

For some reason that seemed impossible. Michael had already invaded, taking up space not allotted for his presence. He had invaded her dreams.

* * *

The telephone on her desk was ringing when Maggie walked into her office on Wednesday morning, a cup of coffee in one hand, a box of cookies in the other. She set the cookies down and reached for the telephone. Michael walked in behind her, carrying two paper bags.

"Hello?" She answered the phone and watched as Michael pulled bagels, cream cheese and a plastic knife out of the bag. He reached into the other bag and produced single-serving containers of orange juice.

Maggie pointed to her coffee and cookies. As she listened to the caller trying to sell her siding for her house, Michael reached for her cookies. She watched as he left the room with her breakfast, leaving behind food that looked terribly healthy...and almost appetizing.

She put the phone down and reached for a bagel. The telephone rang again, startling her. Michael had entered the room and had started spreading cream cheese on the bagels. She picked up the phone, smiling a thank-you to him as she lifted it to her ear.

"Maggie Simmons." She smiled at Michael and lifted her bagel as she mouthed the words "thank you."

"Maggie." A long pause followed. She took a bite of her bagel and waited. "Maggie, my name is Jacob Simmons. I'm your father."

The room tilted and started to spin. Michael's face loomed above hers. She set the bagel down, but she couldn't form words to respond to her caller. Tears that she didn't want to shed welled up behind her eyelids and her throat tightened with emotion.

Jacob Simmons? Just like that, he barged into her life, claiming the title of "father." That word should mean something. Pastor Banks was a dad. She had seen him with his children. She knew what the word meant. Pastor Banks had been more of a parent to her than the man on the other end of the phone.

"Maggie?" His voice should have sounded familiar, but it didn't. She'd never spoken to him, not once in her life.

"Yes, I'm here."

"I know this must be a shock."

Of course, a shock, that's what it was. She was glad he told her how to feel because at the moment she didn't know what name to put on the wrenching pain that twisted inside her.

"Yes, it's a shock." She drew in a deep breath.

"I know this call is a surprise to you, but I'd like to see you," he continued, sounding nearly as personal as the man who had tried to sell her siding not five minutes earlier. She had siding on her home. She didn't need a father, not now. She'd passed the years when she'd needed someone to hold her, to tell her that nightmares weren't real.

"You want to see me? So, you're scheduling an appointment."

"Maggie, this isn't easy."

"No, it isn't easy, is it?" She looked away from Michael's concerned gaze. "It isn't at all what I expected. I always thought that if you called it would be a great moment in my life. It isn't."

"If I could just have a chance to talk to you."

"You've had twenty-six years of chances."

"I know that I've let you down. I know that I hurt you. But I do want to see you."

"Just like that, you want to see me? What happened to the promise you made to my mother, that you would take care of me if something happened to her? Something did happen, she died. And you weren't there."

"I know."

Of course he knew. She squeezed the bridge of her nose and waited for her vision to clear. Michael was sitting on the corner of her desk. She met his clear, compassionate gaze.

"I'm not sure if I want to see you."

"I understand that. But I think we do need to see each other. I've made a lot of mistakes. The biggest was not being a part of your life."

The words sounded so right. It was what she'd always prayed for, what she'd always wanted to hear. But why now?

"Why now?" Only he had the answer to that question.

"I received a phone call from someone who was tracking me down for you."

"I see." Her gaze came up, locking with Michael's, and she knew immediately who had tracked her father down. Her heart didn't know how to respond to that knowledge. "I never contacted you because I didn't want to force you to be a part of my life. I thought your absence said it all."

"I should have been a part of your life."

"I can't talk right now." She scooted her chair away from the desk and walked to the window. "Maybe soon. Let me have time to think about this."

"Can I see you in a few weeks? I'll be in Missouri on business."

She tried to think of a reason she couldn't see him. Several excuses came to mind, but those would have been lies. And she would have been denying God's answer to her prayers. She couldn't say it was too late, but she wanted to.

"Maggie, I'm sorry." He repeated the words he had already told her.

"I believe you." She closed her eyes and rolled her neck, trying to relieve the tension. "I need time to think."

She hung up and when she turned, Michael was still at her desk. He didn't turn away. He didn't even have the sense to look guilty.

"*You* did this." She sat again, touching the bagel, not picking it up. Tears burned her eyes, but she wouldn't let them fall. She didn't need tears, not today, not over Jacob Simmons.

"I did."

"Why would you do this? What made you think you had the right to interfere in my life this way?"

"I want to help." He shrugged. "Maybe it was a mistake. But then, maybe it wasn't."

"This is my dad, not the roof, or coffee, or even Chance. This is a man who has denied my presence since before my birth."

"I know."

He got off the desk and squatted before her, taking her hands in his. She let him. His fingers were strong as they wrapped around her hands, holding tight. The comfort of that touch mixed in with anger. He had stepped into an area of her life that no one else had ever entered, not with this kind of action.

She should feel something other than anger, but she couldn't allow that, not yet. What kind of person did this for someone?

"This is my life, Michael, mine. I'm not sure why you thought I needed for you to come in and fix it."

"Like you try to fix everyone else."

She bit down on her bottom lip. "You can't fix other people, they have to fix themselves."

"Sometimes they need a helping hand." He lifted her

hand, brushing it against his cheek. "Isn't that what you do here for these kids, help them fix lives that others consider broken?"

"And sometimes they need to be left alone. Some things can't be fixed." She pulled her hands free from his. "I'm sure that someday I'll thank you for this, but right now I need time to think. And I need to figure out how to stop being angry with you."

"Fine, I have to go to work. I just wanted to bring you breakfast." He walked to the door, but then he stopped and turned. "You know, you don't make it easy to be your friend."

She opened her mouth to respond, to tell him she hadn't meant it to be that way, but he turned and left, giving her the time alone she had thought she wanted.

Michael watched as the mouse crawled out of hiding, its whiskers twitching as it scurried across the floor to the crackers he'd left for it. It stopped midway across the floor and looked around, beady eyes surveying the room.

"So, my little friend, we're a lot alike, aren't we? You aren't really wanted by most people. Sometimes I feel the same way."

The mouse hurried across the floor, grabbed a piece of cracker and then disappeared behind the bookcase. The telephone rang. Michael looked at the caller ID before answering.

"What?"

"Mike, my friend, I think you still owe me money. And as someone who owes me, I'm trying to think of a way for you to pay your debt."

"I'll send you a check."

"That would be too easy."

"What do want, Vince?" Michael closed his eyes, listening and feeling nothing, not even temptation.

"Pick something up for me."

"This is a setup, isn't it? I go pick up your package, you have someone there to break my legs."

"You've been watching too many movies."

Michael stood and walked to the front door. He looked out, watching as the rain poured down. The grass and trees were brilliant green. The sky had been gray for two days. He hadn't seen Maggie since the day of the phone call.

"Mike, if you cooperate, I'll leave your friend alone."

"You don't have to worry about that, she isn't my friend."

It couldn't have come at a more convenient time, the fact that Maggie was upset with him. Contacting her father had put distance between them. It hadn't been his goal, his goal had only been to help her. It had worked to his advantage, though. If it meant getting Vince to leave her alone, it was worth it. Even if it meant losing her forever.

"Vince, I'm not going to do your deal."

"You'll regret that."

"I regret a lot of things, most of them have to do with you. But this is one thing I won't regret. I'm done playing your games."

A car pulled up the drive. Jimmy. He ended the conversation with Vince and opened the door.

"You look good."

"Thanks." Michael motioned his friend into the living room.

"Do you want to go out tonight?"

"No, I can't. I need to get laundry done, and I have some errands to run."

"Do you ever do anything for fun?"

Jimmy walked into the kitchen and opened the door to the fridge. He helped himself to a can of soda and offered one to Michael.

"No, thanks. And yes, I do have fun."

"Really, what do you do for fun?" Jimmy walked back into the living room. He surveyed the couch and the ancient recliner, choosing the recliner.

"I…"

"Gone on any dates since you got out? No disrespect to the time you spend with the lovely youth worker, but have you met up with any old friends other than myself, or gone out to dinner?"

"No, I haven't." Michael continued to stand in the center of the living room. He caught sight of his unshaved face in the mirror over the sofa. "I'm not exactly the guy that girls want to take home to meet their parents. I'm a felon for life. That isn't exactly the résumé for dating success."

"No, I guess you have a point there. But it wouldn't hurt you to get out once in a while."

"No, it probably wouldn't. I'll work on that."

Jimmy's attention shifted to the corner of the room. He grimaced, his eyes narrowing. "Is that the same mouse?"

"Yeah." Michael hid a smile as the mouse slipped back under the entertainment center.

"Why don't you get a trap?"

Michael shrugged, unsure of the answer. "So, why are you really here?"

"I didn't have a date, either." He smiled, but the gesture didn't reach his eyes. "And I'm worried about my dad."

"Is he getting worse?"

"Today was worse. And when I went to visit, he asked

me to read the Bible. He's worried about eternity and I don't have answers."

"You started at the right place. Keep reading the Bible to him. And call Pastor Banks."

Jimmy looked away, focusing on the window as a flash of lightning lit up the room and thunder rattled the walls. "I thought you might be able to talk to him."

"I could try, but I'm not sure how much good I would be."

"You would do more than you think. No one can deny that you've changed. I give you a hard time, Michael, but I admire what you're doing. You're stronger than you think."

Michael wasn't sure about that. There were days when he might have agreed. Not today. At least he knew he wasn't on his own. Even when he felt weak, he knew that God was there to give him strength.

He wanted to share that with his friend, but he knew it wasn't the right time. Jimmy wasn't ready to hear, not yet.

"I'll talk to your dad." The words were simple to say and the look of relief that passed over Jimmy's face made Michael glad he'd said yes.

It was the one thing he felt good about that day. The other things all seemed tangled in confusion—Vince, church and Maggie.

Michael walked through the church a few days later. A quick glance at his watch and he knew he was late. A chaotic tangle of voices came from the kitchen. He stepped into the room and into the middle of a party. Banners hung from the walls and balloons floated to the ceiling. Chance's birthday party, and he was late. He hadn't planned it that way and he knew he couldn't explain it to Maggie. She couldn't know where he'd been or what he'd been doing.

Maggie looked up from cutting the cake. Her eyes flicked to his and then away. He crossed the room, greeting a few of the kids as he passed through the crowd. Being late served one purpose, it pushed the wedge between them a little deeper.

"I didn't think you'd be here." She cut a piece of cake and handed it to him. "Chance was asking."

"I'm sorry that I wasn't here sooner. I had other appointments. I tried to call, but kept getting your voice mail."

"Don't worry about it."

"Maggie, I am sorry."

She handed him a stack of plates. "Can you serve the cake?"

"I can. And a dish of humble pie if you would take it."

"Stop."

"Forgive me?"

"I've forgiven you. I forgave you three days ago. I even called my dad. I'm going to meet with him when he comes to Springfield."

His heart did a funny sigh of relief. "I'm glad to hear that."

He was glad she had forgiven him, and glad that she was moving forward with her dad.

"We can't talk now. These kids are expecting cake and ice cream, and I have gifts to wrap."

"Okay, I'll serve, you wrap."

Michael took the knife that Maggie held out to him. He finished slicing the cake as she walked away. One of the girls picked up the stack of paper cups and started filling them with ice. Across the room the boys were hitting balloons into the air. It was a safe place for kids, somewhere to hang out.

A safe place. Michael wished he had been involved in a group like this when he was a kid. Here the kids had positive peer pressure. He had watched them and listened to their conversations. Sometimes they were hard on one another, harder than an adult would have been.

"Don't I get the first piece of cake?" Chance sat next to him, the bruise on his face had disappeared.

"No way, girls first," Cathy teased, her face turning pink when Chance looked up, making eye contact with her.

"Girls first, but after me." Chance continued to tease. When Michael set the first piece of cake in front of the teenager, Chance picked it up and handed it to Cathy.

There were no lost causes in God's kingdom. Michael remembered that from the previous Sunday's sermon. Chance wasn't a lost cause, just a hurting kid that needed people who believed in him.

Maggie was back, and she carried a stack of gifts. Michael took them from her and piled them on a table that wasn't being used. In the cool fluorescent lighting of the church kitchen, her face turned pink. She moved away from him and he let her go.

The kids were begging to play darts. The look she shot his way looked like one that begged him to give her space.

"We're only going to play one more game."

Maggie heard Michael's declaration and she couldn't stop the smile that sneaked across her lips. He'd said that three times already. After cake and ice cream he had challenged some of the kids to a game of darts. She had a sneaking suspicion he kept issuing the "one more game" warning because he kept losing and he wanted one more chance at victory.

She glanced at the clock on the wall and shook her head. "No more games. It's time for you all to get home."

A wave of moans answered, but the kids obeyed. They

dropped the darts into the box and with a chorus of good-byes they grabbed their stuff and headed for the back door. Maggie followed them out into the moonlit night.

"See you on Sunday," she called out as they took off in a group.

"They're good kids."

Michael spoke from behind her, making her jump. She managed to stifle the scream, but couldn't do anything about the way her heart tried to race out of her chest. She turned, facing him with all the stability of a soft maple tree in a strong breeze.

"Don't sneak up on me like that."

His hand brushed down her arm and he nodded, as though he understood. "I'm sorry, I didn't mean to scare you. I thought you knew I was here."

"I didn't know."

"I would never hurt you." His eyes sought hers, as if he wanted to convey more than the words said. "I called your dad because I wanted to do something for you. I wanted you to have that, because you do so much for others and you deserve to have something done for you. You don't deserve to be hurt."

She closed her eyes as his words registered in her heart. Of course he knew. He had known about her dad, and he knew about Greg.

"How did you find out?" She opened her eyes and saw that he had taken a step back. Good, because she needed that space.

"I overheard. I was going to get a drink and you were talking to Pastor Banks."

"You heard..." She sighed and shook her head. "You heard everything?"

"Most of it."

"I don't want to talk about this, Michael."

"I know you don't, but you have to understand that what that guy did to you wasn't your fault. And he's only one man."

"I know. In my heart I do understand that. It was a long time ago, really. It's in the past."

She turned to walk away, but his hand on her arm stopped her. It didn't hurt and she didn't feel the dreaded shot of fear that she would have felt a few years ago. All wounds heal, some just take more time than others.

"I know you don't want to talk. But I want you to believe me when I say I would never hurt you. I care about this ministry, the kids and you. It isn't always easy, doing the right thing."

"What does that mean?"

"I don't want to let you down."

"I think I know that. Michael, thank you for calling my dad. It was a shock, hearing his voice, but it meant a lot to me that you would do that." She touched his cheek. "You won't let me down. I trust you."

His eyes closed and his cheek moved into her hand. When he opened his eyes their gazes connected and Maggie wondered if her heart could handle the well of emotion brought on by his touch. Had she ever cared for anyone the way she cared for him at that moment? And was the emotion real, or something created by moonlight and a sultry summer night?

"You don't know what that means to me, Maggie, that you trust me. You make me feel like someone who can be counted on. I want to be that person." He leaned, dropping a light kiss on her cheek. "Thank you."

"You don't have to thank me." She looked down at their

intertwined fingers and for the first time in a long time she felt truly protected. "Just be my friend."

"Of course we're friends."

She closed her eyes as he leaned in to kiss her. For that moment she was the girl that Michael Carson wanted in his life, even if they were only calling it friendship.

Tomorrow she would deal with reality.

Chapter Fourteen

Reality had to be dealt with that night, before emotion had a chance to carry Maggie away on a roller-coaster ride she'd rather not take. For the reality check she went to Faith, who had no trouble keeping her in the real world. Faith would give it to her straight. Before heading across town, Maggie called home. When there wasn't an answer she remembered that her grandmother had gone to stay with a sick friend.

Ten minutes later Maggie was knocking on Faith's door. It took a few minutes for Faith to answer. When she did, her hair looked like she'd styled it with a blender and her clothes looked like she'd pulled them out of the laundry basket. She didn't look at all happy.

"Did I wake you up?"

"Do you think?"

"It isn't late."

"I didn't get any sleep last night. I was making up for it tonight." She motioned Maggie inside. "What are you doing here?"

"Yeah, I know. And you're right. It was sweet. But he also—

"Gran is with a friend."

"And you needed someone to cook for you?"

Maggie followed Faith into the kitchen, the cats chased after them. "I can cook for myself. And since you can't cook, we'd have to order something. I needed a cup of coffee and I knew you'd have some."

"I have tea."

"Traitor."

She sat at the table and Faith settled across from her. The two of them sat in silence as Faith's "little darlings" curled around their legs, Persian kitty tails twitching.

"So?" Faith finally said, hiding a yawn behind her hand.

"My dad called a few days ago."

Faith's eyes widened and her hand came down. "He called. Just like that? And you're just now getting around to telling me?"

"It took me a few days to get a grip on my emotions. And it wasn't 'just like that.' He didn't suddenly decide to call. He had a little help."

"A little help?" Faith walked into the kitchen and filled up the teakettle. "From above?"

"Michael found him and gave him my number." She fiddled with a stack of papers. "It isn't like we couldn't have found each other sooner. He knows where I live."

"So Michael called him. You mean, the Michael who is lumped into that category of men that you think you can't trust?" Her eyes lit up. "How sweet is that?"

"I think it was more interfering than sweet."

Faith rolled her eyes heavenward. "Oh, please. Maggie, Greg was a rat. Your dad was a fink. Do not punish every other man in your life for their mistakes."

"Yeah, I know. And you're right, it was sweet. But he also

knows about Greg." She pulled a tissue from the box on the table, not planning on crying, but just in case it happened.

"How?"

"He overheard a conversation I had with Pastor Banks."

"Nosy, isn't he?"

"I guess. But what do I do now? He knows all of my secrets. He knows about Greg. He found my dad. He cares about the kids at church." She fiddled with the tissue, wrapping it around her finger. "The only thing he probably doesn't know about is my mother."

"What is it that you're afraid of? Are you afraid you'll care too much and he'll let you down? Are you worried about the kids at church? I guess I don't get it. You've met a nice guy and he has done some very sweet things."

What was she afraid of? Maggie thought it was possible that everything that Faith had said could be on the list. At the top of the list was trust. What if she trusted him and he let her down?

"When does the floor fall out? When does he expose his true self?"

"And leave you disillusioned and brokenhearted?"

"I'm not sure if the brokenhearted thing is possible." She hugged the cat that had crawled into her lap. "He doesn't need me, Faith."

"He's a strong guy and he doesn't need to be fixed."

"I hate it when you're right." She stood and let the cat drop gently to the ground. "I should be getting home. Gran will call and she'll be worried."

"Call and tell her that you're here. Why don't you spend the night?"

Her phone rang. She shot Faith a look as she raised it to her ear. Like Faith had anything to do with it ringing.

"Maggie, it's me." Michael hesitated. "Are you at home?"

"No, I'm at Faith's." She slid her friend a look, hoping to silence any outbursts she might make.

"Good. I wanted to make sure you're okay."

"I'm fine." She ignored Faith's knowing look. "Thank you for calling."

"I've been thinking about what you said." He spoke in a rush that stopped her from hanging up. "You said I'm a friend. I want you to know how much that means to me."

She nodded her head but the sob in her throat wouldn't let her answer. Biting her lip, she inhaled and tried to control the sting of tears.

"Maggie, if you're not okay, I could come over." His voice was strong, confident, reminding her that he was a man who could not only take care of himself but the people around him.

"No, don't come over."

"Promise you'll call if you need anything?" A short pause followed. "Even if you doubt me, remember, I'm always a phone call away. I have to go now."

"Michael?" A few tears rolled down her cheeks. She dashed them away with the back of her hand, but more slid down to replace them. Stupid hormones, that was all it was, nothing more. She needed some chocolate and then everything would be okay again.

She closed her phone and dropped it into her purse, for a few seconds avoiding Faith and the questions she would ask. She sat again. When she looked up, Faith was waiting and obviously trying not to be too nosy.

"He wanted to check on me." Maggie explained as she reached for a doughnut from the box Faith had pushed toward her.

"Sweet."

"Is that all you're going to say?"

Faith shrugged. "I'm not sure what else to say. Maybe I should tell you to be careful."

Maggie thought about it, and then she decided that it might be too late for warnings. Her heart was involved. To what extent, she wasn't sure.

The house sat on the corner of a street that Michael didn't care for. He'd been here before, but not for a long, long time. He hadn't planned on coming tonight, but the phone call that came in the middle of the conversation with Maggie changed his plans. Cars were parked in the front yard, people milled around, going in and out the open front door.

He parked a few houses down and walked up to the party. A few people spotted him, recognizing him and shouting that he was back. He wasn't, but he would let them think what they wanted.

A crowd of guys stood in the front door. He shoved past them, bumping past those who didn't seem to know where they were or who was around them. The odor of the place burned his nostrils and gagged him.

He spotted Vince in a corner talking to people that Michael knew were connected. He pulled out his phone, held it to his ear and before he closed it, he snapped two pictures. He was walking through the house in search of Katherine when Vince walked up behind him.

"What are you doing here?"

Michael turned, fixing a smile on his face. "Visiting you."

"That's dangerous, Mike. You aren't really welcome here."

"I'm paying my debt."

"I've got a package you can deliver."

"I'll have to think about that."

"Why are you really here?" Vince's greasy hair fell forward, his gray eyes, glassy and red, seemed to have problems focusing. Hard to believe he had once been an honor student with a promising future. "Are you looking for a fix?"

"You need help, Vince." Michael hadn't planned those words. He glanced over Vince's shoulder and searched the crowd. "And I'm not here for any real reason, except that old habits die hard."

Vince pushed him back against the wall. His arms were thin, weak. Michael grabbed him by the shoulders and spun him around with no trouble. He had Vince pinned when he saw her standing in a corner. "I just saw the reason I came."

"Katherine." He shouted her name above the din. She looked his way, her eyes widening in fear, and then she was gone.

"I helped her out of that joint you took her to." Vince laughed and the laughter turned to a rasping cough.

"I heard. And I'm not going to let you get away with this." He shoved Vince away and took off out the back door.

He didn't find her. But that night the faces he'd seen haunted him. Kids with hollow eyes, gray skin and hopelessness etched into their features. Kids who didn't stand a chance if someone didn't do something to help them.

And Katherine had worn a similar look.

He picked up the phone and called his new sponsor for a reality check. If he wanted to be someone that Maggie could trust, he had to learn to trust himself.

Michael had asked her to trust him. Maggie wanted to, but could she? Especially when he had disappeared after church the previous day, with no goodbye and no explanation for his hasty departure.

The shouts of kids flying kites on the lawn carried through the open office window. Her gaze swung to the clock on the paneled wall. Almost three-thirty. The telephone rang and without taking her gaze off the book in front of her, she reached to answer the insistent ringing.

"Is your grandmother okay?" The voice, slurring and male, sent a chill up her spine. Maggie's hands numbed as she gripped the phone tighter.

"Who is this?"

"Have you checked on her today?" The caller laughed.

Maggie slammed the phone back onto its cradle. Shaking and cold, she leaned forward, burying her head in her hands. The door to her office opened and Pastor Banks stepped into the room.

"Didn't you hear me knock?"

Maggie looked up. "No, I'm sorry."

"What happened? Are you okay?"

She nodded and then shook her head. "I don't know. I need to go home and check on my grandmother."

"Is she sick?" Pastor Banks handed her the cup of ice water on the edge of her desk. "Here, take a drink and tell me what's going on."

Maggie sipped her water. "Someone called. They asked me if my grandmother was okay."

"You don't know who it was?"

She shook her head. "I don't know. No, I didn't recognize the voice. He sounded drunk."

Pastor Banks picked up her phone and dialed. "Betty. I just thought I'd call and say hi. How have you been?"

Maggie listened to the conversation. Pastor Banks paced

the room, stopping at the window. He held the phone with his shoulder and pulled the curtain back to look out. When he turned around, he smiled.

"Sure, I'll tell her. Talk to you later." He set the phone down on Maggie's desk. "She's fine. She wanted to make sure you remembered that she wouldn't be home tonight. She's quilting with friends."

"I just don't understand what's happening."

"Someone's trying to scare you." Pastor Banks sat across from her desk, swiveling in the chair. "Any idea who?"

"The only one I can think of would be Chance's dad. Or maybe whoever has been calling—"

"What's going on?"

Maggie looked up, smiling at Michael, but the gesture not feeling quite right. He stepped into the room and closed the door behind him. Pastor Banks motioned toward the other empty chair. Michael ignored the offer and instead stood near the window, arms crossed over his chest.

"Did something happen?"

"Someone called and asked if Maggie's grandmother was okay." Pastor Banks tilted his head to one side and scratched at the beard he was trying to grow.

Michael sat, his intense eyes pinning Maggie. She looked away, concentrating on the condensation the glass of ice water had left on her desk. She brushed the moisture off the wood. Michael moved the cup.

"Maggie?"

"It scared me, but I'm fine now." She looked up, forcing a smile that she didn't feel.

Part of her wanted to let herself need Michael. The other part, the grown-up part, wanted to sit here and show the world that she didn't need anyone. Hadn't she done a good job of taking care of herself, and her grandmother? She could handle this problem, too.

"I need to go." Michael stood, his usual smile replaced by a concerned frown. "I'll be back in time to help you with the kids. I promise."

Maggie started to ask him where he was going, but he didn't give her a chance. Without a backward glance, he was gone, the door closing with a click of finality as he walked out. Maggie lifted the empty glass and twirled the ice.

"I don't think we should let him go." Her teeth sank into her bottom lip and she closed her eyes for a few seconds of much needed composure time.

"He's a grown man, Maggie. And I think this is something he has to take care of."

"This? I don't even know what *this* is." She piled up the paperwork on her desk, straightened the edges and then picked up the stack and shoved it in a desk drawer. "I have a group of kids waiting to plant flowers."

"Maggie."

Pastor Banks followed her to the door. She turned, positive she didn't want to hear his advice at this point. The fatherly look he gave her pushed away her resolve to be independent.

"Yes?"

"Give Michael a chance. He has to learn to believe in himself, and that will be easier if he has people who believe in him."

"I'm helping him in every way I can."

"I didn't say help him. I said believe in him."

She didn't see the difference. Or maybe she did, but she didn't want to stop and think about word definitions right now. She wanted to ignore the growing turmoil she felt and how it seemed connected to Michael Carson.

What had happened to her nice, quiet life? The answer was simple: Michael Carson had invaded.

"I'm really trying."

"I know you are. Remember that not one of us is perfect, and a person fighting an addiction has a serious battle to fight." He closed his eyes for a brief moment, opened them and smiled. "I guess I don't have to tell you that."

"No, you don't. But maybe I needed to be reminded. But while we're trusting him, he needs to do some trusting of his own. He needs to know that he can talk to us."

"I think he's probably trying. And remember, right now we're just speculating. We're not sure what's going on, so we're drawing conclusions on our own."

"I hope you're right."

Pastor Banks put an arm around her shoulder for a loose hug and then he walked away. Maggie walked out the back door, plastering on a smile for the benefit of the half-dozen teens who were waiting for her.

It would have been easier if she hadn't been remembering her mom walking out the door, promising everything would be okay and she was really going to quit using.

Chapter Fifteen

Michael walked into the church at nine o'clock—hours after the kids had left for the day. He knew Maggie was still here, her car was in the parking lot and a light glowed from her office window.

What would he tell her? He couldn't tell her the truth about where he'd been. He just hoped that in time she would forgive him.

As he walked down the hall he could hear contemporary Christian music at a slightly insane level. The music vibrated with electric guitars and crashing drums. He laughed in spite of the heaviness in his heart.

At the door to her office he stopped and peeked around the corner. She wasn't working. She was leaning back in her seat, pounding on her desk with her pencil. He stepped into her office and she looked up. No welcoming smile turned her lips. She didn't even say hello. He understood. He deserved her anger.

"I'm sorry." He moved close enough to see the red around her blue eyes. Tears. She had cried and it was his fault. He wanted to tell her it would never happen again. He couldn't make that promise. Not yet.

"Of course you are." She looked away from him.

"Maggie, I couldn't help it. I had to take care of something."

She nodded, but he could see that she didn't believe his excuse. If he was in her place, would he? He crossed the room and squatted next to her chair. She didn't move, not even when he touched her arm.

"So, what is your excuse?" She dropped her pencil on the desk and scooted her chair back. "People who don't keep promises always have very good excuses."

He put a hand on her arm to stop her from moving away. How many times in her life had people broken promises to her? He didn't want to be one of those people. She made him want to be the person she could count on.

His prayers lately had focused on that.

"I went to check on your grandmother, and to make sure that call had nothing to do with me. But, Maggie, I can't tell you more than that." He exhaled on a sigh. "And I can't stay."

"Of course not." She pinned him with an angry glare. "Michael, were you with them?"

Them? Did she mean was he doing drugs again? Her distrust hurt. But then, he had hurt her. Maybe they were even. He cupped her cheeks with his hands and forced her to look into his eyes.

"Maggie, you have to trust me."

"No, I don't. You have to earn trust."

"I have earned your trust. I'm sorry about tonight, but this doesn't make me a drug dealer…or your father."

She breathed in, turning her face away from his touch.

He wanted to drag her into his arms and promise her that he would never hurt her. The distrust in her eyes stopped him.

"No, you're not my father." She leaned back from him. "At least you're here."

"And I want to always be here." Another promise he didn't know if he could keep. "Why don't you tell me what is really going on?"

He reached to turn down the stereo and then he sat down on the edge of the desk. Maggie looked away from him, her eyes focusing on something he couldn't see, but what he speculated were flashes of memories she kept locked inside.

"My mom died of a drug overdose. She promised she was clean and that she would stay clean."

Michael sighed, unsure of what words would fit the moment. He could make promises, but she had learned at an early age that promises got broken. He could be the person who didn't let her down. But what if he did? There were no guarantees.

"I'm doing my best to be someone you can count on."

"I know that."

"Maggie, I have to go, and I'd really rather you not stay here alone."

"I'm fine here alone. I've been doing this for a few years now."

"Yes, but…"

"Go, Michael. I really don't need a bodyguard."

What she needed was a friend. The friend that she thought Michael was going to be. Watching him walk away, his words echoed in her mind. He had earned her trust. He wasn't her father. Her heart ached, wanting to give him the trust he needed but not wanting to risk the outcome if he failed.

Would she always be wondering if Michael would fall? She had spent too many years on that carousel with her mother. Her mom would kick the habit, stress would get to her, she'd fall off the wagon.

Michael had something to lean on. He had faith.

She needed to go home. She had been sitting here for two hours, doing nothing, just listening to music, praying and being alone. Why go home to an empty house when she had the empty church?

Empty house, empty church, empty life.

That truly stunk.

She decided that Chinese takeout was in order. She might even call Jacob Simmons again. Another call, another shot at building a relationship. She knew from those few calls that he liked Chinese, too. And he didn't like spinach. Of course, who really did?

She put everything away, including her bad attitude. The coffeepot was off. One by one, she turned out the lights. At the front door she remembered her keys. She had taken them out of her purse and then left them on the desk.

When she got back to the front door, she froze. The shadow that moved across the steps didn't look menacing, but it shouldn't have been there. She reached into her purse for her mace but couldn't find it. Her fingers hit her cell phone, she pulled it out.

"You don't have to be afraid, Miss Simmons." It was Curt. She sighed, relieved, but then not. What had happened to his new foster home?

"Curt, what are you doing here?"

"I was visiting a friend and I saw the light on inside."

"I see. Well, don't you think you should let your foster parents know where you are?"

"Nah, they don't really care." He took a step closer and she could smell the alcohol, which explained the slurred speech.

"I should really be going, though. My grandmother is expecting me." She knew God would forgive that little lie.

A glance in the direction of Pastor Banks's house and her heart plummeted. He was still gone. They'd left a few hours ago for a late dinner and a movie.

"You don't have to go, do you? We could hang out."

"No, we can't do that, Curt." Her heart was racing, pounding, telling her to react. She couldn't. Her feet felt like lead, her hands were shaking. She wanted to believe he wouldn't hurt her, but something in his eyes told her that he might.

He took a step closer. She backed up, her fingers trembling as she tried to turn on her phone. He was smiling at her—a young kid with a lot of anger. The smile didn't reach his eyes. Her heart pounded so hard, so fast, it ached inside her chest.

A single headlight flashed across the parking lot. Maggie's breath caught as she glanced toward the entrance of the driveway. Curt yelled at her and then he was gone, running across the back parking lot and into the dark.

Michael's motorcycle rolled to a stop and he jumped off, running up the steps to grab her. He pulled her roughly against him while her chest heaved for air and tears rolled down her cheeks. His hands were on her back, soothing her, telling her that it would be okay.

"I called the police," he whispered near her ear, his breath warm, his hands holding her steady.

"It was Curt."

"I know, I saw him. I should go after him."

She shook her head. "No, stay here with me. Don't leave me."

"I won't leave you." His voice was gruff. "Maggie, you have to stop staying here at night by yourself. I know you think you're able to handle anything, but this proves that there are some things you can't."

"I couldn't find my mace. I would have used it."

"You didn't have it, and if I hadn't shown up, what would have happened?"

"Don't, please, not right now. Tomorrow you can tell me how stupid I am."

He sighed and then his hand brushed her cheek. "You aren't stupid. I'm just worried. What if I hadn't come back?"

"Why are you here?"

He laughed. "I came back to argue with you some more, to tell you how trustworthy I am."

Trustworthy. She closed her eyes as a chill swept down her back. Yes, he was someone worth trusting.

When she took a step toward him, Michael almost backed away, almost kept the moment from happening. He wanted to be someone she could trust. Hadn't he joked about that only moments earlier? And here she was, trusting him, and he didn't know if he could be that person for her.

What would happen in the next couple of weeks, when it appeared to all that he was falling apart? It was a role he had to play, and one he trusted himself to play. But would Maggie continue to trust? Or would his obvious slipping away shatter whatever had been building between them?

"Michael, where are you?" Maggie's voice, soft and near his ear.

He looked down, smiling at the woman who stood on tiptoe, bringing her face closer to his. "I'm here."

"No, you weren't."

With effort he brushed away the doubts that clouded his

mind. Instead of thinking, he pulled her close, his lips touching hers as her hands rested on his arms.

"Sweet, Maggie, you're so sweet." He murmured the words against her cheek and heard her sigh as he pulled away.

Blue lights flashed, reflecting against the building and breaking into the dark night. The silence that had surrounded them was broken with a short blast from a siren as the two patrol cars came to a stop in front of the building.

Maggie pulled her hand away from his. Before the police officer reached them, she turned, her gaze connecting with his for just a brief moment.

"I really do trust you," she whispered.

"I know."

And for some reason knowing that she trusted him didn't make him feel better.

The law office was having an unusually quiet day. Michael's dad and his partner were both in court. One of the secretaries had taken a vacation day. Michael dropped the phone in its cradle and leaned back in his chair. He linked his fingers behind his head and closed his eyes. The case on his desk could wait, just for a minute, while he relaxed. Instead of relaxing, his thoughts turned to Maggie, as they often did these days.

He didn't want to think about what could have happened to her the other night. He didn't want to think about how she would feel if she learned about what he was doing.

The door to his office opened a crack, taking his mind off the paper and Maggie. He looked up as Jimmy Grey stuck his head around the door and grinned.

"Busy?" Jimmy didn't wait for an answer but stepped into the office, still smiling.

"I guess I'm not." Michael nodded to the chair across from him, knowing Jimmy wouldn't sit. He never sat, he rarely even stood still.

"You've been pretty scarce lately." Jimmy paced to the window and then turned to pace back to the desk. "I called the other day, to see if you wanted to play tennis. You were gone again."

"I don't have a lot of spare time these days."

Jimmy laughed and shook his head of blond curls. "Okay, sure, caseload and church." He actually sat, propping his feet up on Michael's desk. "And a certain youth worker has nothing to do with your busy schedule?"

How did he answer that? Michael tapped his pen on the desk and shrugged, trying to make it look as though Maggie had nothing to do with anything going on in his life. "She's at the church and I'm there."

"Okay, I'll buy that."

"So why don't you tell me why you're here?" Because Michael was sure there had to be more to this visit than a friendly chat about relationships.

"Someone saw you the other night." Jimmy's ever-present smile faded into a frown.

"What is that supposed to mean?"

"They saw you at a certain house, with a certain crowd."

Of course that would happen. Springfield wasn't a small town, but sometimes it felt that way. Everyone knew everyone else, especially when there could be good gossip involved. Michael had expected as much, and even planned for it. He hadn't planned the way he would feel when one of his best friends looked at him with obvious disappointment.

"It isn't what you think."

"I was hoping you could explain." Jimmy leaned forward, all seriousness, his normally jovial self nowhere in sight.

Michael leaned back in his chair. He looked out the window, avoiding eye contact with Jimmy. The thump on his desk rattled his coffee cup and his nerves.

"Michael, what in the…world is going on? You come back telling me that God has made a change in your life. You actually had me thinking that maybe I needed some religion or something, and now you're back there, hanging out with those people."

Religion. Michael smiled and shook his head. "It isn't religion, Jimmy, it's a relationship with God. It definitely doesn't make me a perfect person. And I can't tell you what is going on."

Jimmy stood, his features unreadable. "I figured as much."

"It isn't what you think."

At the door, Jimmy stopped. He didn't look back, but his shoulders lifted on a sigh. "I hope it isn't."

And then he was gone. Another person whose trust in Michael had been shaken.

The door closed and Michael attempted to turn his attention back to the file in front of him. His mind didn't immediately focus on the accident case. When the phone rang, he reached for it absently. Vince's voice on the other end no longer sent a chill of dread down his spine, instead it sickened him. He took a deep breath and pretended to be glad the other man had called.

"Vince, you got my message."

"I must have, I'm calling." Vince didn't sound as positive as Michael would have liked. "So, what do you want, Preacher Boy? If you think I'm going to tell you where Katherine is, you're dead, and I mean dead, wrong."

"You can keep Katherine. I think you know what I want." Michael stood and walked to the window. The view of the city was outstanding, buildings, trees and parks. Lavender-gray clouds loomed on the horizon and the wind shifted, turning the leaves of the trees. A storm was coming.

"Okay, Mike, you want some stuff." Vince paused. "I think I'll make you earn it. I don't like the idea of you spending your hard-earned money."

"Fine, whatever, just get me something."

Vince laughed. "Don't get yourself all upset. Just be ready when I call."

Michael put the phone down and leaned back in his chair. Step one taken care of. There could be no turning back. Step two would take him further into this. Step three would bring Vince to justice and hopefully reveal Katherine's location.

Katherine. He had spent hours looking for her the other day, a day he would have preferred spending with the kids at church and with Maggie. But he couldn't leave a friend in the gutter. Katherine deserved a second chance, a chance like the one God had given him.

That would be step three. And then would be the final step. That would come when everything else was taken care of. Making amends with Maggie.

As Maggie crossed the parking lot, she rummaged in her purse for her keys. Behind her a car started, the church secretary leaving for the day. Maggie turned to wave and then she turned her attention back to the search for her keys.

She felt a little moment of sickness as she looked over her shoulder at the locked building. A mental image of her keys lying on her desk made her groan. Now what would she do? She leaned against the car and considered crying. After a long day, that option really appealed to her.

The ringing of her cell phone intruded into her moment of crisis.

"Hello?"

"You sound happy." Michael's voice was the answer to her silent prayers for help.

"Happy, of course I am. I'm standing in the parking lot of the church, it's hot and I'm tired."

"So get in your car and meet me somewhere cool for dinner."

"Sounds like a great idea, but I would need keys to do that. And I can't eat, I have to go to the mall."

Laughter carried over the lines and Maggie pulled the phone away from her ear. She made a face at the piece of plastic and then held it back up to her ear.

"Where's your extra key?" Michael asked.

"On my key ring." She spoke quietly, hoping he wouldn't hear.

"Good place for it. Isn't Pastor Banks at home?"

"No, they went to visit his sister." She brushed perspiration-dampened hair back from her face. "Could we save chatting for later, when I'm not melting into a puddle on the pavement?"

He laughed again. "I'll be there in ten minutes. Hang tight and don't talk to strangers."

Maggie looked at her watch as she hung up and dropped the phone back into her purse. She could have gone all day without him reminding her not to talk to strangers. Just the mention of it meant that he was still thinking of Curt and what had happened a few days ago. It almost made her worry that someone could be watching. She glanced around, seeing nothing out of the ordinary.

If she had been thinking, she would have told him she would just walk home. It was only a few blocks and the exercise would have done her good. Instead she was stuck here, waiting. And she was thirsty.

She shoved through the clutter inside her leather bag and pulled out a mint left over from her last trip to a pizza place.

The motorcycle pulling into the parking lot ten minutes later sent a rush of conflicting emotions through her. Aggravation seemed first and foremost. He *would* be the one to rescue her from a humiliating situation.

Then another emotion surfaced, feeling a lot like happiness. She figured both reactions were allowed.

He pulled up next to her and took off his helmet. He turned to where the other was attached to the backrest. "Here you go, your chariot awaits."

"You want me to ride on that thing again?"

In answer he pushed the helmet into her hands and shoved his own back on his head. His gaze melted her reserve. "Yes, I want you to ride this thing again. Don't worry, I'm very safe."

She didn't know how to take the safety comment.

"I can't believe this day." She climbed on behind him, wrapping her arms around his waist. He leaned slightly, pulling her forward with him.

"Where do you want to eat?" He asked the question as he pulled from the driveway.

"I thought you were just here to open the building so I could get my keys." She had to yell so that he could hear over the engine as he gunned it and pulled onto the road. "Besides, I really do have to go to the mall."

A few minutes later they pulled up to a light. Michael leaned back and turned slightly.

"I wanted to make up for the other day. I let you down and I'm sorry."

"I forgive you." Her simple words restored his smile. "And you did sort of come to my rescue later. Remember?"

"Purely by accident." He smiled and then turned back around. "Where do you want to eat?"

"Somewhere quiet."

"You wanted to go to the mall and yet you request quiet?"

"Okay, you're right. We can eat at the mall. Go, the light's green."

Michael accelerated through the intersection and made the turn that would take them the few blocks to the mall. Momentarily distracted by Maggie's hands clutching his shirt, he forgot about his fears and the earlier conversation with Jimmy.

But he couldn't let himself forget, not when careless moves like this one could very easily put Maggie in danger. What if Vince saw them together?

What if? What if? He had to get his life back. Regrets swarmed him and doubts circled through his mind. If he had never made the move to talk to Vince, he could have gone on with his life, pretending that that world of darkness and destruction didn't exist. But if he hadn't taken a stand, how many more kids would have fallen victim to meth addiction?

He couldn't let that happen.

He turned into the mall parking lot. Maggie leaned with him as they made the turn, her hands tightening their hold on his waist.

"I really don't like riding this thing." She spoke close to his ear.

He parked and they climbed off. Maggie unbuckled her helmet strap with fingers that shook. He reached to help her and their fingers connected, startling him with a thread of emotion too strong.

"I can do it," she whispered.

"Good idea."

Ten minutes after the helmet incident, Maggie still imagined she could feel Michael's fingers touching hers. Funny how that had happened. It wasn't as if they hadn't touched before. So why had a simple touch like that one seemed to undo them both?

Or maybe she had imagined it? Maybe she had only thought it felt like something more than friendship at that moment. She let go of the thought as they walked out of a sports shop. Whatever had happened, it was best forgotten.

Her cell phone rang as she walked through a shoe store looking for slippers that her grandmother had been wanting for ages. She picked up a pair but they were a size too small.

She put them down and reached into her purse for her phone. The number on the caller ID had become familiar to her over the past couple of weeks. She lifted the phone to her ear, afraid of what his excuse would be this time.

"Hi." She still paused, unsure of what to call him. "Dad" didn't seem to fit.

"Maggie, I'm going to be in town in the morning. I know that's a couple of days early, but I thought it might be good to have more time together."

When they had first started talking, Maggie hadn't expected her father to keep his promise. She especially hadn't considered he would show up early. She sat on a bench meant for trying on shoes. Michael dropped down next to her, stretching his legs and turning his feet so that she could see the tennis shoes he had tried on.

She gave him the thumbs-up.

"What time will you be here?" What else could she say? Michael sat up, obviously listening in.

"Early afternoon. I thought we might get together in the evening. Maybe after dinner?"

Maggie found her voice. "Where do you want to meet?"

"Could we meet at my hotel? We can have more privacy there." He gave her the name and room number.

She dug through her purse for a pen, but couldn't find one. Michael held one out to her. She took it, offering a smile as she jotted the number down on the back of a grocery list she had pulled out of her purse.

"Fine, we'll meet tomorrow at seven." Maggie said goodbye and dropped the phone back into her purse. Looking up, she met Michael's questioning gaze. "My father wants to see me tomorrow."

"And I'm going to be there with you."

"You don't have to."

"I want to, if you want me."

Did she want him to be with her? She was so used to doing things on her own. She couldn't imagine how it would feel to have him there with her. But could she let him take this step with her? How would this bind them together if he was there with her for one of the most important events of her life? And did she really want to go through it alone?

Maggie stuck his pen back in his pocket and then she rested her hand on his shoulder, his very broad and capable shoulder.

"Yes, I want you there with me."

Just don't let me down. She met his gaze, wondering if he heard her silent pleading.

Chapter Sixteen

The blue car followed Michael as he left his dad's office the next afternoon. It slowed when he slowed, took the turns he took and then proceeded to tail him down the quiet paved lane to the lake. He pushed aside the moment of doubt. He had to do this. There was no backing out now.

This was the only way to find Katherine, to get her back for her family.

He pulled to a stop and the blue car pulled in next to him. Michael didn't bother getting out of his car. He waited and the passenger door of his car opened. The man that slid into the seat smiled a greeting.

"You won't regret this, Michael."

That was probably meant as encouragement. Michael had a sneaking suspicion he *would* regret his actions. It seemed as if his entire adult life had been spent regretting. Now he was trying to do the right thing and he even found regret in that. Not because he didn't want to do the right thing, but because he knew it could mean losing the trust of people he cared about.

"Michael, don't back out on us now." Officer Conway pulled a pack of gum from his pocket and took out a stick, offering it to Michael. "I know you have concerns."

Michael took a deep breath and exhaled. "Yes, I have concerns, but I'm not backing out on you. I just want to make sure people I care about won't be hurt."

"We can't guarantee that."

"You have to." Michael looked up, sighing to relieve pent-up emotions. "You have to make sure this goes off without them being hurt."

"Then you're going to have to start distancing yourself from the people you want to protect."

The words sank like weights into Michael's heart. Distance himself from church, from Maggie and the kids? He didn't want to consider that, but he knew that he had to.

"Make it look like you're slipping, like you're falling back into drug use," Officer Conway said, making it sound easy.

"I don't..."

"If you want to protect your church and your friends, you have to. This has to look real, to everyone. Michael, you're an informant, we can't guarantee your safety or anyone else's."

"Fine, I will. But not until tomorrow." Tonight he had to be with Maggie. He needed to see her through this meeting with her dad.

"Okay, I'll give you tomorrow. But then you have to. If we're going to find Katherine, if we're going to get Vince, you have to do this. And make it look good."

For the next ten minutes they discussed the plan. Michael listened, tried to remember all of the details as Officer Conway looked at the pictures in his phone and took the few that Michael had developed. When Conway stepped out of the car, Michael leaned back in his seat and closed his eyes.

He still had prayer. God knew the truth, He knew Michael's heart. Now if God could just convince Maggie to give him a chance and to not give up on him.

The hotel where her dad was staying was located on the south edge of town in an area not yet built up. The parking lot was freshly paved and there were only a few cars. Michael pulled into a space near the office and turned off the engine.

At least he had driven the car today.

"Are you ready for this?"

Maggie turned to look at Michael as she reached to unlatch her seat belt. Glancing away from him, toward the hotel, she nodded.

"Ready as I'll ever be."

"Just try to think of it as a blessing, a long-awaited answer to prayer." Michael reached for her hand.

"You hold on to that optimism for me, will you?"

"Maggie, this is a good thing. This is a beginning for you and your dad."

"I know." She licked lips that were suddenly dry. "Michael, before I forget, thank you for doing this. At first I was mad at you for interfering. Now, well…I should have done this a long time ago."

He leaned over and kissed her cheek. "I should have talked it over with you. I shouldn't have gone behind your back."

She laughed at that. "Like I would have agreed?"

And then she opened the door and stepped out of the car.

"Is it too late to change my mind?" she asked Michael when he joined her.

Michael laughed but held tight to her hand, as if he feared she might bolt. She wondered if that might be his reason for locking his car. But then, he always locked it and set the alarm. And he never failed to put his keys in his pocket.

The temporary distraction for her thoughts ended. She glanced toward the hotel and the man waiting at the front door.

"What am I going to say to him?"

"Start with hello." Michael leaned to whisper, his breath soft on her ear.

They walked through the front door of the hotel and stood in the lobby. Jacob Simmons stood off to the side. It had to be him because he had her hair, her smile. He wore a wary smile on his face as he approached them.

Maggie's throat tightened and she somehow managed to hold back her tears. She couldn't hold back the sob that escaped.

"Maggie." He spoke her name in a low voice, making it sound strained. His lips tightened as he shook his head. "You're beautiful."

"I..." She bit down on her bottom lip. "I don't know what to call you."

He nodded his head, as if he understood that she couldn't call him Dad or even Father. Not yet. But where did that leave them? They were two strangers who just happened to share the same DNA, the same blood.

She looked to Michael, hoping he could help. He smiled his encouragement and patted her arm. "The two of you need time alone to get acquainted. Maybe in your father's room? I'll wait down here in the lobby."

Maggie wondered how many daughters ever had that said to them about their fathers. Getting acquainted should have happened twenty-seven years ago. It should have started with midnight feedings, first days of school and first dates. Instead they were virtual strangers.

It seemed a little too late for closeness. Maggie fought that negative emotion. In God's kingdom did *too late* exist? A prayer had been answered. She needed to concentrate on that and not on lost years.

Unfortunately the lost years would always be between them.

Michael's hand rested on her arm. "Go on. I'll be here when you get done."

Maggie nodded as her eyes clouded with tears. She mouthed the words *"thank you"* and then turned to follow Jacob Simmons onto the elevator.

When they walked through the door of his suite, Jacob pointed to the small sitting room. "Have a seat. I'll make coffee. Or do you drink coffee?"

"I drink coffee." And with that they learned something else about each other. Baby steps, just like those first years of life.

Maggie sat on the sofa and picked up one of the throw pillows. A few minutes later her father joined her. He took the seat across from her.

"The coffee's on. Now what do we do?" His question snatched her attention away from the loose threads that hemmed the pillow.

"I'm not really sure." Maggie tried to smile.

"Could I explain?"

Maggie tossed the pillow to the end of the sofa and crossed her arms over her chest. "Explain what? I just don't see how you could have an explanation."

"I don't have a good one." He admitted with a sigh. "I can only be honest and tell you that I made a serious mistake. I regretted my actions for years, but I never regretted you. I just didn't know how to undo what I had done."

"How can you say that?" Maggie uncrossed her legs and moved to the edge of the sofa. She leaned toward the man sitting opposite her and was glad when he didn't look away.

"If you didn't regret us, then how could you leave and not come back?" Maggie wiped at the few tears sliding down her cheeks. "My mother loved you. Until the day she died she loved you. And even then you broke a promise. Probably the most important one you ever made, and you just broke it, without a second thought."

"I know that I hurt you."

Maggie shook her head. "You *don't* know. You have no idea what I went through, or what happened to my mother." And then the truth. "For years I've blamed you for her addiction and for her overdose. If you had done something to show that you cared. If you had called. Or even answered the message she left for you."

"I know that I failed you. I'm hoping in time you'll forgive me."

"I forgive you. That doesn't mean the pain is gone. I'm working on that now. And I'm working on understanding how you could go on with your life like we didn't exist."

"And that's where you're wrong. You have no idea how I've regretted that decision. You need to know the whole story."

Maggie sat back and with a deep sigh she managed to regain a feeling of almost calm. It came from detachment, from pretending this wasn't really about her.

"Fine, tell me the whole story."

Jacob Simmons nodded, his graying blond hair catching a ray of sunlight, making him look younger. Maggie now understood her mother's attraction to him. She could almost picture them together. Him with his blond good looks and money, and her mom vivacious and full of laughter.

"I met your mom at the lake. I was a senior in college. She had just turned nineteen." His eyes took on a faraway look as he remembered that time. "She looked at me and I fell in love. *Special* doesn't even begin to describe her or the way she made me feel." He paused and for a second Maggie thought tears glimmered at the surface of his eyes.

She remembered her mom like that. Before the drugs destroyed her she had been full of life, finding a lot to laugh about, even in the hard times.

"I loved her and I used her. I knew how my parents would feel about our relationship, but I just had to be a part of her life. I wanted to elope, but she wouldn't let me." He stopped speaking and silence entered the room for several long seconds. "After I graduated and went back home, she called to let me know about the pregnancy. By then I was in another relationship."

"You could have taken care of us. You could have at least been there." Her mother had never even asked for child support.

"I know that now. But at the time I didn't know how."

"That's an excuse."

His eyes closed and he nodded. "Yes, I guess in your eyes it is. That's the way it was, though, and I can't change any of it."

Maggie stood and crossed to the large window that looked out over the hotel pool. When she turned she met the questioning gaze of Jacob Simmons, her father.

"It seems like there should be more to it than this. I

wanted you to have a better excuse, some real reason why you walked away and why you never came back. Instead, it was just to make your life easier."

A cloud covered the sun and the room dimmed. In shock Maggie watched as tears ran down the cheeks of the man she'd spent her life resenting. She swallowed as her anger melted.

"I should have come for you when your mother died. I just didn't know how to tell my wife Nancy the truth."

"Nancy means nothing to me. I don't know a thing about you, about what has happened in the last twenty-seven years of your life."

Maggie crossed the room and sat in the chair next to his. He turned, wiping a hand across his face. She reached for his hand and tried to think what it would have been like to be his little girl, to hold his hand crossing the street. How would it have felt to crawl up on his lap after a bad dream?

Her own tears flowed and he reached to hold her. For the first time in her life, Maggie knew what it felt like to be held by her dad. It should have felt better. The moment shouldn't have been tangled with anger and resentment.

"Why did you suddenly decide to tell Nancy about me?" Maggie pulled away, brushing away the tears that dampened her cheeks.

"Conviction. Your friend called my office and I had to take a good long look at what I'd done. I'd tried to forget, but I've never been able to do that."

"And?" She wanted more than that.

"Some weeks back our pastor preached a sermon about the consequences of our sins. We can pretend sin doesn't exist in our lives, but it's still there and we have to recognize it and how it affects us. The consequences of our sins have to be dealt with. We have to seek forgiveness, not brush our mistakes under a rug."

"So I'm just a sin that has to be dealt with? Is that the only reason you're here?"

He reached for her and she pulled her hand away.

"You misunderstood, Maggie. That was the sermon. I didn't say that's how I felt. The sermon helped me to see that I couldn't deny you. You aren't a sin, but what I did to you and your mother was...is."

"So you told Nancy about me?"

"She said she always knew and it's always bothered her that I've left you alone. She just didn't know how to confront me."

"I see."

"Maggie, you have two brothers. David and Jonathan are in high school."

Brothers. She closed her eyes, trying to make sense of what she'd just learned. She had two brothers and she had no idea what they looked like or who they were.

"Do they know about me?"

"I told them last week. They were upset, not about you, but about what I did. They're looking forward to meeting you."

Maggie closed her eyes and, taking a deep breath, she counted to ten. She tried to relax, and finally she remembered to pray. She should have done that first, before anger got the best of her. Counting to ten never really worked, it just gave her ten more seconds to boil over.

"Maggie, I am sorry and I'd like it if you could forgive me."

"I need some time."

"I would like to get to know you." He let out a long

sigh. "I know that's going to take time. And forgiveness will take time."

It didn't make past rejections obsolete, but his apology brought some healing. Maggie knew that her anger wouldn't disappear overnight just because he apologized or because he now wanted to be a part of her life. Healing the mistakes of the past would take time.

This was a start. And Michael had given this to her, this chance to have a family.

Michael drove Maggie home. Her silence cued him to give her space and so he didn't push her to talk. When she was ready, she would tell him the details of the meeting with her father.

They were pulling up in front of her grandmother's house when she finally turned to face him. Her smile hovered tremulously on her lips and tears clung to her eyelashes. Michael stopped the car and waited.

"I'm not sure how to feel about him."

"That sounds like a normal reaction to me."

She took a deep breath and exhaled shakily. "I want to give him a chance and yet a part of me is still so mad at him."

"What did he say, or do you want to talk about it?"

He listened as Maggie gave him a brief description of the conversation with her father. His heart ached for her as he listened to the story. It could have been so different for her, had her dad been the father she had needed him to be.

"It sounds like a good starting place."

"I suppose it does." She looked toward the house when the front porch light came on. "Grandma is waiting to hear how it went."

"I bet she's been praying all evening." Michael smiled

at the thought. He could almost see Grandma Betty on her knees, intervening on behalf of her granddaughter.

"She's been praying longer than that." Maggie smiled at him and he felt as if his whole life had been leading up to this moment.

He touched her hair, letting a silken strand slip through his fingers. Slowly he leaned forward, touching his lips against hers. She returned the kiss, her lips moving lightly from his lips to his cheek. Her hands moved up his arms, her fingers soft on his shoulders.

One kiss, one moment. He knew that he shouldn't take this from her. He had nothing to give and no future to speak of. She had nothing but distrust.

Slowly he came back to his senses and pulled free from her embrace.

"Goodbye, Maggie."

Chapter Seventeen

"*Goodbye, Maggie.*" The words played through her mind the next day as she sat waiting for him to show up. She hadn't though about it last night, about the note of finality in his tone or the sweetness of a kiss that seemed to signal a parting.

One of the kids asked her a question. She looked up, managed a smile and even an answer. They were all watching, waiting for her to do something. They had planned to go over recipes and plan meals for shut-ins today. With school out, she had a list of activities to keep them busy and out of trouble. She couldn't focus, though. Her thoughts kept slipping back to Michael.

Why hadn't he said something like, "see you soon"? *Goodbye* had meant something, and now her imagination was carrying her away on a wild game of speculation that included him slipping back into a past that he couldn't escape from. That didn't fit, not with the Michael that she knew, the Michael who had made her feel protected. But what else did fit?

The creak of the door brought her around, a lecture

already forming on her lips. Pastor Banks took a step back, raising his hands for mercy.

"Sorry, I thought you might be Michael," Maggie explained.

"Nope, I'm not him. From the look in your eyes, I'm glad I'm not."

"He didn't show up."

"Well maybe..."

"And he didn't call," she continued, ignoring his attempt at excuse making.

Pastor Banks's gaze slid past her and she got the hint. This wasn't a good time for this conversation. She turned to face the group, pasting on a smile that wouldn't fool them.

"So, let's get started." She didn't know where to start, not when her mind was racing, trying to come up with a reason for Michael's absence. Anger mingled with fear, making her stomach turn. She wanted to call his parents or the hospital...or the police. She had already tried calling him and he hadn't answered his phone.

"Let's just shoot some hoops today." Pastor Banks shot her an understanding look. "Hey, school's out for the summer, it's time for some fun."

The kids jumped up from their chairs and raced from the room, Pastor Banks in the center, being adored because he had saved them from her. She didn't mind, not today. Glancing at her watch, she walked to the window, hoping to see Michael pull up.

He didn't.

Michael didn't show up until the next day. He swaggered into Maggie's office without warning. She looked up from her Bible and met his wary gaze. He rubbed a hand across the stubble on his cheeks and grinned.

"Sorry, I just woke up." He fell into the chair across from her desk.

"Sorry?" she repeated, looking at her watch. It was almost noon. "You just woke up?"

He laughed. "You're repeating me."

Sarcasm suited Michael like the dirty clothes he was wearing. Neither of them was his style. Maggie almost told him that, but she kept her lips clamped shut.

"Michael, what's going on with you?" She chose the easier route, the route of counselor, not friend. As a counselor she could be detached from the situation. She could almost convince her heart that it wasn't involved.

She reminded herself that this was why she never got involved. When she tried to fix broken people…well, fixing people wasn't possible. She couldn't save the world.

She couldn't save Michael Carson. An ache, lonely and empty, accompanied that thought. She wanted to save him, to pull him back from whatever he was going to, to keep him in her life, smiling and making her feel as though something special could happen.

He put his feet up on her desk and leaned back in the chair, giving her anger a target. She pushed his feet down.

"Nothing's going on with me," he insisted. Maggie met his gaze, those clear eyes that she had always thought could see into her heart. Something in his look pleaded with her for understanding.

She wanted to give him that. She wanted to believe he was okay.

"Michael—" She broke off in a sob and he leaned toward her. For a moment the old Michael returned.

"I'm sorry, Maggie." He rubbed a hand across his face, across the stubble on his chin, and sighed. "I have to go. I just wanted to tell you that I never meant to hurt you. Pray for me, will you?"

He stood and without a smile, without a backward glance, he walked out of her office. Maggie watched him go and then decided not to let him get away with that. He wasn't going to be her mom, giving up and not fighting. She wouldn't let him be her dad and walk out on her. She jumped out of her chair and followed him.

As she hurried into the hall, she saw him. He picked up his pace as he headed for the back door.

Maggie ran, knowing she had to catch him. She had to pull him off the destructive path he seemed to be taking. He was better than this, she knew he was.

He was getting on his bike when she reached him. She stopped a few feet away, breathing deeply to calm her heaving chest. Michael waited, sitting on the seat. While she tried to calm down, he pulled on his helmet, looking for all the world like he honestly didn't care.

"Please." She put a hand to her chest and took another deep breath. "Please let me help."

His features softened and he smiled. His hand shot out, taking hold of hers. When a car drove by, he flashed a look toward the street and withdrew his hand.

"Maggie, you have to let me go." He started the bike and released the kickstand. "Stand back and let me drive away."

"I thought you were different." She backed away from the bike. "I thought you were someone special."

His eyes closed, briefly, and pain settled like a mask over his features. He didn't try to argue with her. He nodded and started backing out of the parking space.

Maggie stepped back on the sidewalk and watched as he rode away. Brushing away the tears, she told herself that it didn't matter. Michael had to make his own decisions. And she had to protect her heart.

Her heart. She closed her eyes as the truth settled into her heart. Michael was more than a soul she wanted to rescue. He was someone she believed in, and now he was gone.

When she turned around, Pastor Banks was on the church steps. He shook his head as she approached him. His usual smile was nowhere to be found. She needed that reassuring gesture to tell her things would work out. Instead his gaze lingered on the motorcycle driving away from them. She stopped next to him and watched, unsure of what she should do or how she should react.

"We have to let him go, Maggie. He has to find his own way in this."

That wasn't what she had wanted him to say. She wanted words of encouragement. He should be telling her that everything would work out, that Michael would be okay. And that if he wasn't, they would go after him and help him.

"His way is going to destroy him." She looked back toward the road. He was gone.

"Maggie, Michael is a child of God. Do you think God is going to give up on him? And are we going to give up on him?"

Maggie didn't know how to answer that question. Her heart felt tangled in a web of emotion. She cared for Michael, but she wasn't really sure what name to put on the emotion…other than caring.

She had trusted him. How could she have been so wrong?

* * *

A week after walking away from Maggie and life still felt out of control. And Michael still hadn't seen Katherine. He had seen plenty of Vince and his cronies. Michael drove away from the apartment building that Vince had just moved into. As he drove through town, his mind switched gears from where he had been and what he'd been doing, to Maggie.

To missing her. The lonely ache had taken him by surprise. She was a friend, someone who cared about him, of course he missed her. But his heart prodded him to think deeper, to realize that maybe she had become more than a friend. She had made him feel good about himself. And what had he felt about her? Maybe missing her signaled something else, something bigger than friendship.

He wanted to be the kind of man that Maggie could depend on. Would this end any chances that he might have had? Would she write him off as another person who had let her down?

He kept telling himself he was doing the right thing, but the right thing was getting more and more difficult. The right thing almost felt as if it was going to lead him back into a life he had left behind. He didn't want that temptation.

So far he had fought it back. And he had won.

Blue lights flashed behind his car and a short burst of siren warned him to pull over. He slammed his hand against the steering wheel as he pulled into a department store parking lot.

The cop approached slowly, gun drawn. Michael leaned back against his seat, waiting, watching and not knowing what would happen.

The window was down. The cop stopped. "Hands on the steering wheel."

"Fine." He put his hands up.

"I want you to climb out of the car, slowly, hands on your head."

"Can I open the door first? It's hard to open the door with your hands on your head." This part of his life should have been long gone, over. He felt a slow, simmering rage. Even doing the right thing he couldn't catch a break.

"I'll open the door."

"Fine."

Michael stepped out of the car, hands on his head.

"Slowly turn and put your hands on top of the car."

"Got it."

The cop reached into Michael's back pocket for his wallet. Michael waited for recognition. He thought that there should be something. This officer should know what the others knew, that he was an informant. Or maybe not. Maybe they didn't give that information to everyone on the force.

"Michael Carson, you were weaving."

The officer had followed him from Vince's. That put Michael in a suspect category, one he didn't belong in.

"Of course, that's the standard excuse for pulling me over. Would you like for me to walk a straight line or would you like to call Officer Conway?"

"Conway?"

"Call him, please."

"You're telling me what to do? I should take you in now."

"You and what army?"

"Are you threatening me?"

Michael leaned his forehead against the roof of his car and shook his head. Shouldn't someone out there know that he was on the right side of the law? "No, man. I'm not threatening you. I'm sorry. It's been a long day."

"I've had a long day, too. So don't push me." He pulled Michael's hands behind his back and cuffed him. "For precaution. I'm going to call Conway, but he'd better tell me something good or you're going in."

"Trust me." Not that anyone else did.

The cop stepped a few feet back and spoke into the mike on his collar. The whispered words didn't carry. Michael waited, holding his breath, trying to hear something.

At last the cop stepped forward and uncuffed his hands. "Okay, you're in the clear. But remember, I'm not as trusting as some guys. I don't believe old dogs learn new tricks and I'm skeptical about jailhouse conversions. This might be a good time for you to go home and get off the streets."

"I plan on it."

Michael slid into the front seat of his car and rested his head on the steering wheel. Step…something or other, call a friend. He didn't know if he had a friend left in the world.

He did have a friend, and she chose Monday morning to visit his office. She barged through the door just as he turned away from the bookcase behind his desk. At the same time Janet was calling a warning on his intercom.

Maggie stepped into the room, her honey-blond hair back in a clip and blue eyes glittering with…well, wrath. He could have smiled, if she hadn't looked so thoroughly ticked off with him.

"You missed church again yesterday."

"Yes, I did. I'm sorry." He stood.

"I'm sick of that."

"Okay."

"I'd like for you to come back. Whatever you're going through, you can deal with it better at church."

He would have given anything if he could have told her that he wasn't going through anything, at least not what she thought. He hadn't lost faith, not in God, or even in his own ability to stand strong. If anything, he had learned a lot about himself.

His main problem right now was loneliness.

Instead of defending himself he stood there thinking how amazing she looked as she stormed into the room, her eyes flashing fire and determination. The pale blue sheath dress made her eyes look even bluer and the summer sun had lightened her hair.

The most amazing thing of all—she was here to rescue him. And he needed it. Just looking into her eyes he felt like a man who could possibly be drowning.

He put the book down and stepped out from behind his desk. A few steps and he'd be close enough to touch her.

"Are you just going to stand there?" Her chin came up a notch and she took a step forward.

"I guess I am."

"You look like something the cat dragged in."

"Thanks." He rubbed the three day growth of whiskers and then brushed a hand through hair that was definitely getting too long. He knew how bad he looked.

"Is that it? No explanations? No apologies."

"I miss you."

"Of course you do." She wavered. He saw it in the softening in her blue eyes and the way her teeth bit into her bottom lip. "Michael, please don't do this. Don't give up."

"I haven't given up, Maggie. Can you trust me?"

"I'm trying." She closed the distance between them. He could smell the strawberry scent of her shampoo and the light floral of her perfume. "We miss you. I'm not sure what to tell the kids. They've asked if you're coming back."

"I hope so." He itched to touch her, just to hold her for a minute. He took a step back. "Maggie, you have to leave."

"What?"

"You can't be here. You can't be in my life."

Confusion clouded her vision. "Fine, Michael. I only wanted to let you know that we're here if you need us."

He did need her, but he couldn't bring himself to say the words. To make this work, she had to believe he had fallen and then hopefully Vince would believe. He wouldn't be allowed in Vince's circle if they considered him a threat.

"I know you're there. But…right now I don't need you."

A flash of pain shot through her eyes. She looked past him to the window and then she turned and left. He had done the right thing, it just didn't feel like it.

He didn't need her. Maggie sat behind the wheel of her car, still in the parking lot outside the law office. Her throat constricted painfully in response to those words. What a fool she'd been. Of course he didn't need her. Somehow she had convinced herself that maybe he cared and that he might be more than a friend.

His words had shaken her free from that dream and snatched her viciously back into the real world. She was on the verge of becoming her mother—a woman who spent her life waiting for one man to return and make everything all right.

With hands that trembled, she called her grandmother. The answering machine picked up, so she left a message that she'd be at Faith's. Next she called to make sure Faith was home.

A few minutes later Maggie stood in front of Faith's door, unable to knock. She wasn't sure if she could face her friend's sympathy. The door opened as Maggie started to knock.

"I saw you pull in," Faith explained as she motioned her into the house. "Oh, sweetie, I'm so sorry."

"I don't want sympathy." She wanted chocolate. She went to the cabinet were Faith kept her emergency supply of Lindor truffles.

"He doesn't deserve you." Faith reached into the bag of foil-wrapped chocolates and took a few for herself. "He's a jerk."

"No, he isn't."

"You're too good for him."

"Probably."

"He is adorable, though."

"I agree." Maggie walked onto the deck and Faith followed. "Let's order pizza. I'll pay."

"There are back-to-back episodes of 'I Love Lucy' on tonight."

"Sounds good." Maggie opened another truffle. Before she popped it into her mouth she smiled at Faith. "Thank you for always being here for me."

Faith shrugged as she sat. "Are you ready to talk?"

"There isn't a lot to say. I thought I knew him, but I don't. I went to his office to let him know I'm here for him." No tears, she reminded herself. "He told me he doesn't need me."

"And you bought that?" Faith leaned forward, propping

her elbows on the wrought-iron patio table. "You're so naive, Mags. When someone says, 'I don't need you,' then that means they really do need you. It's like saying, 'I don't care.' He's obviously pushing you away for a reason."

"Yes, and the reason is obvious. He doesn't want me in his life. We're not exactly two of a kind."

"Yes, you are. You're both caring people who have survived a lot." Faith stood, but before she walked back into the apartment she patted Maggie on the shoulder. "Give him time. He knows where to find you. And now I think we should order that pizza."

Problem solved. Or at least it was solved in Faith's mind. Maggie wasn't as convinced. She had watched Michael change and saw him pulling away from them. And it was her heart that ached at the thought of losing him for good.

The parking lot was empty. Of course it was. He glanced at his watch. It was after eleven. Nobody would be out at this time of night. Every light in Pastor Banks's house was off and there were few cars on the streets in this quiet section of Galloway.

After his run-in with Maggie earlier that day, Michael had been on edge, questioning every decision he had made. He needed to clear his mind, to get his thoughts together so that he could finish what he started.

He reached into the back seat of his car and grabbed his racquet. After a long night, he needed a release, a way to work off his energy. What he didn't need was a quiet night at the trailer with just his own thoughts and a mouse for company.

His own thoughts would get him into trouble. That would take him on a mental trip, thinking about past mistakes, old temptations and new ones.

Maggie. He missed her. That shouldn't be the driving force in his life at this point. But it was. Or at least it was a big part of what kept him going. He had a friend that he could count on. He had a God who was stronger than any problem he faced. That didn't mean life would be a walk in the park. But as each day went by, he saw that he could overcome.

He felt God's presence. He felt strength when he shouldn't have felt strong. He glanced up at the steeple that gleamed in the pale moonlight. It reached heavenward, tall and steady. He looked up at the brilliant midnight-blue sky twinkling with millions of stars.

God knew the ache he felt, the fear of losing himself in this mess. He wanted to help Katherine and the kids with hollow eyes who were on a path of destruction they no longer recognized as a threat.

In the process, he didn't want to lose what he had gained. He didn't want to lose this place, the friendships that he had built or the trust of these people. Or Maggie. And he didn't want to lose himself.

He walked back to the retaining wall. It was dark, but a nearby streetlight cast a line of orange light onto the pavement. He tossed the ball and when it bounced back he gave it a hard hit that shot it against the concrete, returning it with more force. He hit harder.

A car rattled to a stop. He grabbed the ball and glanced back at the parking lot, groaning as Maggie got out and walked toward him. Her smile wavered. She stopped a short distance away, looking unsure.

"I didn't expect company."

"I didn't expect to see anyone here at midnight."

"What are you doing out this late?" He hit the ball again, swinging when it returned.

"I was at Faith's and then I went to Wal-Mart. I like to go when it's quiet."

Her voice came from a short distance away. He shot a quick look in that direction and hit the ball again. He considered telling God that he didn't need her, that this was a distraction he could do without. He couldn't lie to God.

"You cut your hair."

His hand went to the back of his head and he nodded. He turned to offer her a smile. "Yeah, it was getting on my nerves."

"It looks nice."

"Thank you." He set the racquet and ball down on a bench. She took a few steps toward him, close enough that he could almost reach out and touch her. He was so tired of being lonely. And she was here. He could ask her to go for coffee. She would do it, he knew she would.

"Maggie, you shouldn't be here, talking to me."

"That's the most ridiculous thing I've heard yet. Michael, I'm here for you. Whatever is going on, you can tell me."

What he wanted to tell her was that he could be counted on. Not all men walked away from their commitments. And sometimes things appeared a certain way, but there was an explanation.

She stood in a circle of orange light, darkness on the periphery, making it feel as if they were alone in the world. She stared up at him, waiting for something that would help her to understand. And he couldn't give it to her. He couldn't tell her what he was doing, or why. Doing that would put an end to everything.

He couldn't take the chance that she would tell or that someone else would find out. If it got around. If Vince found out that his suspicions were true, it could all be over. The rats would go back in their holes and the past few weeks would be for nothing. He couldn't tell Maggie anything.

"We're friends, and you can talk to me."

"I don't need you, Maggie." The words slipped from his lips, not even close to the truth, but the only way that he could push her away. It didn't work this time. This time she stood her ground.

"Fine, you don't need me." Anger flashed, wiping away the moment of pain he had seen in her eyes. She squared her shoulders and her chin came up. "Go ahead, then, ruin your life and the second chance you've been given. Toss away our friendship."

"Thanks, Maggie, that's exactly what I needed to hear." He smiled as he said the words, but each accusation she had tossed at him hit the mark.

"I don't want to lose you." Her words hit as sharply as his. "I don't want you to be like my mother, telling me that you're clean and then one day being taken away in an ambulance. She never came back, Michael. I don't want to lose you to this. I can't take losing another person that I care about."

Her voice was thick with emotion and tears were rolling down her cheeks. He took a step forward but stopped short of reaching for her. He started to tell her he wouldn't let her down, but she shook her head, turned and walked away.

It had been his plan to push her away. He had never meant for them both to be hurt like this. He had never realized how much he would want to hold her.

Forever.

Chapter Eighteen

Maggie watched as Chance and a few of the other boys, supervised by Pastor Banks, carried her grandmother's furniture back into the house. After three years of saving, Maggie had finally managed to buy new carpeting for the entire house. It felt good.

And she felt empty. When one of the girls asked Maggie if she wanted a glass of iced tea, Maggie nodded and accepted the plastic cup with a smile. Four months ago she had felt like she had her life all tied up with a neat little bow.

Everything had been in order, including her emotions. Michael Carson had unraveled her well-ordered life. He had forced her out of her comfort zone. And now what?

She was outside her safety zone and he wasn't here, that was what. It made her mad, thinking that way, that he had been the one to push her this far, to make her think she could trust. And now he was gone. Not gone, just missing in action.

"You've got to stop feeling sorry for yourself."

Maggie turned, shocked by her grandmother's words. It seemed like an echo of what she had just been on the verge of telling herself. She was strong. She was a survivor.

Michael. He was strong, too.

It should have been easy to move on. It would have been easy if she hadn't fallen in love. It defied logic, that she could have fallen so easily after so many years of protecting her heart.

"Maggie, it isn't over, you know." Grandma patted her arm with a warm hand. "He needs for you to continue to believe in him. He needs your prayers."

"I'm still praying." Hadn't she recently witnessed a prayer answered? It had taken years, but she now had a father and he was a very real part of her life.

She even felt like she had forgiven him.

Would it take years for her prayers for Michael to be answered? She closed her eyes at the heaviness of that thought. She hoped it wouldn't. But when he did come back to them, would he be a changed person? Someone other than the Michael she had come to care for?

Pastor Banks and Chance walked out of the house, the two nudging each other in a friendly dispute. Chance was another prayer answered. He was coming to church now. His grades were improving. More than that, his attitude was improving.

Michael had helped so much. He had given something to these kids, especially to Chance. For that reason she had to trust him. And there were other reasons to keep trusting. Her heart being the biggest. It wouldn't let her give up.

Michael had parked in a lot across from the church, hoping he would see Maggie. He just wanted to see for himself that she was okay. And he needed to remind himself of what he was working for and why.

For two weeks he had been living in his past. He had

gone places and seen people that he had hoped he would never seen again.

He had been tempted and he had survived.

Leaning against the steering wheel of his car, he peered through the sheets of rain, making out the images of people running from the church to their cars. Only one person captured his attention.

Today she wore a white shirt and a blue skirt, and her honey-blond hair was pulled back in a braid. Her father ran behind her, holding up an umbrella. Jacob Simmons was sheltering his daughter for the first time in her life.

Michael felt the catch in his heart. The empty ache grew. He wanted to jump out of his car and go after her. He wanted to pull her into his arms and tell her the truth. To keep her safe he had to let her believe the lies, the careful web of deception he had spun around himself. Even his parents were starting to believe the rumors.

He could even imagine what people were saying: Michael Carson, prison hadn't taught him a thing. Oh, sure, he had put on a good show for everyone. He had professed faith, gone to church, helped troubled youth, but it had all been an act.

He leaned his head against the steering wheel and took a deep breath. He had at least hoped that Maggie might believe in him. But then, he had done his best to make sure she didn't.

He whispered a prayer that she would heal and that she would find someone to trust, someone who would take care of her. As he whispered that prayer he realized something. He realized that God had already sent someone to love Maggie Simmons. Michael loved her. He wasn't noble enough to want someone else in her life. He sighed, allowing himself to accept that fact. He loved her.

It was more than a need for friendship, more than a desire to have someone there for him. She was more than a partner in ministry. He loved her.

He could even be strong enough for her. He knew that now. He had been tested and survived. He had been tempted and he had withstood the temptation.

But would she want him in her life when he had done everything in his power to push her away? Would she want him, when he brought her pain and made her think of a mother who hadn't been able to stay clean?

Michael shifted into Reverse and backed out of the parking space. He had a job to do, one that he couldn't get out of. He was going to lead the police to a house in the country that was being used for a major drug operation. He had pictures, names and addresses, all of which had been given over to officer Conway. In a few days this would all be over.

And while the bust was going down, Michael was going to try one last time to find Katherine. He had a limited window of opportunity to drag her out of his mess. And afterward? He hoped that Maggie would let him explain. If she didn't? Well, he had learned he was stronger than he thought. He would survive.

He didn't want to think of surviving without her.

A glimpse of red caught Maggie's attention. She glanced toward the street, confirming her suspicions. Michael. He was there, in his car, watching.

"Michael." She felt a catch in her heart as he drove away. It had been two weeks since she'd seen him at the church. Two weeks, and nobody had seen him in that time.

"Maggie, why don't you go ahead and get in the car while I go back to the church for your grandmother?"

Maggie looked up at her dad, at Jacob Simmons. He was actually in her life. And soon he wanted her to go with him to Illinois to meet his wife and to meet her two brothers. He looked down at her, still holding the umbrella as he waited for her to get in the car.

Maybe she should go with him when he left in a few days. It might be good to get away from Missouri and away from thoughts of Michael.

"I need to go after him." She watched Michael's car drive away.

"You can't." He held the door open. "Maggie, I don't know Michael Carson, but it sounds like he's a young man with some problems."

"No, I don't think so. And if he does have problems, shouldn't his friends be there to help him?"

"Not in the rain. Besides he's gone now." He smiled an encouraging smile. "Get in before we're both soaked."

She slid into the back seat. Michael's car had disappeared. That left her to speculate. What had he been doing outside the church? Why hadn't he approached them?

The front door of the car opened and Grandma got in. Maggie's dad closed the door quickly as wind and rain sliced through the opening.

"Maggie, honey, are you okay?" Gran whipped off her plastic rain scarf and turned with a smile in place. "Try not to worry about Michael. I think he'll be back soon."

"I hope so."

On Tuesday afternoon local breaking news interrupted the radio program Maggie had been listening to as she helped her grandmother clean. As the news anchor spoke about a widespread area drug bust, Maggie flipped on the television. The broadcast was live, showing a secluded house set among a thick cover of trees.

Maggie dropped the dust rag on the table and reached for her purse. As she hurried through the house, looking for her lost tennis shoes, her grandmother walked out of the laundry room.

"Where are you going in such a hurry?"

"Gran, I have to go check on Michael."

Maggie walked into her room, thinking her grandmother would follow. Instead she heard the volume on the television go up. When she walked into the living room, her grandmother was sitting in the recliner.

"I think you should stay here and let him come to you."

"He might need me."

"Maggie, you don't even know if he's involved."

Maggie sat, leaning to tie her shoes. "No, I know. But I feel like this has something to do with him. He asked me to trust him. I do. But I need an explanation."

"Did you forget that Faith is on her way over?"

Maggie groaned. "Yes, I forgot. But she might be late. She's working on a new project."

"Maggie, why don't you call Michael? That might be better."

"No, I really want to see if I can find him."

Grandma followed her to the door. As they opened it, Faith pulled up. Maggie kissed her grandmother on the cheek.

"Faith will go with me. I'll be fine."

As she walked down the sidewalk toward Faith, Maggie searched for that confidence she'd felt a few minutes ago. She was going to find Michael. She had allowed herself to lose hope for the last few weeks, thinking that he was slipping and he wanted it that way.

Speculation. She had played the game. She had taken one piece of information and built a story that seemed to fit. But there were pieces missing.

Would a person who was slipping ask someone to trust him, to believe in him? Would he watch from a corner parking lot?

And would someone who believed in him and trusted him let him slip away without a fight? She didn't think so.

Michael sat on his front porch with Katherine. It was shady and cooler than inside the trailer. They had been there for an hour, since Michael pulled Katherine from the house she'd been staying in for the last month. She was shaking, her eyes glassy from the toxic poisons she had been surviving on.

"Katherine, I called your parents. They're going to get you some help. We're going to take you to the hospital." He should have called an ambulance from the house where he'd found her, but she had seemed fine at the time.

Not fine, but definitely not in need of immediate medical attention.

"I can't believe you're doing this to me." Her words were tossed out in an angry wave, but her voice was raspy, not at all strong.

"Yes, I'm a horrible person."

"You're a jerk." She tried to pull free from his restraining hand. He tightened his grip. "You've found religion, so now you think we all need to find some for ourselves."

"I can only pray that you will, but that isn't why I'm doing this. I'm doing this because I care about you. We've been friends for a long time, and I don't want you to die."

"Did you ever stop to think that I want to die?" She

spoke in words barely above a whisper now. "Why did you have to save me? You know that I'm dying anyway."

"You can be treated for Hep C."

"Yes, treated." She chewed on her bottom lip as she looked away from him.

Tires hummed on the paved road. He looked up, expecting company, not expecting to see Maggie's car driving past. Oh, Maggie. He sighed when she slowed, started to turn, but then went on. Maggie.

He held on to Katherine's arm, knowing that Maggie would assume the worst, and he couldn't do anything about it.

"Michael, let me go."

"I can't. You have to get help."

"I don't want help."

"I think you do." He held on to her. "I want you better."

"I know." She leaned her head down. "I want to be better. I just don't know if I can do it."

"I'll be here to help." He kept his hand on her arm, knowing that even now she could be playing him. And he really needed to call Maggie.

As they drove past Michael's, Faith put a comforting hand on Maggie's arm. Deep breath, Maggie shook her head, trying to clear her thoughts and the horrible ache.

"I'm fine."

Faith looked apologetic, she had no reason to be. "No, you're not."

"I'm not my mother. I'm not going to spend my life waiting for one man to show up in my life. I'm not waiting for him to rescue me or make my world right."

"Of course you aren't."

"I was content before Michael Carson and I'll be content without him."

"You were very content."

Maggie pulled to the side of the road as her cell phone rang. She looked at the caller ID and shook her head. "Stop patronizing me, Faith. I know what you're thinking."

"Maybe you should stop jumping to conclusions and answer the phone. Maybe he can explain."

Maggie gave Faith the look, the one that told her friend to stop looking for easy answers. Maggie had come to her senses, Faith needed to do the same.

He was with another woman, probably his friend Katherine. Common sense told her she needed answers, and the answers could only come from Michael, but the part of her that hurt wanted to crawl off somewhere and lick her wounds until she healed.

It seemed impossible, that she had fallen so deeply in love with him. But then, it wasn't really impossible. The Michael who had held her hand, cared about her kids and sent her dinner, was the Michael she had allowed into her life and her heart.

He was the Michael who instinctively knew that healing would begin in her life when she confronted her dad. He had done that for her.

After all of that, shouldn't she do as he asked and trust him? Shouldn't she give him a chance to explain? That seemed reasonable, but self-preservation said that any explanation he gave could be a lie. Maybe it had all been a lie.

Tears burned her eyes as she remembered how it had felt to be cared about by Michael Carson. And how it felt to have him walk away. Stupid tears. She wiped them away with the back of her hand and let the phone ring. It didn't stop. Mozart continued to play in bell tones that rattled her nerves.

"Answer it, Maggie." Faith handed her the phone she had set back down on the console between the seats.

"I can't. Not right now."

"You're being stubborn."

"No, I'm not. It might look like I'm being stubborn, but what I'm doing is protecting myself. My mother spent fourteen years waiting for Jacob Simmons to come back. Until the end she believed his lies."

"Michael isn't Jacob Simmons."

Maggie shifted her car into Drive and pulled back onto the road, heading away from the trailer where Michael was with another woman. "No, Michael isn't anything like my father. What scares me is that I'm a lot like my mother."

And the only way to solve that problem was to take control of her life. She had to move forward and make real changes.

"I think I'm going to take my father up on his offer to visit my family in Illinois. A change of scenery is probably the perfect cure."

For a broken heart.

Michael wasn't going to let Maggie get away with ignoring him, but he had to wait a few days for things to settle down. Katherine's parents had taken her to a treatment facility and Vince was in jail. Michael had started reclaiming his life. He had talked to his parents and then to Pastor Banks. He had explained what he could and apologized for any pain he had caused.

Maggie was the one person he had yet to talk to. He wanted to have the right words to explain. And she had to be willing to listen. When he called her on Friday she didn't answer, not the first call. He wasn't giving up. He called again thirty minutes later. That time she answered. The reaction to her voice took him by surprise. It felt like coming home after a long time away.

It was like rain after a long drought. It washed over him, comforting, refreshing. He had known he missed her, at that moment he realized just how much he missed her.

"Michael." Her voice trembled, or at least it sounded that way to him. He wished he could see her, so he could read her expression.

"Maggie, you finally answered."

"I had to. I wanted to let you know that I'm going to Illinois for a few weeks. I have vacation time I haven't taken for a few years."

"When are you leaving?" His heart thudded heavily at the idea of losing her again. If he had ever really had her.

What if the feelings were one-sided? What if she didn't feel what he felt? Or if she had, what if his actions over the past few weeks had pushed her permanently from his life?

"Maggie, I would at least like a chance to explain."

"You don't have to."

"I do have to. I know that you have questions about what has been going on with me. You saw Katherine at my place. I was trying to help her, nothing more."

"It's okay, Michael. Pastor Banks told me everything. He thought I should know. He wanted me to know that you'll be back with us."

So she knew, and she was still leaving? His heart plummeted.

"Maggie…"

"Michael, you have to find your way. That's what you've been doing. You had things you felt a need to take care of. Now I have things I have to take care of. We all make choices. You have to find your path and the direction God is taking you."

"Maggie, I can't have this conversation on the phone." He needed to see her, to hold her.

She didn't answer. At first he thought she had hung up, but then she spoke again, her voice strong. "There's no need for that. We can talk when I get back. I left some materials on my desk, some books to help you plan activities for the kids."

"That's it, then?"

"That's it. I'll see you soon. 'Bye for now."

And then she was gone.

Maggie was proud of herself. She didn't cry until she clicked her phone closed and dropped it in her purse. After that the tears rolled down her cheeks.

Being strong shouldn't have felt so bad. She had told herself that this was the right thing to do. She needed time away, time to regroup and decide where her own path was leading. Michael needed time to regain his footing. He didn't need her to help him with that. What he'd done for the police proved that he was strong.

She had to prove to herself that she was just as strong. At first the thought of losing Michael had felt like the end of the world to her. And that had scared her. Those feelings had made her think of her mother's love for Jacob Simmons, a love that had held her mom captive until the very end.

Maggie could move on. She was moving on.

Only her heart didn't agree. Her heart was telling her that a forever love wouldn't be such a bad thing. She knew better. It would be a bad thing if the love was one-sided.

She picked up the phone to call the airport. If she was going to Illinois, she needed to make this call. She would get her plane ticket. That would finalize the process.

A car door slammed. Maggie put the phone down and walked to the front door. Grandma was quilting with friends. Faith was visiting her parents for the day. She had a sneaking suspicion that she knew who would be at the door, and her heart clued her in to the fact that she wasn't as willing to walk away as she thought.

She peeked out the window. Michael was heading her way, looking like someone about to storm the gates of the castle.

She opened the door as he lifted his hand. "Michael, I don't—"

"No—" he put his hand up "—you're going to listen to me. I won't let you walk away from me without telling you this."

The fight left her. "Okay, I'll listen."

He reached for her hands and then he took a step closer.

"You told me to find my own path." His voice was husky and shaky with emotion. Maggie felt her heart quiver, and start to cave in response to his touch.

"Yes."

"Maggie, you might not see this, but I do. You said I have to find my own path, and I have. *You're* my path. Every time I want to hear something funny, if I need someone to lean on or a friend to share with, I think of you. You're the person I want to turn to. You are my path. These last few weeks were miserable, but I had to keep you safe. To do that I had to distance myself. But you were never far away. You were always with me. Thoughts of you kept me going."

"Michael, I missed you." She didn't know what else to

say. She had planned on fighting him, on keeping her distance from a broken heart.

"Maybe God's plan has always been about the two of us."

She closed her eyes, trying to imagine that and wanting it to be true. "Maybe."

"Maggie, I want to be the person who doesn't let you down." He half laughed at that. "I guess I'm not off to a good start. Maybe now is a good time to accept that sometimes I might let you down, but not because I want to or mean to."

"Am I missing the first part of this conversation?"

"Yes, I had it with myself on the way over here. It started with me realizing how much I need you in my life and how imperfect I am. And it ended with me realizing that I never want to let you down, but because I'm human, I probably will."

"None of us is perfect."

"No, we aren't. But we have a God who is, and He's my reason for walking a little straighter and trying a little harder. And you're the reason that I wake up every day, knowing I can walk that line."

Maggie's heart tripped all over as he said those words.

"I'm not perfect, either." Her words came out in a breathless rush. "I spent a lot of time thinking the worst. I wanted to jerk you out of the mess you seemed to be making of your life."

"I love you for that, for wanting to rescue me."

"You love me?" With breathless wonder she stepped into his arms.

"I'm sort of hoping that you feel the same way."

"I do." She leaned into his embrace, resting her forehead in that comfortable place on his shoulder, a place where she fit so perfectly. "I love you. I've missed you so much."

"So much it hurt?"

"How did you know?"

"Because I felt the same way." His tender gaze held hers in its grasp, the way he had held her hand just moments ago, melting her heart in the process. "And it hurt when I knew you had stopped trusting me."

A flash of pain shot through his eyes.

"I'm sorry. But I didn't stop trusting, not really. I was hurt because you kept pushing me away."

He pulled her into his arms. His gaze swept over her face as he lowered his head and his lips touched hers, grazing them lightly and then returning for something deeper, something that answered all of Maggie's questions about Michael and what she felt for him.

She pulled back, brushing her cheek against his as his arms captured her and held her close.

"I love you, Maggie. You helped me realize that I'm strong enough for myself and strong enough for you." He whispered the words against her ear.

She turned into his embrace. He held her lightly, giving her the freedom to lean back and look up into his eyes. "I love you, too. And I don't ever want to repeat another three weeks like the ones we've had. I felt lost without you."

"Trust me, Maggie, I won't ever let that happen again. If I have my way, we'll be together forever."

"I trust you."

He kissed her again, with the sun setting behind the deep green of the trees and the sky a delicate lavender and coral backdrop. And he promised he'd do his best to never let her down.

She believed him.

Epilogue

Four months later...

Michael stood at the front of the church and if he tried, he could convince himself that this day was like any other. But it wasn't. Today the church was crowded with friends and family who would witness Maggie Simmons and Michael Carson becoming husband and wife.

His wife. His heart reacted to that word, to the amazing truth. Maggie was going to be his wife. Pastor Banks stood at the front of the church.

The music started and emotion welled up in his throat. He didn't know if it would be possible to feel even more than he already felt, not without his heart exploding. And what if the guys saw his tears?

They were walking down the aisle. Jimmy walked with Faith, and he could tell from her grin and Jimmy's pained look that Maggie was wrong in thinking their two friends would make a good couple.

Next came Chance with Cathy.

The wedding march started and the guests stood. Could a person's heart explode? Michael thought he might find out. Instead tears started to trickle down his cheeks as Maggie walked toward him, her hand on her father's arm.

Late-afternoon sun poured through the stained glass in the front door of the church, creating a halo of golden light behind his bride. Her smile reached out to him, and he saw the tears that streaked down her cheeks and the tears in Jacob Simmons's eyes.

Not sad tears, happy tears, rest-of-his-life tears. Michael's breath caught as she stopped and her dad gave her hand over. To have and to hold, forever.

Michael ignored the crowd and the questioning look that Pastor Banks shot at him. He couldn't wait for the service to end to kiss the bride. As their lips touched, soft and sweet, Michael thanked God for knowing the right path.

Dear Reader,

Trusting Him is the story of redemption and new life. Maggie Simmons has faith in God, but has trouble trusting people. She would like to keep things simple, and stay within her comfort zone. When Michael Carson steps into her life, she's pulled from that circle of safety, but finds unexpected love. Fresh out of prison, Michael has a new life and he's looking for a second chance. Maggie has to make a choice. Will she be a person who holds Michael's past over his head, waiting for him to fall? Or will she trust him?

We all have had to make choices at some point in our lives. Sometimes we find it difficult to accept that people have changed. We wait for them to fail, rather than helping them become the person God intended them to be. Second chances, and new beginnings, are all a part of God's plan. We only have to seek Him to find the right path.

God bless you on your journey,

Brenda Minton

QUESTIONS FOR DISCUSSION

1. Maggie found it easy to trust God in most areas of her life. As *Trusting Him* progresses she gives more areas of her life to God. Why do you think she found it easier to trust God with some fears and insecurities, but not all?

2. Why do you think it is important for Michael to be in church and building those new relationships? What are some temptations he could face?

3. Maggie is illegitimate and unclaimed by her father. How do you think that affected her relationships with others and with God? What traits does an earthly father have in common with our Heavenly Father? What are the differences between the two?

4. In Michael's case, do you think that letting go of his past and forgiving himself are important steps in healing?

5. There were people in Michael's life who were unwilling to believe he had changed, but there were also people who believed in him. Who encouraged Michael? How can our positive attitude encourage someone to keep trying?

6. The kids in the church group came from different backgrounds. What did Maggie give to these kids? Why would that make a difference in a young person's life?

7. Did the church limit ministry to the message spoken from the pulpit or the lesson taught in a Sunday school classroom? Do you think the life lessons, mentors and activities would make a difference for the teens?

8. Maggie found it easy to allow the kids into her life, but not Michael. Why? What do you think helped her to trust him?

9. In moments of weakness, Michael recognized that he would be more open to temptations. Why? And what methods did he use to overcome them?

10. While Michael sought Maggie's trust, he kept secrets from her. Have you ever kept secrets from a loved one? What was the outcome?

Love Inspired

Celebrate Love Inspired's 10th anniversary with top authors and great stories all year long!

Look for

Love's Healing Touch

by Jane Myers Perrine

Diagnosis: Love

Dr. Ana Ramirez took notice of orderly Mike Fuller's quick skills and impressive bedside manner. So when she proposed a simple cup of coffee with Mike to talk about his future, she never expected to find herself wishing she were a part of it....

Steeple Hill®

www.SteepleHill.com

Available October wherever you buy books.

LI87450

REQUEST YOUR FREE BOOKS!

2 FREE INSPIRATIONAL NOVELS
PLUS 2
FREE
MYSTERY GIFTS

Love Inspired®

YES! Please send me 2 FREE Love Inspired® novels and my 2 FREE mystery gifts. After receiving them, if I don't wish to receive any more books, I can return the shipping statement marked "cancel." If I don't cancel, I will receive 4 brand-new novels every month and be billed just $3.99 per book in the U.S., or $4.74 per book in Canada, plus 25¢ shipping and handling per book and applicable taxes, if any*. That's a savings of 20% off the cover price! I understand that accepting the 2 free books and gifts places me under no obligation to buy anything. I can always return a shipment and cancel at any time. Even if I never buy another book from Steeple Hill, the two free books and gifts are mine to keep forever.

113 IDN EF26   313 IDN EF27

Name	(PLEASE PRINT)
Address	Apt. #
City	State/Prov.	Zip/Postal Code

Signature (if under 18, a parent or guardian must sign)

Order online at www.LoveInspiredBooks.com

Or mail to Steeple Hill Reader Service™:
IN U.S.A.: P.O. Box 1867, Buffalo, NY 14240-1867
IN CANADA: P.O. Box 609, Fort Erie, Ontario L2A 5X3

Not valid to current Love Inspired subscribers.

Want to try two free books from another series?
Call 1-800-873-8635 or visit www.morefreebooks.com

* Terms and prices subject to change without notice. NY residents add applicable sales tax. Canadian residents will be charged applicable provincial taxes and GST. This offer is limited to one order per household. All orders subject to approval. Credit or debit balances in a customer's account(s) may be offset by any other outstanding balance owed by or to the customer. Please allow 4 to 6 weeks for delivery.

Your Privacy: Steeple Hill is committed to protecting your privacy. Our Privacy Policy is available online at www.eHarlequin.com or upon request from the Reader Service. From time to time we make our lists of customers available to reputable firms who may have a product or service of interest to you. If you would prefer we not share your name and address, please check here. ☐

LIREG07

Love Inspired

TITLES AVAILABLE NEXT MONTH

Don't miss these four stories in September

SOMEBODY'S BABY by Annie Jones
Josie Redmond had raised her twin sister's baby as her own, and now the child's father was in town seeking his son. But when Adam Burdett saw Josie with little Nathan, he discovered it wasn't just his child he was interested in.

A MOMMY IN MIND by Arlene James
A Tiny Blessings Tale
A tiny baby stole Lori Summer's heart and made her petition to adopt. Before the papers were signed, though, the teenage mother changed her mind. The teen's lawyer Ramon Estes believed in his case, but longed to get to know his opposition in a more personal way.

A TREASURE OF THE HEART by Valerie Hansen
She needed stability, so Lillie Delaney headed to her tiny hometown to find it. But everything there had changed. She turned to Pastor James Warner for guidance, only to find a handsome motorcycle riding rebel who showed her that the Lord does indeed work in very mysterious ways....

LOVE'S HEALING TOUCH by Jane Myers Perrine
In the busy hospital emergency room, Dr. Ana Ramirez admired orderly Mike Fuller's quick skills and impressive bedside manner. So she proposed a simple cup of coffee to talk about his future, never expecting to find herself wishing she were a part of it.

LICNM0807

SOL GORDON, Ph.D.
When Living Hurts

The plain fact is that
  Life, in large part, is made up of things to worry about. . . .

Life can be unfair, unlucky, uninteresting, unnerving,
for large parts of the day
or for years.

Real people have bad moods,
periods of depression,
fall in love with someone who doesn't love them.

Life can also be full of joys, pleasures, and excitements.
They may not last long, but nevertheless they are real.

Most other self-help books want you to pretend that you
are the only reality. This book does not pretend. It acknowledges the pain of the real world, but it also says that
by being helpful to others . . . by reaching out beyond
your own pain, you can renew and revitalize yourself.
  Wisdom, daydreaming, and risk-taking introduce
    you to options that you never felt possible.

I don't have all the answers, not even most of them,
but I try to attend to many of your questions.
Make up your own mind,
especially about controversial issues
hopefully in ways that enhance your own well-being.
                                    —from *When Living Hurts*

A lively what to do book for yourself or someone you care about who feels discouraged * sad * lonely * hopeless * angry or frustrated * unhappy or bored * depressed * suicidal

QUANTITY SALES

Most Dell Books are available at special quantity discounts when purchased in bulk by corporations, organizations, and special-interest groups. Custom imprinting or excerpting can also be done to fit special needs. For details write: Dell Publishing Co., Inc., 666 Fifth Avenue, New York, NY 10103. Attn.: Special Sales Dept.

INDIVIDUAL SALES

Are there any Dell Books you want but cannot find in your local stores? If so, you can order them directly from us. You can get any Dell book in print. Simply include the book's title, author, and ISBN number, if you have it, along with a check or money order (no cash can be accepted) for the full retail price plus $1.50 to cover shipping and handling. Mail to: Dell Readers Service, P.O. Box 5057, Des Plaines, IL 60017.

WHEN LIVING HURTS

Sol Gordon, Ph.D.

Published by
Dell Publishing
a division of
The Bantam Doubleday Dell Publishing Group, Inc.
1 Dag Hammarskjold Plaza
New York, New York 10017

Laurel ® TM 674623, Dell Publishing Co., Inc.

ISBN: 0-440-20051-2

Reprinted by arrangement with Union of American Hebrew Congregations

Printed in the United States of America

February 1988

10 9 8 7 6 5 4 3 2 1

OPM

I write for people of all faiths, little faith, no faith, and for those still searching for a faith. I write to encourage you to stand for *something;* otherwise you may fall for anything.

"Believe that life is worth living and your belief will help to create the fact."

—WILLIAM JAMES

"The secret of wisdom is kindness."

—CHARLES B. HAYWOOD

"If I am not for myself, who will be for me?
And if I am only for myself, what am I?
And if not now, when?"

—HILLEL

Contents

Did some terrible thing happen to you when
    you were a child?
What was the worst thing that ever
    happened to you?
Do most people fall short of your
    expectations?
Do you have disturbing thoughts?

2

If You or Someone You Know Is Suicidal

3

Sex and Love Worries and Facts

7

WHEN LIVING HURTS

Introduction

This is a book for people who want to help people who are in trouble.

It is also for those who are themselves lonely, depressed, or suicidal.

My basic message is that we are all our brothers' and sisters' keepers and that living well is the best antidote (revenge) for feelings of hopelessness, helplessness, being unloved, unfairness, and tragedy. This book focuses on how to cope appropriately with disappointments and imperfections (in an imperfect world).

Most other "how-to" books tell you—

—not to worry. (When's the last time someone told you not to worry and you stopped?)

—not to feel guilty. (If you've done something wrong, why shouldn't you feel guilty?)

—that you can be anything you want to be. (You should live so long.)

—to get rid of unrealistic expectations. (How does one know in advance that one's expectations are unrealistic?)

—That if you eliminate shoulds, musts, perfectionistic tendencies, worries, and other imperfections you'll be happy. (So, what else is new?)

The plain fact is that life, in large part, is made up of things to worry about: not only personal things, but the state of the world—hunger, overpopulation, torture, crime-infested cities, disasters, personal tragedies, despair.

Life can be unfair, unlucky, uninteresting, unnerving for large parts of the day, or for years.

Real people have bad moods, periods of depression, fall in love with someone who doesn't love them.

Life can also be full of joys, pleasures, and excitements. They may not last long, but nevertheless they are real.

Most other self-help books want you to pretend that you are the only reality. This book does not pretend. It acknowledges the pain of the real world, but it also says that by being helpful to others . . . by reaching out beyond your own pain, you can renew and revitalize yourself.

Wisdom, daydreaming, and risk-taking introduce you to options that you never felt possible.

I don't have all the answers, not even most of them, but I try to attend to many of your questions. Make up your own mind, especially about controversial issues . . . hopefully in ways that enhance your own well-being.

Fragments of an Autobiography

Sometimes a present situation is grim. There is nothing one can do except allow (gracefully) the passage of time. My own childhood was filled with years of a schooling I hated, a loneliness I didn't understand, and parents I didn't appreciate. There were times when I lived with it, with some crying and trusting that some day . . . I contemplated suicide and imagined how everybody would be sorry. It was hard not thinking about irrational ways out.

I began to feel better in my late teen years when I realized there is nothing wrong with being unhappy every once in a while. Lord knows there are lots of times and situations when unhappiness is the most appropriate response.

I figured out that it was not hard to tell when unhappiness has an important component of irrationality. Irrational unhappiness comes equipped with symptoms like
fear of high or closed places,
pains without disease—malfunctions or lesions,
chronic constipation,
gross loss of appetite, or
sexual compulsions that don't get you any place.

Rational unhappiness is mostly grand, dignified, private, a bit heroic, unselfish, free of irrational guilt or pride, and ends up being a learning experience.

What To Do If You or a Friend Needs Help

Do you have a right to feel bad?

In *The Right to Feel Bad—Coming to Terms with Normal Depression* (New York: Dial Press, 1984), Lesley Hazleton writes:

> To be fully alive means to experience the full range of emotions, to struggle with the downs as well as to enjoy the ups. Life is certainly difficult and even unpredictable—full of meaning and purpose at one time and utterly meaningless and purposeless at another, sometimes so desirable that we wish to freeze

it at a certain point and remain there forever, and at other times so undesirable that we may find ourselves wishing we had never been born. But it also has its own dynamics. There is no real happiness without the experience of depression to balance it. If we are not capable of depression, we are not capable of happiness either. In a very real sense, depression keeps us alive.

I bet you never thought of depression this way. I recommend Lesley Hazleton's book.

Are you feeling depressed?

Feeling bad, down, or miserable is one of humankind's most common ailments. We are not talking about people who are depressed for weeks—even months at a time. That could be a sign of a serious emotional disturbance.

Ordinary depression strikes everyone from time to time. But some of us suffer from it more often than do others. We won't dwell on temporary upsets such as grief upon the death of a loved one, or a bad mood. Those are reality situations that don't usually last long and don't cause symptoms like fears and physical problems.

The depression we are concerned about results from irrational ideas, such as blaming yourself for something you were not responsible for—all the "should ofs," "could ofs," or "would ofs" in your life. Mainly, depressions occur because, for one reason or another, you feel inferior. Perhaps you often or relentlessly compare yourself unfavorably with others.

Sure, there are always some people who are luckier, richer, more handsome, or smarter than you are.

Yet did you ever think about this? Each person is unique. There is no one in the world who is exactly like you. Could it be that we are all on earth for a special mission or purpose? The great Eleanor Roosevelt once said, "No one can make you feel inferior without your consent." So if you want to avoid depression, you must begin to feel better about yourself. Of course, this is easier said than done.

It's important to deal with depression because it can lead to serious problems, such as headaches, backaches, fears, obsessions, nightmares, insomnia, or a chronic state of feeling inferior. There is hardly anything more exhausting than feeling inferior. (Some of you now know why you are tired most of the time.)

A lot of people try to solve feelings of depression in the wrong way. They eat too much or too little. Or they think alcohol or drugs can numb those feelings. These may make you feel good for a little while, but then you feel worse than ever. You have a hangover; you feel bloated, terrible, alone, and miserable.

What should you do if you're feeling depressed? Start by learning something new.

**THERE IS HARDLY ANYTHING MORE
ENERGIZING
THAN LEARNING SOMETHING NEW.
IT'S THE FIRST STEP IN
GETTING OUT OF A DEPRESSION.**

Here are some suggestions to get you started.

1. Write a letter to someone who would be surprised to hear from you.
2. Go to a park, a museum, a play, or somewhere you rarely think of going.
3. Watch a program on TV that you

wouldn't ordinarily watch—like a PBS documentary.

4. Go see a serious movie.

5. Don't watch TV for a whole day (better yet, don't watch for a whole week). Find out what radio has to offer *aside from* your favorite music.

6. Bake bread or cookies from scratch.

7. Write down all the things you really like to do. Don't stop until you've written down at least a number equivalent to your age. If you are twenty years old you should be able to write twenty things you really enjoy. Then, without giving it much thought, *do* one of the things on your list.

8. Daydream without feeling guilty.

9. Fix or build something.

10. Write a haiku (a seventeen-syllable poem arranged in three lines of five, seven, and five syllables).

11. Purchase a magazine you haven't read before, like *Ms., Rolling Stone,* or *Psychology Today,* and read at least two articles in it.

12. Create your own psychodrama. Act out a *scene* for at least twenty minutes that you would like to play in real life. Be very animated and enthusiastic.

13. Get a dog or a cat.

14. Make a decision to collect something (stamps, coins, cactus plants).

15. If nothing else works, try exercise.

This list is a start. Of course, we know that in the long run there is no substitute for feeling good about yourself through having a sense of purpose or mission in your life . . . a sense that life is worthwhile because your life is meaningful!

> **IF YOU HAVE AN INTEREST,**
> **PEOPLE WILL BE INTERESTED IN YOU.**
> **IF YOU ARE DEPRESSED,**
> **YOU WILL BE DEPRESSING TO BE WITH.**

You'll start feeling better when you put a little effort into learning something new; when it feels good to do something for someone else; when you begin to plan ahead instead of worrying ahead; and best of all, when you don't have to compare yourself to anyone else.

How does feeling better feel? Energized and optimistic.

If you've been depressed for a long time

And especially if you are not sure why . . .

Get yourself a complete medical examination; something may be physically wrong with you that affects your mental state. Then see a psychiatrist. Medication could help, but it's rarely the whole answer. Get into therapy (with a psychologist or a social worker). You may be able to confide in a professional even better than someone you know. They are trained to listen without taking revenge or getting hurt. We can't always say that of friends. A warning—don't stay with a therapist you don't like. Think twice about continuing to see someone if you haven't experienced a significant improvement after about ten sessions. I'm not saying to quit therapy, but I'm saying that research in this field suggests that for most people some improvement is evident early on in the treatment. In addition, read carefully the sections of this book that are pertinent to you.

What to say when you are leaving a depressed person

"You can count on me."

Shake hands or embrace and say with a smile . . . "Hey, just because you are unhappy is no excuse to make yourself unhappier."

Are you lonely?

The loneliness that is most painful is when you feel desperate—when it reflects a low self-esteem. The worst of it is when you begin feeling hopeless and alone.

Strangely enough, the loneliest people often feel the most desperate when they are in crowds. Some of the loneliest people I know are married and have families.

Loneliness is a state of mind.

Well-adjusted people often enjoy being alone—even savor the precious moments when they are alone, to read, reflect, or just relax. It is their choice.

It's a different matter if you are alone without wanting to be. Here, too, it's a state of mind. Being alone can always be put to good use. There are lots of things you could do when you are by yourself.

Read.
Write—keep a diary.
Be nice to yourself.
Eat and dress well.
Treat yourself to leisurely baths.
Clean your apartment.
And you know what? It's okay to talk to
    yourself. (You can figure out a lot of
    things that way!)
Call a cousin whose company you enjoy and
    suggest getting together.
Plan a strategy for meeting people.
Do volunteer work.
Get a hobby.
Join a club.

**IF YOU SHOW INTEREST IN OTHERS,
OTHERS WILL BE INTERESTED IN YOU.**

I know, I know—all this is easier said than done.
All the excuses
I have no friends.

I have no money

I'm not attractive. (There is someone for everyone.)

For some people loneliness will last a long time. I was lonely most of my childhood. I wasn't good at athletics. Kids made fun of me because I was a redhead and I was clumsy with everything. I survived by daydreaming and reading books. And then as I got older, in the late teens, I went to libraries and museums where I talked to people, and it was there I met one of my best friends.

Look under "Things To Do" for a list of books to read and tapes to study while you are passing from a "loneliness" stage into a "pleasurable aloneness" stage.

Sure, some of you are not into reading. That's okay.

You could move into fitness and exercise to build your body. Or you can experiment with meditation or yoga.

You could even find out more about your religion.

A review! And three messages!

Loneliness is a temporary state.

Use the time to be nice to yourself.

Don't be mean to your family.

It's nobody's fault that you are lonely.

Message one:

Take emotional and intellectual risks.

Unless you are willing to risk rejection, you won't have the chance for acceptance.

Message two:

Try to do the right thing for *yourself.*

You can't live according to other people's expectations.

Message three:

If you feel attractive, you'll attract people.

If you feel unattractive, you'll give off bad vibrations.

Things to do

For those who are into reading, try:

Whoever Said Life Was Fair, by Sara Kay Cohen

The Aquarian Conspiracy, by Marilyn Ferguson

When Bad Things Happen to Good People, by Harold S. Kushner

The Trouble with Being Human, by Eugene Kennedy

Coping Better: The Handbook of Rational Self-Counseling, by Maxie C. Maultsby, Jr.

For novels that deal with the purpose of life, try:

The Color Purple, by Alice Walker

The Snow Leopard, by Peter Matthiessen

The Book of Laughter and Forgetting, by Milan Kundera

Zen and the Art of Motorcycle Maintenance, by Robert Persig

Siddhartha, by Herman Hesse.

I would also recommend novels by E. L. Doctorow, Kurt Vonnegut, Herman Melville, Saul Bellow, Virginia Woolf, Amos Oz, I. B. Singer, Ernest Hemingway, and Elie Wiesel.

Russell Baker's autobiography, *Growing Up,* is inspirational. So is Eudora Welty's, *One Writer's Beginnings. An Orphan in History,* by Paul Cowan, could be important for anyone concerned about Jewish identity.

* * *

Don't feel like reading? Then get the magazine *Psychology Today*. It always lists self-help tapes. Order ones by Albert Ellis, David Burns, William Glasser, Rollo May, Jack Gibb, and Jean Houston. Look carefully at the titles and decide which are most appropriate for your present situation.

Hooked on drugs or alcohol?

No matter what your problem you can't solve it with alcohol, speed, coke, crack, or grass. Even if you remain functional, you'll become less productive, as well as nasty to people who care about you. You'll spoil any chances of a good sex life—to say nothing of an intimate relationship. (Did you know that most males have their first experiences of being impotent after having drunk too much or taken drugs?)

People who are hooked characteristically—

—lie a lot.

—can't be trusted.

—are overconfident ("Don't worry, I can handle it.").

—have poor judgment (That's why it's so dangerous for them to drive.).

If you can't stop on your own (or your friend can't), a Crisis Intervention Clinic will inform you of where you can get help. Once you are addicted, or a chronic user of any drug, it is extremely difficult to stop without professional support. Getting help is an act of courage. Not getting it leads to despair and hurting the people you *should* care about the most.

Here is something else you must know. Just getting off the stuff will not automatically solve any of your problems. You'll still need time, patience, energy, and motivation to make friends and develop interests. The most difficult period is the first three or four weeks after stopping. This is a period of high anxiety and tension. It's the crucial time to learn something new, discover a hobby, try a new sport, exercise a lot, or get involved in helping others who are worse off than you are. Above all, don't expect to be perfect (you'll make mistakes), and, indeed, don't expect anyone to appreciate what you are trying to accomplish.

Learning to cope with this transitional period of anxiety is just as important as stopping substance abuse—otherwise you may start again.

The main thing is to get help *right away.* Alcoholics Anonymous (or any of the other 'Anonymous' groups) is a good place to start.

If you don't like the way you look

Maybe you *are* too fat or too skinny or too tall or too short, or some part of you is not just "right"—thighs, nose, breasts, penis. Maybe it's your imagination or lack of information. Perhaps you can't change anything about your appearance, but you can change your attitude about it.

This is the first thing you need to know. People who accept themselves are attractive to other people—period. It's not that short, fat, or "unattractive" people can't "find" a mate or a friend—it's that people who hate themselves and express it in being (not looking) unattractive, shortsighted, or fatuous tend to repel rather than attract others.

* * *

If you are overweight, it's all right to diet. But it's not all right to literally starve yourself to death—a condition called anorexia. It's not all right to binge and then purge yourself (vomiting* or overmedicating with laxatives) —a condition called bulimia, or bulimarexia.

The point is that even when you lose weight you still have to learn how to make friends.

Sometimes people worry about parts of their body for no rational reason at all. Males worry about penis size. Yet you can't tell the size of the penis by observing its non-erect state. Some penises that appear small erect to five and a half inches or more, while some that appear large erect to less. Besides, size of penis is totally unrelated to sexual gratification.

Do you think your vagina is too small? No such thing. You could be psychologically tense or tight, but it can't be too small.

---

* The use of the drug syrup of ipecac for this purpose is very dangerous to one's health.

* * *

You can easily blame your appearance or some physical "defect" for any problem you have, but it's not fair to yourself. Haven't you noticed that *personality* is more important than looks?

**THERE IS SOMEBODY FOR EVERYBODY WHO FEELS
REASONABLY GOOD ABOUT THEMSELVES.
IF YOU HAVE AN INTEREST,
SOMEONE WILL BE INTERESTED IN YOU.
BUT IF YOU ARE BORED, YOU WILL BE
BORING TO BE WITH.**

Are you bored or are you boring?

Everyone is bored now and then. That's of no particular significance. It's only when boredom becomes a style of life that you have to get off your dead end.

There is nothing more uninteresting than a bunch of people standing around talking about how bored they are.

Here is a list of the most boring things you can do:

1. Run yourself down. Tell yourself and others how worthless and rotten you are.

2. Tell friends, when they ask how you feel, all the details of your rottenness.

3. Tell people you're horny.

4. Boast about things that everybody knows you haven't done.

5. Watch more than two hours of TV a day. Have you noticed—the more you watch, the more bored you get?

6. Talk about only one subject (sports, sex, stock market.) It's okay to have one main interest, but if that's all you talk about, people won't listen.

7. Always come across as Pollyanna-ish ("Oh, everything is wonderful!") or cynical and sarcastic.

8. Relentlessly tell people you're tired.

9. Talk too much. It's not as boring to talk too little—as long as you participate by listening.

10. Be sure of everything.

11. Complain a lot.

12. Be paranoid and suspicious of everyone's motives, always thinking, "What do you want to know for, anyway?"

13. Relate to people without ever risking being intimate (which also means without risking rejection).

14. Be superdependent on what other people think of you. They get the message that they can't talk frankly with you.

15. Begin your approach to people by saying, "I don't want to trouble you, bore you, or take up too much of your time." It's fake humility.

16. Be unwilling to try new experiences.

17. Be a super-miser. You don't want to do the most interesting things because you "can't afford it." It will be *forever* before you can afford it.

18. Persistently analyze the motives of everyone's behavior.

19. Be a gossip. (Super boring.)

20. Nearly always wait to be asked; hardly ever ask.

21. Almost always be serious and humorless; or almost never be serious and always kid around.

22. Relieve tension *mainly* with drugs or alcohol.

23. Almost never tolerate being alone.

24. Lead an unexamined life.

25. Spoil other people's stories (because you've said, thought, or heard them before).

26. Put on a slide show that lasts more than ten minutes.

27. Announce how self-sacrificing you are and what ungrateful slobs the rest are.

28. Complain that there's nothing to do; or talk endlessly of future plans that usually don't pan out. . . .

How to move out of boredom

The process of not learning is exhausting. A big disadvantage of being bored is that it's very tiring. It's no accident that when employers really want something done, they ask their busiest employee to do it. The more you are learning and doing, the more alert you are, and the more time you have to do all the things you want to do.

By the way, when you are bored you need to be especially careful about taunting, tormenting, and hurting other people. Boredom is often one of the biggest factors in senseless delinquent acts and other evils.

The best medicine for *getting out* of boredom is to do or learn something new or different. This will give you a first-class rush, which you can then seize on to keep going.

You'll become alert, energized, stimulated, and more confident, too. Now is the time to do things: it doesn't matter whether it's cleaning the house, getting a ball game started, baking a cake, doing all the odd jobs you've been putting off, or finally starting the big project you've been dreaming about.

While it may seem difficult to get out of a bored state, if you are willing to take a chance and follow the suggestions below, it may not be as hard as you think.

1. Go to the refrigerator or cupboard (many of you do this anyway when you are bored or upset) and eat or drink something with sugar in it. You'll feel better, but the physical effect will last only about two minutes. Ordinarily you might want to eat more and more, but then you might end up feeling worse than when you started. Here's the gimmick: Once you have taken something sweet you have only two minutes in which to learn or do something new or different.

2. Read an article that will give you some new information.

3. Prepare a dish you haven't made before and try it out on somebody.

4. Buy something you can't quite afford but that you've saved for and have been wanting for a long time. I'm not talking about going on a buying spree, which is useless and usually results in guilt feelings.

5. Renew a friendship you've neglected for a long time. Risk its working or not working out.

6. Go out to an interesting place to eat.

7. Let people know you are in a good mood.

Do you have a disability?

If you are not yourself disabled in some way, you very probably know someone, a relative or friend, who is. According to the American Coalition of Citizens with Disabilities, about thirty-six million Americans today

—roughly one in six—suffer serious physical, mental, or emotional impairment.

Being disabled involves all kinds of difficulties—social, emotional, sexual, and, of course, economic. Part of the problem is that disabled people are often excluded from the mainstream of life by *the rest of us.*

As a psychologist who has worked with disabled people, I have some advice to people who are not disabled: Make an effort to befriend a disabled person. Do this not from pity, but with empathy and compassion, as an aspect of being a decent human being. Form your friendship on the basis of a common interest, or by helping the person to develop an interest in something you already enjoy. Once a relationship has been established, don't treat the disabled person with exaggerated delicacy or sensitivity. This is likely to do more harm than good. In particular, don't hesitate to convey frankly what pleases and displeases you. For example, you may find that your new friend is "overdoing it," or misinterpreting your friendly interest for love. If this is so, the sooner and more decisively you straighten things out, the better.

Here is another important point: It's all right to start out feeling uncomfortable. Very few people can be fully comfortable at first in the company of someone who is blind, deaf, or cerebral-palsied. By acknowledging your discomfort, you can bypass pity, shame, guilt, rejection, or withdrawal. Talk about your discomfort, and then your friend may be able to explain, directly or indirectly, how to deal with it.

Now a few "messages" to a person who has a disability:

1. "No one can make you feel inferior without your consent."

2. If you have interests, someone will be interested in you.

3. If you are chronically bored, you will be boring to be with.

4. If you have nothing to do, don't do it with anyone else around.

5. Most important: Our society does not give you "points" for being disabled. You need to work hard to make friends and to prove to everybody that you are a person first

and that your disability is secondary to everything that is important to you.

Please note: If you have a disabled child, read our book *One Miracle at a Time* by Irving Dickman and Sol Gordon (a Fireside/Simon & Schuster paperback).

You can't please everybody!

Are you the type who tries to please everybody?

Well, you can't. You can only *try* to keep your own life in order, not everybody else's.

What pleases one friend or parent or teacher may displease another. What you do isn't always understood or appreciated. You need to please mainly yourself—be your own person, and in that process you'll find that some people, not all (maybe not even many), will like you. People who try to please everybody end up pleasing nobody.

So why not do the best you can, even if the best you can isn't good enough for some people.

What really counts in relationships is intelligence, imagination, character, luck, good will, and, sometimes, who you know.

So you might as well get to know people.

Are you very angry?

The legitimate purpose of anger is to make a grievance known. If that isn't done appropriately, anger can easily be turned into hostility, revenge, or even violent rage.

Just blowing off steam often doesn't result in relief because it doesn't take into account the person you are angry with.

It is still a good idea to count to ten before you express your anger, and sometimes it is a good idea to sit down and say, "Now whose problem is it?"

I agree with expert Carol Tavris, who says that if the object of the grievance is not confronted it matters little whether the anger is kept in or let out. The recipients of rage also have hurt feelings. Silent sulking, however, is about the worst response. It's a passive way of expressing hostility that can hurt even more than saying what is bothering you.

Try to avoid turning anger into an attack.

Stick to the issue—don't wipe out the whole person.

Don't say, "I hate you." Say, "I am angry about what you said or what you did to me."

Anger is a legitimate emotion. Violence, as authority Carolyn Swift suggests, is a response of weak, ineffective, inadequate people (villains) rather than of effective, strong, competent people (heroes, heroines).

A conference on anger, sponsored by the Institute for Mental Health Initiatives (September 1984), concluded:

> Anger, appropriately used, can provide an opportunity to make grievances known, solve problems, correct an imbalance of power in a relationship, and restore hurt pride. Anger contains the potential energy for change. On the other hand, anger transformed into unresolved hostility can result in serious physical ailments, severe emotional conflicts, greatly diminished ability to function at school or work, as well as suicide.

Are you teased, or bullied, or excluded a lot?

If this has lasted a long time, and especially if you don't have friends to help you out, you must do everything you can to put a stop to this intolerable situation.

Even if you have to be dramatic and say you won't go to school.

Tell your parents, teacher, principal, counselor, or rabbi/minister. Say you are afraid of being hurt and it's up to them—teacher, principal, parents—to see to it that it doesn't happen.

Sometimes the worst of it occurs in a particular place, such as gym. Insist upon a change. Get a doctor's excuse if necessary. Nobody should have to tolerate an unsafe situation in a school. It's supposed to be a safe place for everyone.

Sometimes a good technique is to approach the people who are teasing you (individually, if you can). "I would appreciate it if you would stop teasing and hurting me. I am weaker than you are and it's not fair that you take advantage of someone weaker. It feels really bad to be excluded." A direct approach, being polite and serious, often works. It's an act of courage, not weakness, to acknowledge that you can't deal with a situation alone.

These suggestions are worth trying, even if you think they won't work.

Do you feel empty inside?

. . . like there is nothing there?

It's a terrible feeling and it gets much worse if you do nothing, sleep a lot, or just mope about. You might—

—eat too much

—drink too much

—pace up and down

—do drugs

—watch too much television

—compare yourself with others

These don't fill the void. The only thing that can help is facing reality. This might make you very anxious.

But take heart. The first sign of getting better is anxiety. It means that something *is* there, that you are . . .

EMPTY NO LONGER.

You need to take care of yourself. Go for a walk, a swim, or an exercise. Call up a friend, someone you have neglected. Keep trying until you find someone who would be pleased to hear from you.

Talk about what's troubling you to a friend or some person you think you can trust. Fill the void with ideas, alternatives, faith, in the possibility that life circumstances can change. Prayer, if you are up to it, can help.

You can feel much better even if nothing changes except that you have made an effort to fill the empty spaces.

*Do you feel overwhelmed by guilt?**

Guilt is good to feel if you've done something wrong. But there are two kinds of guilt.

Mature guilt helps you organize yourself and enables you to respond in a more rational manner to similar future situations or temptations. Mature guilt can enhance your self-im-

---

* My son, Josh, hates the word guilt. He much prefers I call it remorse.

age provided you don't overdo it and let it degenerate into a destructive guilt.

Immature guilt disorganizes and overwhelms a person. You can usually tell whether your guilt is immature. It stems from an overreaction to something you did wrong, but more commonly from something you did not even do (perhaps it was something you thought about doing). More often than not, this kind of guilt is a way of expressing hostility against yourself, resulting in feelings of depression. At the same time the depression can be used as a weapon against the person about whom you feel guilty. Almost everyone, at some time or another, suffers from immature guilt. The process of turning it into mature guilt can be a growing and maturing experience.

WHY TRAVEL HEAVY
IF YOU CAN TRAVEL LIGHT?

Did some terrible thing happen to you when you were a child?

Let's say someone you cared about took advantage of you sexually. The first point you have to remember is that it *wasn't* your fault, regardless of the circumstances—even if you didn't tell anyone or you agreed to it or liked it. All mental health specialists agree that it's never the child's responsibility or fault if an adult commits such an act.

Or maybe you did something wrong. Maybe you made a mistake. But now it's over. Why punish yourself more? The best way to recover is to admit your mistakes and talk it out with someone you trust. Be helpful to someone who had similar experiences.

If you had bad thoughts and something happened that upset you, remember your bad thoughts didn't cause anything to happen. You cannot alter accidents or natural events (like death) with your thoughts.

Get on with your life. Your upset or depression is now harming a lot of other people (your friends? marriage?). Not fair. What you do with your life influences a lot of other people whether you like it or not.

Life does not exist for anyone without disappointments, upsets, accidents, tragedies, and loss.

What was the worst thing that ever happened to you?

Now, answer these questions:

Did, or could, anything good come out of it?

Did you learn anything from it that could help you now or in the future?

Every mistake can become a lesson.

Even tragic events can become lessons.

Why allow the ghosts of the past to determine what you can do today?

Do most people fall short of your expectations?

Is it possible that your standards are too high? Unrealistic? Unrealizable?

Unreasonable expectations are the main reasons that—

—so many marriages end in divorce.

—so many parents are angry with their children.

—so many children are disappointed in their parents.

—so many love affairs break up.
Think about it!

WE ALL HAVE OUR LIMITATIONS.

Do you have disturbing thoughts?

YOU ARE NOT YOUR THOUGHTS.
YOU ARE WHAT YOU DO

You can, at times, get some insights about
yourself from your thoughts and dreams and
fantasies.

You can use your imagination to write po-
ems and love letters.

BUT ONLY WHAT YOU DO WITH YOUR
THOUGHTS DETERMINES WHO YOU ARE

Remember, *all* thoughts, turn-ons, fantasies,
and dreams *are normal*. They could come to
you voluntarily or involuntarily from your unconscious. Some are subject to your control—
most are not.

*Guilt is the energy for the involuntary rep-
etition of unacceptable thoughts.*

If you realize this, then it doesn't matter how weird or frightening your thoughts are. It is normal to have violent thoughts, such as imagining your friends dead. It is normal to imagine having sex with someone you're not supposed to have sex with. Your thoughts will pass and nothing will happen. Your thoughts will not control you.

But if you allow your thoughts to paralyze you, or if you permit them to explode into violence, then your thoughts are not responsible.

You are!

You say you can't help it. It may feel that way because you didn't realize that all thoughts are normal. They can become abnormal only when they influence—

—how much time you spend unproductively.

—how you respond to these thoughts by compulsive or impulsive behavior.

—when your thoughts are repressed and translated into symptoms such as fears and psychosomatic disorders.

* * *

If you want to know more about rational thinking, I recommend you read *A New Guide to Rational Living,* by Ellis and Harper.

It's possible that just by reading this section, you'll feel greatly relieved. Remember the Zen expression: "When the mind is ready, a teacher appears." It is also possible for a bad situation that has lasted for years to change in minutes. Many people have experienced this. It usually evolves around an insight, a love affair, or doing something useful. But this may not be happening to you right now.

If it's reached a point where your thoughts have become painfully unseparable from you, seek help.

If You or Someone You Know Is Suicidal

How to get help urgently

If you're feeling really bad or thinking about suicide, you may not be in the mood to read a whole book. Read this part and after that turn immediately to the table of contents and read the brief sections that refer to you. Then confide in someone. Talk about what's troubling you. It is important, even if you have to reach out to several people before you get the response that gets you on track to feeling better. Try a friend—or a parent—

first, even if you are sure they won't understand. Then get to someone you can trust—a doctor, counselor, teacher, minister, rabbi— or call a crisis intervention center anytime, day or night. They will help you. (See the "Where to go for help" section.)

It's all right if you feel hopeless—just start out by saying, "Help me, I'm feeling really bad." This is the first step in getting better— finding someone who will know how to respond in the unique way that will reach you. By the way, it doesn't matter if you've tried this kind of advice before and it didn't help. This time it could. And, besides, time is on your side. In time you could change your mind about a lot of things.

Now, if it's someone you know who is in trouble—perhaps someone you care about has confided in you—turn immediately to the section "What to do if someone you care about is suicidal" (page 66). Follow that with "Dying to live the good life?" (page 62).

If you feel the danger of suicide is imminent, don't leave the person alone. If possible, you or another person can call the police and report that there is a suicide attempt in progress. Make sure you give the address and telephone number. Get as close to the person as he or she will allow and talk. "Let's talk. For my sake. It's important for me. If I can't persuade you not to kill yourself, you can go ahead with it later. Please, let's talk. It's possible that I don't understand how you feel. Explain it to me." Push gently for a discussion about options and alternatives.

How to help someone who is in a panic or having what's sometimes called an anxiety attack

Anxiety is experienced as an overwhelming state of tension or fear (often in anticipation of some unknown danger, or in anticipation of not being able to handle a scheduled task or performance, which should not be confused with normal stress or tension before an event). Attacks may be accompanied by such physical signs as rapid heartbeat, sweating, trembling, nausea, difficulty catching your breath,* in addition to intense fears of losing control, going crazy, and even dying.

---

* If the person is panting and out of breath, one way to help him or her stop is to have the person place a small paper bag

Here's what to do:

Say something like this—"Listen, you are having an anxiety attack. If you've had one before, you know you'll get over it. If it's the first time, it's real scary. But it is not dangerous and it will pass. [How do you know? the person asks.] I read about it in a book. [What causes it?] It's not important to figure it out now.

"Here's what you are supposed to do. Just sit down, close your eyes and tense up, then relax every part of your body. Start with your toes, feet, legs . . ." (Progressively move up and name the other body parts—suggesting that the person visualize the body parts in his or her mind.)

"I'll stay with you. Now listen—I know that all sorts of ideas will come into your mind. This is common. It happens to a lot of people. [How do you know?] It was clearly stated in this psychology book that I read. What you are going through is not comfortable (may

around the nose and mouth and breathe into the bag until the panting stops. Breathing the same air over and over for three or four minutes helps the person control the panting by increasing the carbon dioxide in the blood to normal levels, calming them down.

even be terrifying), but it is not, I repeat, not, dangerous."

Please note: This is a first-aid procedure. Don't try to talk them out of the anxiety attack by suggesting it's nothing to worry about. Nor will this relaxation approach solve the basic problem. If intense physical pain is present, emergency medical help may be indicated. If it does turn out to be, as you suspected, an anxiety attack, talking with a counselor or psychiatrist could be suggested at a later time.

When the acute phase is over, the two of you could decide together what's feasible for now or what to postpone for another time.

IT'S A GOOD FEELING
WHEN YOU KNOW
WHAT TO DO
TO HELP SOMEONE IN TROUBLE

Dying to live the good life?

Depressed sometimes? *Everybody,* but everybody, gets depressed every once in a while. Almost all occasional depressions are normal. Have you ever thought about suicide? Did you know that almost everyone has?

About thirty thousand people kill themselves every year. As a statistic by itself it makes no real impression. (How about if I told you that several hundred thousand make serious suicide attempts every year?)

Do you know someone who has killed himself (herself)? Probably yes. Isn't it painful to recall—to visualize—that person? Wouldn't you like to be in a position to help someone (even yourself) who is seriously considering suicide?

First about depression: We live in a world that expects us to be happy virtually all the time. Many parents say, "I don't care what you do with your life, as long as you are happy." Of course, we are not always sure that they really mean it. Ads in the media try to convince us that their products will make us happy. The truth of the matter is that life is not that way at all.

Life has many disappointments: deaths of people you love, tragic illnesses, prolonged periods of bad weather, betrayals, feelings of worthlessness and despair, times dominated by cries of "why me?" and wallowing in pools of self-pity. Most people discover ways of dealing with depression and become convinced that times will be better, even if at the moment of crisis it does not seem that way.

Normal depressions follow a bad event. Sometimes it may turn out that what was wrong was your perception—your way of looking at it. For example, your friend gave you the impression that he had deceived or compromised you—but then you discover it was not true.

Normal depressions don't last a long time. Normal mourning after a death can seem like an eternity, but during this time you allow your friends or parents to comfort you.

A more serious and what is commonly called a neurotic depression is usually related to accepting blame for something you didn't do, or feeling guilty for irrational reasons.

Sometimes, in response, people eat too much, use drugs or alcohol excessively—but it doesn't help. It only makes the depression last longer and get worse.

The most severe forms of depression occur

whether good or bad things happen. They can lead the body to function improperly. Significant changes in appetite and sleep are most common. This type of depression seems to have an organic base and can often be relieved with appropriate medication.

People who seriously consider, or do, commit suicide as a result of any of these depressed states haven't learned appropriate ways of dealing with disappointment. They feel there is no way out or that their agony will last forever. They feel there is no one who really believes in or understands them. For them, life is no longer meaningful. Many haven't understood that life without frustrations, depressions, and profound periods of mourning simply doesn't exist for anybody. But mostly it's inconceivable for them to imagine that—

—things always change.

—time heals.

—they have many options.

A lot of experts pretend they can describe a suicidal person, but they can't. Every person is unique, and so are the reasons for wanting to end it all. Suicidal intent, however, is always a cry for help.

Anyone who is suicidal requires professional help and, sometimes, antidepressant medication. But psychiatrists, psychologists, and social workers can't "cure" a depressed person without the help of friends and family.

Let me convey a bit of personal philosophy that can be helpful. Don't go around looking for *the* meaning of life.

**LIFE IS NOT A MEANING;
IT'S AN OPPORTUNITY
FOR MEANINGFUL EXPERIENCES.**

Disappointments are part of everybody's life.

Expect miracles in your life, otherwise you won't notice them when they happen.

The first miracle surfaces when you don't have to compare yourself with anybody else.

What to do if someone you care about is suicidal

Listen. Don't argue or attempt to prove that what he or she is doing doesn't make sense. Respond by saying things like:

- It must be so painful for you.
- As long as you are alive, things can change.
- I'll help and always stick with you.
- I care about you.

Don't say:

- You're being silly (or stupid).
- Let's forget about it.
- Let's have some fun.
- Let's go to a movie, or a dance.

Don't suggest drinking or drugs. By lowering inhibitions and muddying thinking, they make a person reckless or could even lead to suicide.

Don't be afraid to talk with your friend or brother or sister about what they are thinking about or planning to do. You could ask, "Have you ever felt like life's not worth living?" It's not that you are putting ideas into their heads. If they are considering suicide, it's good for them to talk about it. *Direct questions about suicidal intent do not provoke suicidal behavior.* Ask them, "Have you ever wished you were dead?" "Are you thinking of suicide?" "Are there some things you've thought about or done that you've never told anyone?" Then find out how urgent the crisis is: "How do you plan to kill yourself?" "Have you bought the pills (knife, gun, etc.)?" "Have you been thinking about dying for a while now?" "When do you think you'll kill yourself?"

If the crisis is urgent (they know how they plan to die, have the means, and are ready to act), *do not leave them.* Go with them to a parent, a counselor, a minister, a rabbi, a suicide prevention clinic, or whatever support system is best at the time. If the person refuses to meet with anyone, call someone secretly for help. *You cannot bear the burden of that responsibility alone.*

If the suicidal thoughts are serious (remember: they should always be taken seriously) but not urgent, work with that person. Find out what's troubling them.

Usually, something has ignited a serious crisis: rejection by a lover, the death of a close family member, an impending divorce, or the loss of employment.

It doesn't matter if *you* think what they are upset about is trivial or not much in comparison to the troubles you have. It's how *they* feel that counts.

Accept the feelings. Don't tell them not to worry. Don't trivialize the event by saying things like: "You'll get over it," "It's nothing," "You think you have troubles . . ." Don't try to amuse them out of the hurt.

1. Be a friend, just sympathize.
2. Be sad with them.
3. Be with them.
4. Go for walks (don't sit around).
5. Jog together.
6. Exercise with them.

1. Don't take them to parties, or to be with people who are having fun. (Most really sad people become even more depressed when they are around people who are having a good time.)
2. Don't try to give easy answers or solve the problems all at once.
3. Ask your friend: "Is this the worst thing that's ever happened?"

"What are some ways of dealing with it?"
Help the person list their alternatives. Consider the following responses:

"I know you feel that there's no point in living without her (him), but it's well known that people can fall in love many times. It's not true that you can really fall in love only once. It's not fair to force another person to love you. What if someone you didn't love anymore tried to force *you* to love her [him]? Don't misunderstand me, I know it's hard, and it's okay to feel bad and be disappointed."

You might also say, "It would be good if you would allow yourself to cry," or "I know your folks don't understand you. They care, but in their own way. When you have a family of your own, you'll do it differently."

Don't lay on a heavy guilt or religious trip.

Earl A. Grollman, in his excellent book *Suicide*, cautions that the suicidal person is already carrying the burden of "punishing guilt feelings." If we say that suicide is immoral, this may add to the suicidal individual's guilt and depression. For such a person, Grollman says, suicide isn't a theological issue, but a result of terrible emotional stress. On the other hand, you might suggest, "By killing yourself all you'll do is put a big guilt trip on everybody, your family, me." The main thing is for you to encourage your friend to talk, to reveal and confide.

Any suicidal intent or inference should be taken seriously. These inferences might include comments like:

- I won't be around much longer.
- Soon nobody will have to worry about me.
- I have nothing to live for.
- Nothing works for me.

Don't say things like: You have everything going for you. Instead, respond with caring messages:

- I appreciate how you feel.
- If you think I don't know how you feel, tell me more about it so I can understand you better.
- I know it sounds hopeless, but things can change—even things that last a long time can change in minutes.

Don't tell lies like: She (he) really does love you, or Everybody is your friend.

Be a friend. Stay with the person as long as possible. Make a definite appointment for the next visit. Say, "Call me any time—even in the middle of the night." Go out for a meal together, or an ice cream. The act of sharing a meal can lift depression, if only for a while. Make a pact with your friend—what she will do, what you will do, when you will meet— and compare notes. Let him know you will see him through this.

And don't let your friend glorify death without responding: "Listen, pal, if you kill yourself, it's over. Only the survivors suffer, and for the rest of their lives."

And, besides, unconsciously everyone who thinks about suicide (listen, it's not unusual to think about it, even seriously) feels that they will be rescued at the last minute. Often it doesn't happen and they die, or they botch up the attempt and remain crippled for the rest of their lives.

With some depressions doctors can help. In some crisis situations, it's surprising how a change in a parent's usual response can bring immediate relief. What doesn't work is blame, resentment, or hostility.

Convey that you care. Everybody needs someone who believes in them. Respond to cries for "revenge" with: "Listen, my friend, there is only one revenge, and that is living well."

Nobody ever fully recovers from the sadness of a child or a close friend or sibling who commits suicide. It is difficult not to be haunted by a dreadful feeling of "What did I do wrong?"

So many people who commit suicide, or think they want to, or try to, do so because of a sense of hopelessness, and sometimes because they feel life is without purpose or meaning. They may feel that threatening to kill oneself is heroic.

It is not heroic—it's a failure to connect meaningfully with people who could or would like to love and believe in them. Sure, your friend may need professional help as well. Be sure to tell your friend—not all therapists are good for every person. If you don't like or trust that professional the very first session, find someone else. There is nothing wrong with you if you don't like the first therapist who is available, no matter how important or famous that person is.

What do you do if you are told in confidence that someone you care about is considering suicide? Do you tell anyone? Yes! Find a way to tell his or her parents, the spouse, counselor or minister or rabbi that you are worried. The more worried you are, the more explicit you should become.

There is nothing easy about all this. Sometimes the best you can do isn't good enough. *Blame* makes everything even worse.

You can't keep a suicidal intent confidential

You can't always trust your own judgment about whether it's serious or not. You could easily be thinking:

- He is not the type.
- Her carrying on is just an attention-getting device.
- I can't believe she is serious.
- He seems much better now.

Many suicides are committed after the depression has lifted and the person has regained the energy to go through with the suicide. She may have already decided to kill herself and therefore comes across as having nothing more to worry about. *This calm period must be treated with urgency.*

If your friend refuses to secure help, a starting point for you is calling a crisis center. Give him this book to read. Encourage her to tell another close friend or relative.

Please realize that we're not expecting you to be the therapist and resolve the problem. At the same time, you may be the only person your friend confides in, and the only person who can help. By determining the seriousness of the crisis, motivating that person to seek help, and by showing your support, you can make a real difference.

If they say to you, "Leave me alone," you can be sure that they very seldom mean it.

**THE CRUCIAL PART TO UNDERSTAND
IS THAT SUICIDAL INTENT IS ALWAYS
TEMPORARY.
IT CAN BE REVERSED.**

Can you tell the difference between a cry for help, a wish for attention, and depression?

You can't always, but here are some points to consider.

Francine Klagsbrun, in her excellent book for parents and counselors entitled *Too Young to Die—Youth and Suicide,* writes:

> Friends, relatives, teachers, co-workers . . . make up the front line of defense against suicide. . . . And, they must help, even if they believe the suicidal person is manipulating them or using threats of suicide to gain attention. A person who must resort to suicide to get attention has lost the ability to communicate in normal ways. *The person needs attention* [emphasis added]. Without it the next cry for help will be shriller, more desperate, more dangerous.

In any case, it's better to err on the side of concern than to be sorry later.

When you get right down to it, there are two main categories of suicide. The impulsive kind with no chance of return and the slow, not entirely intentional kind, often with equally grim results. The second kind may include:

Driving while intoxicated
Drug addiction
Alcoholism
Dieting (to an extreme—sometimes called anorexia)
Eating too much (when accompanied by self-induced regurgitation, it is called bulimia)
Smoking
Suicide attempts
Sexual promiscuity
Violence and crime
Retreat into despair

Suicide warning signs

The signs could also indicate depression, physical illness, or a temporary, and even an appropriate, response to loss. They include:

Expressing feelings of hopelessness
Becoming uncommunicative
Having explosive outbursts

Loss of appetite or excessive eating

Losing interest in activities once considered enjoyable

Exhibiting loss of energy or extreme fatigue

Pacing relentlessly

Sleeplessness

A preoccupation with the notion that "nobody understands"

Talking about death

Moodiness and sudden bursts of crying

Increasing isolation from friends and family

A tendency to become more active and aggressive than usual (unlike suicidal adults, who tend to become apathetic when severely depressed)

A serious drop in grades for those still in school or college

Giving away valued possessions

Increased interest in getting his or her "life in order"

Talking about suicide

A sudden and intense interest in religious beliefs and the afterlife

A profound depression in response to recent loss, such as a divorce or death

in the family, or a close friend moving away

A previous suicide attempt

Even though the vast majority of people exhibiting one or more of the above signs will
not attempt or commit suicide, or end up
mentally ill, they do represent, for the most
part, *changes* in behavior that warrant serious
concern. Why take chances?

Here is something to think about:

In some cases you may find yourself in the
position of having to get direct help for someone who is suicidal and refuses to go for counseling. If so, do it. Don't be afraid of appearing
disloyal. Many people who are suicidal have
given up hope. They no longer believe they
can be helped. They feel it is useless. The
truth is, they *can* be helped. With time, most
suicidal people can be restored to full and
happy living. But when they are feeling hopeless, their judgment is impaired. They can't
see a reason to go on living. In that case, it is
up to you to use *your* judgment to see that
they get the help they need. What at the time
may appear to be an act of disloyalty or the
breaking of a confidence could turn out to be

the favor of a lifetime. Your courage and willingness to act could save a life.

—Excerpted from *Suicide in Youth and What You Can Do about It.* Prepared by the Suicide Prevention and Crisis Center of San Mateo County, California in cooperation with the American Association of Suicidology and Merck Sharp & Dohme.

"Whoever preserves one life, it is as if he preserved an entire world."
—*Scriptures*

Why are so many young people killing themselves these days?

We don't really know. We do know that the suicide rate among young people between the ages of fifteen to twenty-four has tripled in the past thirty years, resulting in between five thousand and six thousand deaths a year. In addition, several hundred thousand young people make serious suicide attempts every year. We do know that many of the suicides come from homes where there has been divorce or separation. But thirteen million children under eighteen have divorced parents.

We would have to make the same comparisons for all the other reasons experts give:

Not getting along with parents
Drug and alcohol abuse
Overwhelmed by loss of parent or close
friend
Feeling useless
Feeling unloved and unlovable
Rejection by a girlfriend or boyfriend

One expert, Charles H. Haywood,* challenges those who put most of the blame on parents:

Suicide is an act of violence preceded in many disturbed individuals by feelings of hopelessness, helplessness and alienation, preoccupation with trivia, cynicism, inability to control moods, irregular and destructive health behavior patterns, absence of creative dreaming, unbearable loss or threat, and the availability of the means to kill oneself.

---

* Charles H. Haywood is executive director of Crisis Intervention Institute in Buffalo, New York. Quoted from *The New York Times,* November 28, 1984.

Dr. Haywood also believes uncontrollable rage, organic problems, or hormonal imbalance may be factors in suicide. (A complete medical evaluation is always indicated for people who are suicidal.)

The five characteristics most experts agree upon are the following:

1. Depression or a feeling of hopelessness are the most important factors in suicide.

2. Almost all are preventable.

3. Many people who took their own lives declared in some way their intention of doing so. Suicide attempts of any kind should always be considered a "cry for help."

4. Almost all suicidal people have mixed feelings about it—they want to and they don't. Suicide is sometimes impulsive but it may also be an act of desperation or a wish for revenge.

5. People who kill themselves often feel that their families don't understand them. It usually comes at the end of a long period of multiple difficulties.

However much a person feels intolerable emotion or unendurable pain, it will pass, it will change. It's temporary. When you get right down to it, each suicidal person is unique and each one is too young to die. As long as the person is alive, there is time for everything, including figuring out why he or she wanted out.

**WHY DO SO MANY YOUNG PEOPLE
WANT TO END IT ALL?
WHAT'S THE RUSH?
THEY'VE GOT A WHOLE LIFETIME
AHEAD OF THEM.**

You really want to know in a few words? They haven't learned to cope with *disappointment.* We are a society that's into instant gratification. If they feel bad, they take a pill, a drink, they try to escape. If they can't get relief right away, their bad situation turns easily into despair.

Everybody has to learn to cope with disappointments and even tragic happenings. It's part of living.

If someone we love doesn't understand this,

it's up to us to convince them. There is no greater *mitzvah** than to save a life.

> *"Although the world is full of suffering,*
> *it is also full of the overcoming of it."*
> —*Helen Keller*

Are you dying to be the center of attention?

What's the point of being the center of attention if you are dead? You'll never know about it.

You think the only way to get people to listen to you is to make a suicide attempt. (You might actually die or botch up the job so you'll be crippled all your life.)

It's just not a good way of getting attention. Suicide is romantic only in novels. In real life it's deadly.

What if I think life isn't worth living?

How can you tell? Moods and feelings change. Every bad situation is temporary.

---

* *Mitzvah* is a Hebrew word that means a commandment but is usually translated as "good deed."

End it all? Try life. You can always change your mind. But wait until you've lived at least half of it.

And then ask yourself the ultimate question: Was it worth it after all?

Strange as it may seem to you now, in almost all cases the person says yes. You better believe it!

In the meantime? *Try* courage.

Sex and Love Worries and Facts

This section is mainly for young adults but everyone, especially parents, can profit from it.

Are you worried about sex?

For starters, I don't think teenagers* should have sexual intercourse. They are too young, too vulnerable, too readily available for ex-

* A teenager is someone under eighteen. After that, make up your own mind about sexual intercourse.

ploitation. Ninety percent don't use contraceptives the first time they have sex. They don't realize that the first experience of sex is usually grim (almost no girl will have an orgasm—the boy gets his three days later when he tells the guys about it). But if you are not going to listen to me, use protection. It's not romantic just to let it happen. It's stupid.

AIDS alert (as well as other STDs— sexually transmitted diseases)

Everybody engaging in sexual intercourse should, in addition to contraception for the female, insist that the male use a condom. (Unless, of course, you are married and sure of your partner and want to conceive a child.) AIDS is a fatal, mainly sexually transmitted disease, which, however, is not transmitted by casual contact. The AIDS virus present in blood, semen, and vaginal secretions can be transmitted by sharing needles used to inject drugs; anal, oral, and vaginal sex; as well as by contaminated blood. For more information call the AIDS hotline in your area. Read "The Complete Guide to Safe Sex," published by

Specific Press for the Institute for Advanced
Study of Human Sexuality.

Sex fantasies

What about your fantasies?

All thoughts, all wishes, all dreams, all fantasies, all sexual turn-ons, no matter how
weird, are normal.* Often these feelings
come from the primitive unconscious and we
have no control over them. If you realize that,
these thoughts will pass and nothing will happen. If you feel guilty about your fantasies
they will recur. *Remember, guilt is the energy
for the repetition of unacceptable ideas.* They
could be obsessive and explode into behavior.
Remember, thoughts and turn-ons are okay,
but not exploitive behavior. It's okay to have
thoughts of sexual seduction, but it's not okay
to exploit someone.

Of course, the ultimate fantasy is falling in
love with someone whose fantasy is falling in
love with you. This sometimes happens in reality. The ultimate turn-on, however, is associ-

* A complete list of books about sexuality is available upon
request by writing to Ed-U Press, 7174 Mott Road, Fayetteville,
NY 13066, or call (315) 637-9524.

ated with intimacy—really getting to know and trust someone you are in love with.

Masturbation

Masturbation is a healthy, normal expression of sexuality for both males and females. It is not physically harmful no matter how frequently you do it (males, by the way, do not use up their supply of sperm; it is replenished and available all their lives). You can, however, live a healthy, normal life never having masturbated. But it's difficult to be healthy if you feel guilty about masturbation. If you don't like it, don't do it. But it's normal—almost all males and most females masturbate.

It's always better if a behavior is voluntary. For example, eating is normal, but if people eat too much because of anxiety (not because they are hungry), eating becomes involuntary (compulsive). The same is true of drinking alcohol. But if you must have a compulsion, please choose masturbation. Nobody has ever died of overmasturbating; however the leading cause of death in this country is related to compulsive eating and alcoholism (compulsive drinking).

Dying for a fake orgasm

Some young people have been experimenting with putting a rope around their necks and masturbating—falsely believing you get great orgasms that way. Not true. You may get a pleasurable sensation for a second or two but most people don't realize how easy it is to lose consciousness when pressing on the neck. Sometimes just turning the wrong way will cause loss of consciousness.

But what is true is that every year more than five hundred teenagers reportedly kill themselves without intending to do so in just that way.

Some teenagers have been experimenting with butyl nitrite (sold under such labels as "Rush," "Thrust," "Heart On," or "Hardware"). You might get a thirty-second high—but may experience dizzy spells, blacking out, irregular heartbeats, and permanent damage to brain tissue. Butyl nitrite in combination with drugs such as alcohol is even more deadly—last year several teenagers died as a result of.

Really great orgasms can be achieved by masturbating (and fantasizing at the same time), but only if you do it without guilt. Masturbation can be relaxing and there are no harmful side effects, either for males or females. But if you feel guilty about masturbating, you'll find that instead of reducing tension it will increase it. If you have an impulse to hurt or exploit someone or yourself in a sexual way, masturbate instead (privately, creatively, and with lubrication, if you feel like it), and you'll be surprised how your impulse will disappear. It may reappear, but now you know what to do. If the whole thing really bothers you, or you feel you are not in control, get counseling.

Homosexuality

We don't know why people are homosexual, but about 10 percent of the population is homosexual. First thing to remember: A few homosexual experiences and having homosexual thoughts don't make a person homosexual. Being approached by a homosexual doesn't say anything about you. The only fair definition of homosexuals is: Persons in their adult lives who are mainly attracted to, and/ or have sexual relations with, members of their own sex.

As far as we know, people don't choose to be homosexual—they just are. That's one of the reasons why it's not okay to be anti-gay.

There is nothing wrong with being a homosexual. It's just hard to be one in our society. If you feel you are homosexual and you are comfortable about it, the only problem might be to "come out," or let people know—such as your parents. Some parents and friends understand and "coming out" strengthens the relationship. Some parents and peers don't understand and might flip. You may want to wait until you are past eighteen and in college. Even then it's not easy.

If you are unhappy about the possibility of being homosexual, I would recommend psychotherapy with a therapist who is accepting of homosexuals. Only with such a person can you get the understanding and help you need.

Anyone who feels homosexual but is concerned about it should read *A Disturbed Peace* by Brian R. McNaught. Recommended books for parents whose child is homosexual (or who are worried about the possibility) are *Now That You Know: What Every Parent Should Know about Homosexuality* by B. Fairchild and N. Hayward (New York: Harcourt Brace, 1979) and *Are You Still My Mother?* by Gloria Guss Back (New York: Warner Books, 1985).

Pregnancy

Pregnant? It's bad news if you don't want to be, but it's not the worst thing in the world. Talk to your parents. Almost all parents will help. If you feel you absolutely can't confide in your parents, then go to a Planned Parenthood Center or a Family Planning counselor. If you are opposed to abortion, go to a Birthright Clinic. It is your choice (according to the law) to make a decision whether to have an abortion or to go through with the pregnancy. Counselors who believe in choice will not try to talk you into anything but will help you to make your own decision.

More than a million women have abortions every year in the United States. But if you feel it's wrong, that's all right, too. You could also consider giving up the child for adoption.

Here's the point: Don't do anything to hurt yourself because you've made a mistake. Why punish yourself twice? If you've made a mistake, turn it into a lesson, not a tragedy.

Virgin rights

Even though about 40 percent of females and about 60 percent of males are likely to have sexual intercourse before finishing high school, virgins have rights, too (even if they have become a minority).

Despite massive societal support for virgins, this group is rapidly becoming more maligned and more vulnerable.

I believe that committed virgins should not be intimidated by peer pressure. Our society, for its very survival, depends upon people who have the courage of their convictions.

As a psychologist, I am frequently asked if it is normal to wait until marriage. I, of course, reply yes. I could be very sanctimonious and stop there, but I add: "If you are going to wait, I trust that you won't expect simultaneous orgasms on your wedding night. Otherwise you might ask yourself the question, 'For this I waited?'"

Sex is pleasurable as an aspect of a caring, intimate relationship. *But* if I were to list the ten most important characteristics of a good marriage, I would say:

1. Love, sensitivity, caring, and respect for each other.
2. A sense of humor.
9. Sexual intercourse.*
10. Sharing household tasks together.**

How can you tell if you are really in love?

Most people confuse sex with love. Yet there are people who have enjoyable sex and don't even like each other, and there are couples who love each other and their sex lives

---

* Remember, too, people who boast the most about their sexual exploits are the biggest liars.

** Are you wondering what happened to 3, 4, 5, 6, 7, and 8? We need to leave room for your own ideas about what's important.

are far from adequate. About the dumbest thing anyone can do is marry for sex—or "chemistry" as it is often called. Even well-intentioned adults say things like this to young people: "If you have sex before marriage you'll have nothing to look forward to in marriage—there'll be no surprises in marriage." I say, if that's the only surprise in marriage don't marry. It's not worth it.

Some say love is blind. I say it's blind for only twenty-four hours. Then you have to open up your eyes and see whom you are in love with. Love at first sight? Maybe—but better take another look. The plain fact is, if you feel yourself to be in love, you are. But there are two kinds—mature and immature. It's not difficult to tell the difference. Mature love is energizing. Immature love is exhausting. If you have an immature relationship you have a tendency to be tired; you procrastinate a lot; you don't do your schoolwork or your job well; and you avoid your domestic responsibilities ("Me? Wash the dishes? I can't do that, I'm in love!"). You have what is called a hostile dependent relationship. You can't stand to be without the person you're supposed to be in love with. ("I miss him—I miss her—end-lessly.") But when you are together you fight and argue most of the time. Mood swings and accusations of jealousy, even violence, charac-terize the relationship. Some people even confuse love and hate: If someone beats you up or forces sex upon you, that has nothing to do with mature love; you may think it's "love," but it's really stupidity or neurosis or dependency or fear. In an immature relation-ship, one person usually questions over and over again, "Do you love me? Do you really love me?" I advise the other partner to say no. You'll have your first real conversation that way.

Immature relationships are characterized by promises. "Don't worry, honey, when we get married I'll stop fooling around with other women [men]." But you might as well know now—a bad situation is *always* made worse by marriage. Immature relationships reveal insensitivity and selfishness by one or both mates; or one person is trying to meet the needs of the other and neither is satisfied. Love feels like a burden.

Sally says she has a headache, but Don is

angry and replies: "You have a headache on my day off, you have a lot of nerve." In a mature relationship, Sally's headache is responded to by, "I'm sorry you have a headache, honey. I'll get you an aspirin; there's always tomorrow."

Mature relationships are full of energy; you have time to do almost everything you want to do. You don't shirk responsibilities. When you are together you enjoy each other. You might argue sometimes but not that much. You want to please each other.

How can you tell if it's infatuation or mature love? The first month you can't (in the summer it takes two months). Infatuation and mature love appear and feel exactly the same. Then, when the relationship settles in, all or some of the above signs will appear and you will be able to tell if you are *really* in love.

Some good general rules: Sex is never a test or proof of love. You can't buy love with sex. So many females have sex because of the possibility of love, but many more males have sex because of the possibilities of sex. A large number of males find it easier to make out than to make conversation. I'm not anti-male, and I know that anything I've written about males is also true of some females. It's just that many males are programmed by society (not born) to exploit females.

So until such time as men and women stop playing games with each other—women had better be "good" at those games!

Of course most relationships start out with many elements of immaturity, but with a lot of caring and effort they become mature (and some start out mature and drift into anger and hostility). The key here is that mature relationships are an evolving—not always easy or magical—process.

Dying for love?

Don't!

If you really love someone—your parents, your friends—don't kill yourself. No matter how they treated you, if your love at any time was real—I mean honest, good—why punish them so severely? It's not right. They don't deserve it. It's not fair. You don't deserve it.

When Scott Difiglia, a teenager from Plano, Texas, committed suicide because his girlfriend rejected him, he wrote a letter explaining that he couldn't live with himself any longer. He concluded:

> I am really sorry for letting everybody down. Mom and Dad, I really love you a lot and I am really sorry. Thanks for putting up with all my shit for so long.
>
> All my love forever,
Scott

Sorry, Scott, what you did had nothing to do with your love for Kathy or your parents, however sincere you felt about it. Real love *always, always,* means you care more about the people you love and their needs than about your own. Selfishness and self-hatred did you in.

Sure, we mourn for you, Scott,* but we mourn for your family and Kathy even more.

---

* See a powerful article about Scott in *Rolling Stone*, November 8, 1984.

For Young People Who Have "Problem" Parents For Parents Who Have "Problem" Children

If you don't get along with your parents

It is possible that your parents don't understand you.

It is possible that you are more adequate than they are.

It is possible that they don't care that much for you.

But in 90 percent of the cases parents do care—at least one parent does. They do love you. But sometimes they don't know what's right for you or how to express it. Sometimes they are so preoccupied with their own troubles that they lose sight of you. All parents have periods of time when they honestly don't understand their kids.

If the problem is not very serious, ask them to read the section entitled "A message to parents of teenagers—Don't turn off your kids." But before that, you read "A message to teenagers—Don't turn off your parents."

If you feel you can't talk with them or even if you think they just don't understand you, it's still important for your parents to at least listen to you. You may need to do something dramatic to get them to pay attention to you. Cut out the messages on the following page and leave them around where your parents can find them. Pick the time carefully. And then risk telling one or both of your parents how you feel. Don't hold back anything. It's possible that it won't work. But at least you tried.

It's not that you should give up. There may be other opportunities. But you may have to manage without parental support. It's possible. Don't take revenge. They may need your

Dear Mom
I'm in deep trouble
I need to talk to you
I want you to listen to me
* without criticizing me*
It's important

Dear Dad
I'm in deep trouble
I need to talk to you
I want you to listen to me
* without criticizing me*
It's important

forgiveness. Remember what we've said before. The best revenge is living well.

If you don't have the parents you want now, when you become a father or mother, become the father or mother you would have liked to have had.

A message to parents—Don't turn off your kids

No, you don't have to compromise your values.

No, you don't have to shift from old-fashioned (which most parents are) to being what people call progressive, liberal, or "with it."

Yes, you may have to improve your communication skills.

First there must be a recognition that adolescence is not a disease or a terrible stage that all young people go through. Many young people even enjoy their adolescence.

Teenagers need to be appreciated and accepted as part of family decision-making, including letting them in on problems—even serious ones, such as unemployment, fatal illnesses, and impending divorce. Teenagers feel rejected when they are excluded from family conferences. Parents need to be available for listening to the problems of their teenagers and for taking their problems seriously.

Advice

Never, never make fun or mock a teenager's love affair. Young people's feelings are as strong as those of mature adults, but are generally of shorter duration. It doesn't matter one bit if you know for sure that it won't last.

Please don't say things like: "You'll get over it," "When you get older you'll laugh about it yourself," or "It's puppy love."

It's all right not to like your child's lover or disapprove of his or her friends. State your feelings, especially if the relationship seems to have a bad effect on the child's attitude or schoolwork (for example, if the child is using it as an excuse to get out of responsibilities).

You can simply state that in your opinion good relationships are "contagious." They make people feel good about themselves and are energizing. People in good relationships do well in school and can afford to be responsive to their parents.

Nevertheless, even if this is not happening and you are not pleased, you should be polite to your teenager's friends.

THE MOST IMPORTANT RULE IS NEVER, NEVER, BREAK OFF COMMUNICATION WITH YOUR CHILDREN NO MATTER WHAT THEY DO.

This does not mean that you can't express how you feel about a particular situation. And try not to be known by your child as having a standard response to almost all crisis situations.

I asked my college students to recall a single sentence that most characterized what they considered as inappropriate parental responses to a serious problem they had. A surprisingly large percentage of students, even those who claimed they got along reasonably well with their parents, recalled sentences like:

From mothers

- Life is tough all over.
- Count your blessings.
- Where did I go wrong?
- Go ask your father.
- Shut off the noise box.

From fathers

- Life isn't fair.
- Moderation, moderation.
- For crying out loud.
- Go ask your mother.
- Life is too short to be miserable.

If you want to have a serious talk with your child, please don't start with the following expressions (which are guaranteed to turn off young people):

- When I was your age . . .
- It's about time you got good grades or straightened up your room.
- That's not your idea, is it?
- Wipe that smile off your face.
- After all we've done for you.
- What will the neighbors say?
- Are you telling me the truth?
- Act your age.

- As long as I don't know about it.
- Get off your high horse.

And please—in response to a teenager's concern—don't tell him or her not to worry. When's the last time someone told you not to worry and you stopped?

You may have a teenager who does a lot of things wrong—they don't clean their rooms, they don't take their homework seriously, or they watch too much television.

Try to make a point of dealing with one thing at a time. Concentrate on only one or two issues and, temporarily, let everything else go. This is usually successful if, at the same time, you try to improve the quality of the relationship by being involved in experiences together.

Telling teenagers all the "not to's"—don't smoke, drink, get high, have sex, or stay out late—doesn't help much unless we are able to help them discover how to feel good about themselves.

Most children appreciate that their parents mean well and, in fact, getting along with parents is the best indication of good adjustment.

Not surprisingly, the area of a teenager's disobedience is of perhaps greatest concern to parents, who often label a certain behavior rebellious, spiteful, ungrateful, or spoiled. Concerns are magnified when the misbehavior occurs on a daily basis.

First of all, it's very rare for a youngster to be in trouble with his/her parents over just one issue: usually it's a combination of things. Many parents tend to talk too much and complain about the whole spectrum of problems instead of concentrating on just the one or two crucial ones.

Suppose that the main problem is a teenager who chronically stays out late and does not return at the prescribed time, such as midnight. After promising to be on time, the teen comes home an hour late without even having telephoned. The parent is waiting up, furious that promises have been broken, worried about the child's welfare. The child is approaching the front door, putting the finishing touches on the lie he/she has made up to explain the lateness (a broken-down car and a traffic jam are perennial favorites).

After having a good time with friends, the

teenager's tension and anxiety have been building in anticipation of the prospective fight that awaits at home. The parents' own anxiety has built to the boiling point from hours of fretting, and from the memory that the child has been late practically every Saturday night for the past two months. In the fight that begins as soon as the door is opened, no constructive communication takes place. The parents' anger is interpreted by the teenager to be saying: "We don't trust you; you are a louse for making us so upset." Often the punishment administered is too severe for the offense. If grounding works, fine, but it usually creates even more dissension.

Next time, say just one line: "I'm very disappointed that you didn't keep your promise," and then leave the room. This is sure to generate guilt. It should be noted that if you had a prolonged shouting match with your teenager, any guilt he/she felt would be dissipated by the fight.

There is nothing wrong with generating guilt in a teenager who has misbehaved—it's nonsensical to argue that all guilt is undesirable. Irrational guilt that overwhelms a person is not helpful, but rational guilt, which organizes a person and helps to avoid repetition of undesirable behavior, can be a constructive force.

Let me state here my opposition to physical punishment under any circumstances. It tends to create even more anger and alienation and intensifies the conflict. Few things turn kids off more than a slap across the face.

Sometimes parents forget that adolescents need models more than critics and want their parents to respect their integrity, privacy, and ability to be involved in family matters. Above all, perhaps, they want love so they can return it, and information that can lead to self-acquired wisdom.

If your child shuts you out anyway, knock gently on his (her) door and say softly, "Honey, I love you. I want to talk!" or "Do you need a hug?" or "Can I give you a hug?" or "I need to give you a hug."

Persist even if the kid says "Go away."

Don't wait for a crisis to tell your child you love him/her. Kids, even teenagers, need occasional hugs and kisses without any special reason (even if at first they seem not to like it).

Mention every once in a while, "Listen, if anything happens, you make a mistake—no matter how dreadful—I'd like to know about it. If there is ever a crisis in your life, I'd like you to test me. I'll never reject you. I'll help you, and if I forget and don't respond appropriately you remind me."

If you tell kids they won't ever amount to anything, or they are stupid, they might believe you.

Don't give your children the impression that they have only one option: "If you don't go to college" or "if you don't pass math, you're doomed." Better to say: "Here is what I'd like [or what I think would be good for you]. If it's not going to be, we'll help you find something else."

Please don't make comparisons with your other children and, above all, allow your children to express unhappiness, disappointments, and sadness without making them feel unworthy or guilty or that you lack empathy or understanding.

The main responsibilities of parents to their children are to—

—love them.

—nurture them.

—promote their self-esteem.

—help them turn their mistakes into lessons.

The children can then become independent adults and still feel affection and love for you.

Please note: All parents who read this mean well, make mistakes, and love their children. Whatever happens, *blaming* yourself or your spouse is not helpful. Jerome Kagan, a noted psychologist, stresses in his book *The Nature of the Child* (Basic Books) that we have, in our society, greatly overemphasized the role of parents as *the* determining factor in influencing how children develop. Parents are important, of course, but so is the fact that children are born differentially fearful, irritable, and alert. Peers and the media influence children.

Mothers seem to blame themselves for whatever happens. They also seem to receive most of the praise if things work well. I recommend that mothers read Lynn Caine's book *What Did I Do Wrong? Mothers, Children, Guilt* (Arbor House).

For parents who have "out of control" children, I recommend contacting Toughlove. For a group in your area, call (215) 348-7090 or write to Toughlove, Box 1069, Doylestown, PA 18901.

A message to teenagers—Don't turn off your parents

One of the most difficult concepts for many young people to face is that their parents are really good people. It doesn't matter that parents tend to be old-fashioned. They mean well even if they don't always make sense to you. To you parental restrictions may seem like hostility—to them it represents their concern for you.

But whether you like it or not, getting along with parents is more often than not an essential aspect of becoming a reasonably well-adjusted adult. We do recognize that in some cases young people are better adjusted than their parents. For them it is still possible to manage in life, but it takes a lot of courage.

Before we discuss improving communication with parents, consider the implications of the following idea: *Young people who don't*

*get along with at least one parent are usually
the ones who don't feel good about themselves.*

So if you've had some hard times with your
folks lately, or especially if you feel they are
not listening to you, here are a few surefire
suggestions appreciated by almost all parents:

1. Make it a point (or a sacrifice) to spend a
couple of hours a week with your parents.
Talk to them about anything, or just watch TV
with them, but be sure to talk to them during
the commercials.

2. Every once in a while ask a parent who
works outside the home: "How are things going?" (If he or she answers "Fine," say: "I
mean, I'd like to hear about your job/busi-
ness.")

3. Ask one or both parents for their advice
about something not too crucial so you can
easily follow their suggestions.

4. Experiment with telling the truth about
aspects of your life that you have not been
truthful about. If necessary, start by saying: "I
worry that if I tell you the truth you'll be very

upset" or "When I tell the truth, the whole thing gets blown up out of proportion."

5. Clean up your room at unexpected times.

6. Compliment them on things they do well.

Another way to conceive of improving relationships with parents is to embark on a one-month politeness campaign—which can be especially effective if you want something (a car, more money, more freedom for staying out late, almost anything except permission for sexual intercourse or a motorcycle).

Make it a point to be polite without sounding sarcastic. It may require some pretending. It helps if you can say at appropriate times: "Good morning," "Thank you," or "I'm sorry. I didn't mean to upset you." If possible, at least once a week, without being asked, say: "I'll be glad to take out the garbage." "Can I do anything to help? I've got an hour to kill." Chances are, your parents will flip. You might even overhear them ask each other if they should send you to a psychiatrist.

It's important not to fall into any of the

traps they may set. For instance, their response might be: "You want something from us." Your polite response should be: "Of course. You always said I should work for something I wanted."

Or they could say, "What's gotten into you?" or, "What took you so long to decide you're human?" Your response: "I haven't been very considerate before. I'm trying to change to see if being considerate will get me anywhere."

Let the experiment run for at least a month and then evaluate the results. If you have been working toward something you want, ask for it in this way: "I'd like to talk with you about something, but please at least hear me out before you say no." You may discover in the process that politeness makes life much easier for you, even if you don't get what you want. Politeness, however, is not a sure method of getting closer to parents—it can be a way of keeping your distance, which simultaneously allows you to discover your own way. You may decide to close the gap or keep up a polite relationship, but that's up to you.

Of course, it's like playing a game, and it

sounds very contrived, but it's still a good way to break through a period of non-communication. It's a "pause that refreshes" and permits a more positive relationship to develop.

Did a divorce or separation—or living with a stepparent—mess you up?

Divorce or separation affects millions of children living at home or away at college. For a large number, their situation, as a consequence, was improved. Living with one loving parent was a relief after surviving years of two parents fighting, arguing, and even abusing each other and, sometimes, you. Unfortunately, many others from broken families have found themselves in really bad circumstances—and for a lot of reasons, such as:

1. Feeling deprived.
2. Economic hardship.
3. A lot of added responsibilities that they are not too crazy about.
4. Missing the absent parent.
5. Being caught up in the middle—sometimes forced to take sides.

6. Having been their parent's best friend and confidant, they resent another person coming into the picture. They feel angry and, in some ways, abandoned.

7. They were so worried about the divorce or separation that it affected their schoolwork and their friendships.

8. They feel guilty in a way that isn't constructive.

9. They are in a stepparenting bind that seems grim to them.

If any one or more of these or related issues have affected you, here are some things you can do and ideas to think about:

First and foremost, you must recognize that *it's not your fault.* If your parents break up, for whatever reason, *it's not your fault.* You can't be responsible even if a parent in an angry, impulsive moment blames you.

Life may be tough right now. Life may seem unfair. You may feel depressed, but that's not a reason to punish yourself twice. It's bad enough that you don't have the family life you want but that's surely not reason enough to do failing work at school, to be rotten to the people you live with, or to do things (like drugs) that are self-destructive. You need to resolve that you won't, of your own free will, allow a bad situation to get worse by hurting yourself. *Now* is particularly the time to protect yourself, to be nice to yourself. Try at least to be polite to the parent or stepparent you don't like. Dislike could also change with more knowledge or even just forgiveness on your part.

In any case, however distant it seems, you will soon be working or in college. You'll soon be able to make your own decisions, live your own life, marry, and have children of your own. The *only* way you can do all these well is by preparing yourself now. Get the grades you want, and earn the money you need.

You may have to postpone some pleasures. You have to avoid inadequate "solutions," such as alcohol. . . . Yes, you need to practice patience. You need to tolerate more frustration so that when you are old enough you can have the opportunity to do things better your time around. That's what life is about for a lot of people. That doesn't mean that in the meantime all aspects of your life will be grim.

By no means. You can still have relationships. Try to develop at least one intimate friend. You need someone you can confide in.

Develop an interest in at least one thing you can be passionate about. Be helpful to at least one person more vulnerable, more handicapped than you are. Make a commitment to at least one cause.

By reaching out beyond your own (perhaps even really bad) situation, you could be a source of comfort to others and, strangely enough, an inspiration to yourself.

You will feel energized!

God Concerns

Are you disappointed in God?

First you need to know that God can't do everything. We can't ask God to change the rules of nature for our benefit. God does, however, help those who stop hurting themselves.

Rabbi Harold S. Kushner expounded on these ideas after a personal tragedy in his wonderfully warm, deeply religious book entitled *When Bad Things Happen to Good People* (Avon Books).

Rabbi Kushner says that God may not prevent calamity, but God gives us strengths and the perseverance to overcome it.

> Prayer cannot bring water to parched fields, nor mend a broken bridge, nor rebuild a ruined city; but prayer can water an arid soul, mend a broken heart, and rebuild a weakened will.
>
> —*Gates of Prayer*

*Yes, hope for a miracle
but, as a Jewish sage suggested,
don't depend on one.*

Have you lost faith in your religion?

It's understandable if you think that faith can alter natural events and that belief in God means that God will arrange a good life for you. But God can't do that for you. Only you can try to do it for yourself.

It is, however, appropriate to agonize over this issue. Talk over with your rabbi, priest, or minister why it is that your religion hasn't helped you feel better about yourself. You might get some surprising answers.

A meaningful religious belief should have

the role of helping you feel better about yourself and others.

This is what I think:

There is a way for everyone

People who want to
mock God
    say there is only
    one road to heaven,
Lord knows
    a one way sign is a
    dead end
    leading to nowhere,
Lord knows,
    there are infinite ways to find
    your own way.

John Donne, a Roman Catholic priest, theolo-
gian, and philosopher, suggests that we give
up the search for certainty and go on a voyage
of discovering and understanding. He feels
the question is not "Is there a God?" but
rather "What is God?"

IF YOU FEEL YOURSELF IN NEED OF PRAYER

When heavy burdens oppress us, and our spirits grow faint, and the gloom of failure settles upon us, help us to see through the darkness to the light beyond.

To You, O Lord, we turn for light; turn to us and help us.

When we come to doubt the value of life because suffering blinds us to life's goodness, give us the understanding to bear pain without despair.

To You, O God, we turn for understanding; turn to us and help us.

When we are tempted to suppress the voice of conscience, to call evil good and good evil, turn our hearts to the rights of others and make us more responsive to their needs.

To You, O Lord, we turn for guidance; turn to us and help us.

And when we become immersed in material cares and worldly pleasures, forgetting You, may we find that all things bear witness to You, O God, and let them lead us back into Your presence.

To You, O God, we turn for meaning; turn to us and help us.

—*Gates of Prayer*

MEDITATION

Looking inward, I see that all too often I fail to use time and talent to improve myself and to serve others. And yet there is in me much goodness, and a yearning to use my gifts for the well-being of those around me. This Sabbath* calls me to renew my vision, to fulfill the best that is within me. For this I look to God for help.

Give meaning to my life and substance to my hopes; help me understand those around me and fill me with the desire to serve them. Let me not forget that I depend on others as they depend on me; quicken my heart and hand to lift them up; make fruitful my words of prayer, that they may fulfill themselves in deeds.

—*Gates of Prayer*

---

* Or, day.

What Is the Purpose of Life?

Does life have a purpose?

Martin Buber, reflecting the philosophy of the Baal Shem Tov, the great Chasidic master, suggested that every person born into this world represents something new, something that never existed before.

All of us have the task of actualizing our unprecedented and never-recurring potentiality and not the repetition of something that another has already achieved. Everyone is unique for, if there had ever been anyone like you, there would be no need for you to be in the world.*

Wow, I was so blown away when I read the Baal Shem Tov's powerful endorsement of *purpose* for each of us that it immediately reinforced my belief that I not only was unique and special but also had a mission. And, while I would never be fully secure as to its exact nature, I *knew* that I was on the right track when these words came to me:

> *Everybody*
> *is*
> *unique.*
> *Compare not*
> *yourself*
> *with anybody else*
> *lest*
> *you spoil*
> *God's curriculum.*

And what's more, my being a writer didn't depend on anyone else agreeing that I was one. If you are on the right path one person is

* Read *The Way of Man According to the Teaching of Hasidism* by Martin Buber (The Citadel Press).

a majority. (Marilyn Ferguson's *The Aquarian Conspiracy* set me thinking along these lines.)

Viktor E. Frankl has explored in depth the meaning of life in his remarkable book *Man's Search for Meaning* (Touchstone, revised 1984).

Frankl, a psychiatrist and Holocaust survivor, argues that the meaning of life is ever changing. One can discover these varying meanings in three different ways:

1. By creating a work or doing a deed—by some achievement or accomplishment.

2. By experiencing goodness, truth in nature, culture, and most likely by loving another human being.

3. By transforming a personal tragedy into a triumph—turning one's predicament into a human achievement.

Frankl concludes that, at its best, human potential will always allow for:

1. Turning suffering into an achievement.

2. Deriving from guilt the opportunity to change oneself for the better.

3. The transitory nature of life itself pro-

vides an incentive for action. There is never a good reason to be *stuck* in any suffering aspect of your life. The potential for change is always present.

Frankl's advice to all of us?

> Don't aim at success—the more you aim at it and make it a target, the more you are going to miss it. For success, like happiness, cannot be pursued; it must ensue, and it only does so as the unintended side-effect of one's personal dedication to a cause greater than oneself or as the by-product of one's surrender to a person other than oneself.

In this context Frankl is referring to "surrender" as giving of ourselves to a loving relationship.

IT'S NOT GIVING UP, IT'S GIVING TO! IN THE GIVING, YOU SHALL RECEIVE!

If someone asks you what you are about these days, could you give a response that approximates one of these?

- I'm in love.
- I'm an artist.
- I'm working for a nuclear freeze.
- I'm into my schoolwork.
- I'm a big brother to a handicapped child.
- I've joined the Audubon Society.
- I work as a volunteer at the Children's Hospital.
- I'm excited about my home computer.

Without a sense of purpose, life doesn't seem very exciting or meaningful. That's why so many people end up filling the emptiness of their lives with despair and addiction to TV, sex, violence, drugs, alcohol, and passivity.

How does forgiveness work?

Let's take a cue from a Holocaust survivor, Rabbi Arthur Schneier:

I can say that if anything, as a result of the Holocaust, I have been strengthened. Instead of just taking my energy and being bitter and resentful, I was able to harness this energy for positive bridge-building, with people of other faiths, with people of other ideological persuasions. That is the price I must pay for my survival.

Rage would be destructive and render survival meaningless. Forgiveness frees you to be your own person. It is energizing. It offers you another opportunity to be optimistic. You become the hero. Give it a try.

Start by forgiving your parents, or a friend, or someone you love a lot who has rejected or betrayed you. Often they mean well, even if they hurt you. Don't they say "I'm doing it for your own good"? Yes, sure! But sometimes they know not what they do.

Hate is exhausting.

With forgiveness love is possible again.

And listen—just because you feel unloved now doesn't mean you are unlovable.

If you can't forgive someone who did you in, or if you don't like the idea of forgiveness

I do not believe that everyone must be forgiven for every act. We may not want to forgive the rapist, the mugger, the people responsible for the Holocaust, but we should, for our own mental health if nothing else, forgive the people who hurt us without malicious or conscious intent. Or those who realize their mistakes and ask forgiveness. Who among us feels free to cast the first stone? How about those we feel we can't forgive— the rapist, the mugger, the murderer?

This is where our response or attitude counts. We may want to put some energy into punishment or rehabilitation for those who are enemies of society.

But why give the rapist the ultimate victory by punishing yourself for years? What for? Sure, you'll be hurt, upset, need support for recovery. But recover fully you must—you must shout out: "I'm alive! I'll protect myself. Enough of suffering. I'll help others. I'm determined that this terrible event will not destroy my life. I will live well!"

A young friend of mine who made three suicide attempts before he was twenty-one (now, at thirty-five and very much alive, vibrant and creative, he thrilled that he didn't kill himself) objected to my emphasis on forgiveness. He wrote:

> As I explored my spiritual being, I have succeeded in overcoming self-hatred by working with unconditional love, unconditional acceptance, and compassion. These concepts keep me spiritually equal to others and do not presume—which forgiveness does—that I'm better than anyone else.

His view is that compassion, not forgiveness, is the key. I'm not sure. Something to think about!

Is it ever too late?

It's never too late

to try again
to grow again
to share again
to risk again
to feel again
to change again
to love again
to be enthusiastic again

to read *Winnie the Pooh* for the first
time.

When someone you love has died

There are no rules. There are no stages you
must go through. My friend Marian Leavitt
says, "Every death has a life of its own." Self-
blame spoils the mourning.

I have been comforted by this meditation.
Perhaps you will be, too.

It is hard to sing of oneness when our world is
not complete, when those who once brought
wholeness to our life have gone, and naught
but memory can fill the emptiness their passing leaves behind.

But memory can tell us only what we were,
in company with those we loved; it cannot
help us find what each of us, alone, must now
become. Yet no one is really alone; those who
live no more, echo still within our thoughts
and words, and what they did is part of what
we have become.

We do best homage to our dead when we
live our lives most fully, even in the shadow of
our loss. For each of our lives is worth the life
of the whole world; in each one is the breath
of the Ultimate One. In affirming the One, we

affirm the worth of each one whose life, now ended, brought us closer to the Source of life, in whose unity no one is alone and every life finds purpose.

—From *New Union Prayerbook*

How is hope renewed?

When we talk about our feelings
When we confide in someone
When we realize that we can influence our
    lives
When we develop relationships
When we realize that all moods are tempo-
    rary
When we do *mitzvahs** and practice for-
    giveness

How can you tell when hope is happening? You'll feel energized and optimistic. When you realize we (the people who care about you) are not complete without you!

---

* Good deeds

More Fragments of an Autobiography

Sometimes it takes
    a death of someone close,
an awareness,
    "there go I
    by the grace of God"
(I could have been gassed in the Holocaust),
a recovery from a terrible illness or accident,
    surviving a catastrophe
or a "simple" mugging

to discover how marvelous it is
    just to be alive
    with all our imperfections

Some people are lucky
  They know this without
  being reminded by tragedies

As I got older and preoccupied myself with philosophy, I read a lot. I read Iris Murdoch's *The Sovereignty of Good.* (Apart from being a philosopher, she's also one of my favorite novelists.) Her main theme is that we need a moral philosophy in which the concept of love can once again be made more central. She also suggests that philosophy is often a matter of finding a suitable context in which to say the obvious. The central theme of her work is that the only thing of real importance for her is the ability to see things clearly, to respond to them justly (which is inseparable from virtue).

I've been reading *The Road Less Traveled* by M. Scott Peck (Simon & Schuster, 1978). Peck sees life as a series of problems that require resolution, and the difference between mature and immature people depends on successful and unsuccessful resolution of problems. He puts a heavy focus on discipline, and he helps us appreciate that the process of confronting and solving problems—a lifelong process—is painful. For him the whole process of meeting and solving problems is what makes life meaningful. It's problems that call forth our courage and wisdom. Carl Jung suggested, "Neurosis is always a substitute for legitimate suffering."

My friend Gloria Blum says, "There are no mistakes, only lessons."

I struggle with conflicting thoughts. They are not harmonious, and they don't all make sense. How does one find peace in a dreadful world?

But we go on with our daily lives, of course, occupied with unimportant things, of course. We don't spend time thinking about most things that are worth thinking about. Even the Talmud says to us, "Just as the hand held before the eye can hide the tallest mountain, so the routine of everyday life can keep us from seeing the vast radiance and the secret wonders that fill the world."

There's a need to be healthy. There's a need to have energy. If you're not well, all you have time and energy for is getting better. I still derive enormous comfort from William James, who said, "Wisdom is learning what to overlook." It's a matter of struggling with priorities, finding out what's important, what's your particular mission in life. The Baal Shem Tov understood what I am trying to discover more about. God has created us in His special unique way. Not one of us is like anyone else, and we have this responsibility for finding out what meaning life has for us, knowing full well that it's a lifelong process. How can we put to use our uniqueness to develop ourselves, and in the process be useful and helpful to others? Many people today are depressed mainly because they feel useless.

Surely, we have to do our daily tasks. If truth be told, most of the daily tasks we do are boring. I suspect that all really meaningful and joyous experiences in life are of brief duration. But what do we do in the meantime? I think we have to do more mitzvahs.

I think we need to cut down on our fear of vulnerability by exposing ourselves to uncertainty—and by taking risks.

We don't need the answer. As Gertrude Stein suggested on her deathbed, we need the question. We need to find the way to the question. If the way is not clear, we need to make our own.

I read this stunning book—*Number Our Days:*

"I had a dream the other night when I was writing up my notes about Jacob's death, Shmuel. A man of great wisdom, a doctor, told me I had a fatal disease. 'You cannot remedy it,' he said. 'There is nothing I can do for you except to give you this advice: Do your work as well as you can. Love those around you. Know what you are doing. Go home and live fully. The fatal disease is life.' "

"This is very interesting," Shmuel said. "The Jews do not have much of an idea about afterlife. Everything is how you live here. You should be good to others. You should pay attention to your history. You should always be wide awake so you can be responsible for what you do. God wants more of the Jews than to survive. The Jews must *choose* to be alive. So for once, I would have to say you had a very Jewish dream."

—From *Number Our Days* by Barbara Myerhoff (New York: Simon & Schuster, 1979)

Then the philosopher Robert Nozick wrote in *Philosophical Explanations* (Cambridge, Mass.: The Belknap Press of Harvard University Press, 1981) that there is the benefit of knowing people who bring out the best in us, who inspire us to grow in new and positive directions.

But Fishkin asks if there are limits to our moral obligations *(The Limits of Obligation* by James S. Fishkin, New Haven: Yale University Press, 1982).

Eleanor Roosevelt answers:

No form of love is to be despised.

Then I read *When Bad Things Happen to Good People* by Harold S. Kushner (New York: Avon Paperback, 1981), and I'm still wondering.

Often I'm preoccupied with how to fit the Holocaust into my life. I know it must not be forgotten, but why does a single death like that of Joanne—or David or Owen—sometimes distress me more?

Yes, I live my life almost fully and with energy and with the support and love of a patient wife. But there are some regrets and personal distresses and genuine disappointments. Suffering is personal and cannot easily be shared.

> *My survival?*
> > *a sense of humor*
> > *a sense of purpose*
> > *a sense of mission*
> > *a sense of meaning*
> > *a sense of beauty*
> > *a sense of nonsense*
> > *a common sense*
> > > *passion for* bittersweet
> > > > *plays*
> > > > *ballet*
> > > > *movies*
> > > > *music*
> > > > *art*
> > > > *novels*
> > > > *chocolate and*
> > > > *intimacy*

June 12 is my birthday. Send bittersweet greetings.

What's a mensch?

First a mensch
Without aspiring to
be a
mensch
being alive is a
burden.

We all start out human
No way can we be more so
or less so.

We are at all times
struggling with the good and the bad
parts of ourselves.

Our free will represents the heart
of becoming a
mensch.

A mensch is someone who
aspires to be
a good person
and is
most of the time.

*A good person is
someone who accepts the biblical injunc-
tion to
Love Thy Neighbor As Thyself.*

*This is not easy, especially for those
who don't love themselves
the best way to change
is by being nice to others
then you may at least
feel good about yourself.*

*If you bless others
you can then bless yourself.
If you can afford to see good in others
you'll come to see good in yourself.
But there is still a catch*

*Not everyone is in harmony with your tim-
ing.
Not everyone is receptive to your kindness.*

*A really important obligation of a mensch
is to do
mitzvahs.*

A mitzvah is a good deed.

One does mitzvahs without intent
*   upon receiving a return.*
But mitzvahs always
accumulate returns in your favor
eventually.

A mensch is a good person
who has faith in humanity
and expresses it with love and unselfish
motives.

My mother (blessed be her memory)
used to say to us in Yiddish
Zug a Gut Vort—Est cost nit mare.
(Say a Good Word—It doesn't cost more.)
She was a mensch.
My life is a struggle to become one.
The hardest part of becoming a
mensch is forgiveness.

Eighteen slogans, poems, and things

New journeys, experiences, and people call
forth a *new you.* Why eighteen? In Hebrew,

the word *"chai"* means life and its numerical value is eighteen. *Chai* is my favorite number.

1. The existential question is coming to terms with life—not death.
2. You cannot find yourself through:
   - drugs
   - dieting
   - complaining
   - getting laid
   - jogging
   - eating
   - making a fast buck
   - violence

not
   - at discos
   - bars
   - cults
   - movies
   - races
   - parties

nor
   - in front of the TV

only by letting yourself
   - be tried and tested in relationships with people.

3. An untested find (a sure cure, prejudice) soon becomes a farce or a weapon used against people who don't share your views.

4. People who feel good about themselves (most of the time) are not available for exploitation, nor do they want to exploit others.

5. Not everything in life can be understood or resolved. All of us have some areas of vulnerability. Sometimes the best we can do isn't good enough. Some of us live in places where the winters are cold and long. That's why it's good to be optimistic.

6. Really marvelous experiences occur infrequently, are of brief duration, and are rarely on schedule.

7. "It is characteristic of wisdom not to do desperate things" (Henry David Thoreau).

8. You can get full with food but fulfillment comes only with love.

9. If you have a tendency to put yourself down, struggle against it. It's really boring to be with people who think they're boring.

10. Each individual is a unique being beyond the reach of diagnostic categories—an artist overflowing with the will and freedom to shape his or her own fate (fashioned after Otto Rank).

11. It's easy to be a hero in someone else's situation.

12. Intimacy is joyous and sad. It is sharing, open-ended, and taking your mind off yourself momentarily.

13. In order to perfect oneself, one must renew oneself day by day (Chasidic saying).

14. Love is where it's at and that's a fact (a refrain from a not-yet-composed popular song).

15. "All the way to Heaven is Heaven." (St. Catherine.)

16. "Honesty is not necessarily self-disclosure. It is saying *only* what you mean." (Sylvia Hacker.)

17. Suffering may not enhance your life but recovery will.

18. Vibrations are real.

Fortunately Not Every Day Is Important

Alone
　　　feeling sorry for

the plants
unwatered
like my love
in the Fall of
life
I
    seek the sun
among withered flowers
and brief encounters
where friendship lingers
not for long.
I am loved
not enough to still the
Exile. I lit two candles to
Find
    The way. No one noticed
What is a way to a
Jewish holiday?
Then
God
    responded, somewhat impatiently
I thought,
"For Heaven's Sake, Water The
Plants, And Get On With It."

Thoughts and things to do for the next eighteen days

Day one: Letting go of the ghosts of the past will permit you to have the life you're ready for today.

Day two: Let go of any thoughts that don't enhance you.

Day three: Give someone the benefit of the doubt.

Day four: You don't have to prove yourself to anyone today.

Day five: Say no when you mean no. This frees you to mean yes when you say yes.

Day six: Unselfishly offer a friend some of your energy.

Day seven: If you've wronged someone, ask that person to forgive you.

Day eight: Today say only what you mean.

Day nine: There is nothing you need to do first in order to be enlightened.

Day ten: Share a dream with someone.

Day eleven: Grow, by coming to the end of something and by beginning something else.

Day twelve: Set yourself a simple task and complete it today.

Day thirteen: Express your appreciation to someone.

Day fourteen: Realize that maturity is the capacity to endure uncertainty.

Day fifteen: Teach someone something new.

Day sixteen: Turn one of your mistakes into a lesson.

Day seventeen: Forgive someone today.

Day eighteen: Seek peace in your own place. You cannot find peace anywhere except in yourself.

If you still don't feel better about yourself

Seven Steps to Self-Esteem

Everybody has troubles, but people who feel inferior seem to have more than their share.

Everybody is unique—special—and has a particular mission in life. One of our sages is reported to have said on his deathbed: "God will not ask me why I was not like Moses—He will ask me why I wasn't myself."

Are you making these mistakes? The seven cardinal ones!

1. Comparing yourself unfavorably with others. There will always be people who appear to be handsomer, richer, luckier, and better educated. What's the point? We are all created equal in the eyes of God. We are all created different to serve God in a special way.

2. Feeling you won't amount to much unless—

- someone falls for you
- marries you
- needs you

- you earn a lot of money
- your parents are satisfied with your achievements

You have to be *someone* to become attractive to someone else. You have to be accepting before you can please someone you care about. If you don't amount to anything before someone wants you, you won't amount to much afterward, either.

3. Thinking you must please everyone. You must first please yourself . . . and thereafter only those people you care about. People who try to please everyone end up pleasing no one.

4. You set unreasonable goals for yourself. Lower your standards to improve your performance. You can always advance beyond today—tomorrow, if you want to.

5. You are looking for *the* meaning of life. Life is not a meaning, it is an opportunity. You can only find *the* meaning of life at the end of it. Life is made up of meaningful experiences —mainly of short duration, but repeatable.

6. You are bored. If you are bored, you are boring to be with. It is especially unattractive to bemoan how you don't like yourself or that

you have nothing to do. If you have nothing to do, don't do it here.

7. You decide your fate is determined by forces outside of yourself. Mainly you are in control of your life.

People who feel good about themselves are attractive to others because they don't exploit others and are not available for exploitation. They also share some of the following characteristics. They:

Are enthusiastic
Have a sense of humor
Have interests
Like being helpful
Are unselfish
Don't make fun of anyone
Have a *sense* of their own special mission
Can begin again
Turn their mistakes into lessons
Are optimistic
Are willing to take risks
Know how to listen

How can you get to be this way? Well, you can start by creating a miracle for yourself. Recognize that you are unique. Stop comparing yourself with anybody else. Believe that you're good enough to stand on your own merits.

It's easy to get caught in the trap of comparing yourself with others. There's always going to be someone who is smarter, wealthier, more successful, or better-looking than you are. But the success of others has nothing to do with you. They can't be you. Only you can be you.

One final note. If you have children, raise them to like themselves. That's the most important thing. Don't criticize them for things they can't change. Don't force them to excel in areas where they have no interest or talent. Praise their uniqueness in small ways every day. Children who like themselves grow into adults who like themselves.

"Be grateful for luck. Pay the thunder no mind—listen to the birds. And don't hate nobody."

—*Eubie Blake*

* * *

"Life was meant to be lived."
—*Eleanor Roosevelt*

"When the mind is ready a teacher appears."
—*A Zen expression*

"Wisdom is learning what to overlook."
—*William James*

*"Nothing in life just happens. It isn't enough
to believe in something; you have to have stamina
to meet obstacles and overcome them, to struggle . . ."*
—*Golda Meir*

*"A person will be called to account on judgment
day for every permissible thing that he or she
might have enjoyed but did not."*
—*Jerusalem Talmud*

* * *

*"It is the characteristic of Wisdom not to
do
desperate things."*
—*Henry David Thoreau*

*"Friendship is born at that moment when
one person
says to another, 'What! You, too? I thought
I was
the only one.' "*
—*C. S. Lewis*

Repeat over and over again: "I shall either
find a way or make one." Or, in Latin, if you
prefer, *"Aut Inveniam viam Aut Faciam"*

And then say:
*"I will be gentle with myself
I will love myself
I am part of the Universe."*
—*Joseph and Nathan*

*"One person of integrity can make a
difference."*
—*Elie Wiesel*

Where to Go for Help

If you are in trouble now, dial your local telephone operator (just dial 0). Ask for the Crisis or Help or Suicide hot line in your area. If it's an emergency, say "This is an emergency." Please, if you get a busy signal, try again. Just imagine for a moment that someone else is in even more trouble than you are (even if you don't think this is possible). Experiment with patience or call the operator again and request an alternative number. Ask if there's a Contact or a Samaritan crisis number in your community, or look at the front pages of your telephone book for the section on Emergency lines or Community Resources.